HATTIE'S PLACE

Katherine P. Stillerman

ISBN: 0988828723
ISBN 13: 9780988828728
Library of Congress Control Number: 2015904248
Katherine P. Stillerman, Winston Salem, NC

In Memory of Nonnie

1

Hattie Robinson sat on her front porch swing in stunned disbelief as she read the letter that had come in the morning mail, just one week before her graduation from Greenville Female College.

May 1907

My dear Hattie,

I am deeply grieved by what I am about to tell you in this letter. In recent weeks, I have become entangled in certain affairs that must be resolved before I can commit further to our relationship.

I am not at liberty at this time to share the particulars with you, but suffice it to say that I must call off our engagement and our plans to marry on August 3. As a result, I am certain that you will understand why I cannot be in Greenville for your graduation as we earlier planned.

You are a wonderful Christian woman and deserving of a man much worthier than I. I hope someday to be able to explain to you the extraordinary circumstances that have led me to cancel our marriage. Until then, I will cherish the memory of our relationship and will think of you as you were that night

I saw you in the choir at First Baptist Church and knew at once that you would be a kindred spirit.

Yours in Christ Jesus Our Lord,
Will

Will Kendrick's words struck like a backhanded blow to the face. Pain and humiliation would soon rise, and she would feel their mighty sting. However, in the no-man's-land between recognition and understanding, the only thing Hattie could think to say was, "'Christ Jesus Our Lord,' indeed. I doubt Jesus had anything to do with this." Why did people always invoke the name of the Lord as if that would help everything to make sense?

She might as well face facts: the only man she had ever loved had jilted her. She would be forced to tell everybody that the wedding was canceled and her plans ruined. A melodrama played in her mind of an endless line of classmates, church members, and family filing by like grief mongers, crowding in to bestow sympathy on a poor, wretched soul. She could read the pity in their eyes and hear their whispers—"Poor little thing, she's just had her heart broken." Hattie shuddered and forced that image from her mind.

Blinking back angry tears, she stuffed the letter deep into her pocket. With her most convincing and determined voice, she made an oath to herself as she sat on the swing, rocking back and forth in a nervous vigor. "I will not be the object of anybody's gossip or pity. Mama always said, 'When adversity comes, you either rise above it or allow it to suck you under,' and that is exactly what I will do—rise above it. I will take charge and make a plan. I will put up a strong front and announce the news to the whole family tonight at dinner. But first, I need to get over to the college and try to find a job to support myself." Hattie paused to smooth her skirt and hair, drew herself up to full stature, took two cleansing breaths, and began the brief walk from her house on East Washington Street to the dean's office at the Greenville Female College.

She found Dean Judson, in deep concentration, pouring over the *Journal of Pedagogy* on her desk. Mary Judson had been Hattie's favorite teacher and had strongly encouraged her to pursue postgraduate work. Motioning for Hattie to enter, she marked her page and removed gold wire-frame glasses, revealing intelligent eyes that now focused as intently on her student as they had upon the article she had been reading.

Hattie took a chair, pulled it close to the desk, and got right to the point. "Dean Judson, do you know of any teaching positions open in the area that I might be able to take?"

The dean's brows arched in surprise, and she paused briefly before responding. "Why, yes, Miss Robinson, I do, but I thought you and Mr. Kendrick were to be married soon and that you would be returning to Louisville with him in the fall. Besides, the jobs I am thinking of require the candidate to be single."

Hattie shrugged with chagrin. "That is just it. My circumstances have changed, and I have decided not to marry Mr. Kendrick."

"I see. I always thought a lot of Mr. Kendrick and considered the two of you a good match. But things don't always work out like we expect, do they?"

Hattie loved that Dean Judson never pried or offered judgments. She exhaled and bowed her head slightly. "No, ma'am, they certainly do not."

Dean Judson continued, "In that case, you may be in luck. I had a request come across my desk just yesterday." She reached for her glasses and began shuffling through a batch of letters from the in-basket on her desk. "Here it is. It's for an elementary teaching position at Calhoun School, in Pickens County. School starts over there on September third, and they are anxious to fill the position as soon as possible. Reverend James Fitts is the acting principal. Would you like for me to contact him and recommend you for the position?"

"Yes, please."

"But, Miss Robinson, since your plans have changed, would you want to reconsider and stay on for another year at the college to pursue the advanced normal course as we discussed earlier?"

Hattie sighed. "No, ma'am. As much as I would like to do that, I can't put that burden on Mama. Since Papa died, she has been raising all of us alone. Papa's last wish was for all us children to be educated, and our little one-room school in Anderson County only went up to the eighth grade. That's why he moved us all to Greenville after he got sick—to make sure we would be near Furman and the Female College."

Dean Judson nodded.

"The older girls are out of the house now. Maudie is married and living in Atlanta, and Minnie finished secretarial school and is holding down a good job here in town. With me graduating this year and Lottie finishing up next year, that still leaves Lillie and the three boys for Mama to educate. Plus, the boys are growing like weeds and they're just about to eat us out of house and home."

Dean Judson smiled sympathetically. "Your mother certainly has her hands full, and I think it is commendable of you to want to lighten her load. Given your circumstances, a fresh start in different surroundings may be just the thing for you as well. I will contact Reverend Fitts today and let him know of your interest in the position."

Hattie thanked her profusely and left the dean's office for home. As she descended the stairs that led to College Street, she fingered the letter, which she had thrust into her pocket, and withdrew her hand as rapidly as if she had touched a hot ember.

Perspiration had dampened her blouse, and she removed her jacket to cool down as she began rehearsing the speech that she would make to the family. If she hurried, she could slip inside the house and have a few hours to pull herself together in the upstairs room she shared with Minnie, who would not get home from work until late afternoon. She walked around the gravel driveway of their comfortable two-story home and entered through the screen door in back, where she thought she could go up the rear stairway to her room unnoticed. Mama would probably be in the kitchen, but she could give her a quick hug as she passed through and run on up to her room without having to say anything.

She was caught off guard when a familiar voice called out from the dining room, "Is that my namesake?"

"Hey, Aunt Harriet," Hattie answered. It was Mama's sister, her favorite aunt, who must've come for a visit. She could smell the coffee brewing.

"Don't you disappear up those stairs until you come in here and give me a big hug and tell me all about that Will Kendrick. I've brought something real pretty for your trousseau."

Hattie could feel her heart pound and her resolve weaken as she forced a smile, brushed past her mother—whose back was to her at the sink—and made her way to the dining room. Harriet slid her chair back and got up to greet her. As she enfolded Hattie in outstretched arms, she stopped suddenly and looked at her niece with a concerned expression.

"Hattie, honey, your arms are all clammy, and you are as white as a sheet! You look like you've seen a ghost."

Mama's ears perked up and she dried her hands and joined them in the dining room. Hattie was determined to stay strong and deliver the lines that she had prepared—albeit not until that night at the dinner table. "No, I'm just fine. It's just that there has been a change of plans. Will and I are not getting married after all, and I have just been over to see Dean Judson about lining up a teaching job for the fall. She says there is an opening over in Calhoun at the elementary school and is pretty sure they would take me on."

"What on God's green earth are you talking about?" Mama's typically mellow voice raised an octave. "Just this morning at breakfast, you were going on about how Will was coming for your graduation and you couldn't wait to see him. I had already made arrangements with the Easleys next door for him to stay in their guest room while he was here. And now you're talking about going to Pickens County to teach?"

Hattie's eyes welled up and she broke into tears. She retrieved the letter from her pocket and thrust it into her mother's hand. "Here, you read it," she said, her voice quavering. "It's all there."

Aunt Harriet sidled up to Mama and read over her shoulder. The taller of the two by several inches, she and her sister shared family traits from their mother's side: the oval face; straight, prominent nose; deeply set eyes; and a full head of dark, wavy hair that both women had worn long in their youth, but as matrons had gathered and tamed into neat buns. They were alike in temperament as well. Hattie had inherited her aunt's height, and she could have passed for Harriet's daughter.

Mama was the first to speak. Her voice had lost its edge and had now become calm and soothing. "Oh, suga', you've had your first real heartbreak, and there is nothing in the world that hurts any worse."

Harriet nodded sympathetically and added, "That's the God's truth. But I just want to know one thing: where does that Will Kendrick get off sending you a letter instead of showing up in person to tell you face-to-face two months before your wedding day? I say, if he doesn't have any more character than that, good riddance. You don't need a man like that!"

Hattie laughed through her sobs at her aunt's indignation.

"Well, Harriet," said Mama. "I am sure that Hattie will come to feel that way, but she will shed a lot of tears before she does. You go on and let it all out, honey. The sooner you do, the sooner you will be able to forget about Will Kendrick and move on. But why didn't you say something right away?"

"Oh, Mama, I didn't want anybody feeling sorry for me," Hattie wailed. "I can just hear it. Down at the church and over at the college and everywhere I go, they will be talking about me getting jilted and giving me that look of pity and gossiping behind my back. And Lottie and Lillie will be all smug and say, 'I told you so,' because they never liked Will from the start."

"Hush now, Hattie, and don't be so dramatic. You did the right thing in telling us. You are not alone in this. I will take care of Lottie and Lillie, and we can get the word out at the church that it was a mutual decision between you and Will, so as to preserve your dignity. You can let everybody at the college know that you have decided to teach a year, which is the truth. Time is the only thing that will heal your heart, but you will rise above this."

"Your mama's right, Hattie, and I think a year of teaching would be just the thing to do. Lord knows, it will keep you busy, and you will be so tired at night you won't have time to think about being lonely. If the job in Pickens County works out, I am sure I can help you find a place to board. My dearest childhood friend married a man from Calhoun, and they live on a beautiful estate right outside of town."

"Oh, that's right. Elizabeth Cahill," said Mama as she gathered the soiled coffee cups on a tray. "She married Charles Barton. She went to the Oak Grove School over in Anderson County when we were living on the farm there. She is a lovely person and would be a wonderful role model for Hattie. I'd feel really good about her being over there."

"If you like, I'll make contact with her right away. I feel sure that she and Charles would be happy to have you, Hattie."

"Thanks, Aunt Harriet." Hattie mustered a smile and gave her aunt a peck on the cheek. "Mama, I'm gonna go on upstairs for a little while before everybody gets home. I'll be down in time to help you set the table for dinner."

The arrangements for Hattie to work in Calhoun fell into place seamlessly. Prior to graduation, Dean Judson confirmed the position, with the agreement that Hattie would arrive before Labor Day to sign her contract and begin school on the opening day.

Elizabeth Barton had responded by return mail with a letter saying that they would be delighted to have Hattie as a boarder and that, in fact, she would be teaching at least one of their boys.

Hattie kept busy during the summer, helping Mama with the garden and the chores. Coming to terms with the breakup had been almost unbearable at first. Each dawning day, when the eastern sun slipped through the slats in the louvered shutters that covered her bedroom window, fingers of light poked at her sleep and stirred her from dreams of Will, the wedding, and their new life together. The cruel fingers poked until they roused her consciousness and along with it the disappointment and heartache for a dream that was not to be.

She had reread Will's letter so many times that it was beginning to tear along the folds, but she was still unable to make sense of that one phrase: "I have become entangled in certain affairs that must be resolved before I can commit further to our relationship." What could he possibly have meant by that? The words haunted her like the lyrics of a song that kept popping into her mind unexpectedly. If he had only told her the reason for the breakup…

Night after night, she lay awake considering the numerous possibilities, and the only one that made any sense to her was that Will had gotten cold feet about the wedding because he had either fallen for someone else or fallen out of love with her. But why so suddenly? Nothing in his previous letters suggested that his feelings for her had changed. In fact, each one expressed his increased devotion as well as his excitement that they would soon be reunited. The wording in his last letter was so formal and cold, almost as if someone else had written it. It was a perplexing mystery.

As difficult as it had been, the weeks passed, the summer eventually drew to a close, and Hattie discovered that her grief was beginning to subside. When the dreaded August date that would have been her wedding day finally rolled around, it came and went like any other.

Had she and Will married as planned, she would have been leaving Greenville and moving to Louisville to make a life together with him. Now, she would still be leaving Mama and her family, but she would do it alone. The thought of being completely independent for the first time in her life both excited and terrified her. She wondered what the Bartons would be like, if she would be successful as a teacher, and what new experiences her life in Calhoun would bring.

2

Hattie arrived at the Calhoun depot on the three p.m. train from Greenville and walked the short distance from town to the Barton estate. She had shipped her trunk on ahead and carried a small overnight bag.

The sun slipped behind a billowing cloud and brought a few blessed moments of relief from the heat and humidity. Tenant farms lined the dusty road that wound up and down the gentle piedmont hills. Across one of the cotton fields, she could see the land rise to the status of mountains, stretching out to the west. The bolls were heavy and ready for picking, and she waved as a farm boy driving a horse and wagon bulging with freshly picked cotton approached and passed on the way toward town and what she supposed was the direction of the nearest gin.

Past the tenant farms and farther back from the road sat an impressive two-story home with large, white columns. On beyond that, less than a quarter of a mile farther and on the same side of the road, was the entrance to the Barton estate, a brick mansion that stood at the end of a winding driveway lined with boxwood—well established and full. Hattie was winded when she reached the front door and stopped briefly to collect herself.

She set down her overnight bag, retucked her blouse and finger styled her hair, which had become frizzy from the cloying humidity.

Drawing two cleansing breaths, squaring her shoulders and raising her chin, she elevated herself to her full height of fifty-four inches. This centering exercise, which she'd learned in elocution class, had become an ingrained habit.

With all of the confidence she could muster, Hattie approached the stately entrance and grasped the brass door knocker, then rapped three times. She heard footsteps, followed by the turn of the lock, and then the door opening to reveal a tall black woman dressed in a starched servant's uniform and standing straight as a sentinel. When she saw the young girl before her, she softened and greeted Hattie with a voice like honey poured on a hot biscuit.

"Oh, Law, you must be Hattie. I'm Georgia. I help out here in the house and cook for Mista' and Miz Barton. Come on in out of that heat, chile, and let me take that bag. Miz Barton is right in the sitting room with Richard. She expecting you."

Hattie followed Georgia through the entrance and into the parlor, where she found a slender, elegant woman holding a small boy who favored her in complexion and coloring. They resembled a Madonna and child, a lovely picture. The woman glanced up and smiled warmly.

"Hattie Robinson, I'm so glad you are here." With one arm around the child on her lap, she reached out with the other and pulled the chair closer to hers. "Come on and sit down. We'll get you settled in your room after you've cooled off and rested. I was just reading Richard a few nursery rhymes before he goes down for his nap.

"Georgia, can you bring some tea for Hattie? And go ahead and put her bag in the blue room where she will be staying. Her trunk arrived yesterday.

"Honey, you look so much like your mother when she was your age. But you have your father's beautiful green eyes." Elizabeth took Hattie's hand and squeezed it. "Oh, Hattie, I was so sorry to hear that he had passed. How is poor, dear Sallie doing without him? She was so devoted to him, and he to her. You know we all grew up together over in Anderson County. Your aunt Harriet and I used to tag along after the older ones to the point we made ourselves a nuisance. I always looked up to Sallie, and when she and James started courting, I couldn't take my eyes off of them."

"Mama is getting along okay. She stays busy with the boys, and we older ones try to help out as much as we can. Little John had his third birthday last week and he is such a happy baby. Mama is determined to keep things as normal as possible. She doesn't ever want him to feel like a poor little fatherless child." Elizabeth's manner was so gentle and empathetic that Hattie felt she might be able to tell this woman anything.

"Well, I know that you girls have been a great comfort to her. And that precious little John! I had not realized that he and Richard were so close in age."

Elizabeth Barton pulled the toddler closer, lifted a bare foot to her lips and began kissing each ticklish toe as Hattie had seen her mother do with her babies a hundred times. Richard giggled and threw his arms around her neck with delight. He snuggled into her, and she tucked her shawl around his legs as he thrust the book of nursery rhymes into his mother's hands and demanded, "Weed."

"Not now, darling. I'm talking to Miss Hattie." Richard sighed and rested his head on her chest.

Elizabeth stroked his dark ringlets as she continued talking. "Charles and I thought that after we lost little Rose, and I had such a time recovering, we had completed our family. Then Richard came along and brought laughter back into our lives. He has been such a joy! I know that Sallie feels just that way about John. It really is your children who keep you going." As she spoke, Richard's lids grew heavy, and the black fringe covering the deep blue eyes met in sleep.

Georgia came in with a fresh pitcher of tea. "Lawd if he's ain't a sleeping angel."

Elizabeth shifted Richard to her shoulder and began to stand. "I'll just take him on up to the nursery and get him settled. He sleeps so much better when he can stretch out. You finish your tea, Hattie, and I'll be back down in a few minutes to show you around."

"Miz Lizabeth, you betta' give me that child and let me carry him. You know you ain't 'spose to be lifting him and climbing up steps like you been doing. Docta' Wheeler say with your condition you not 'spose to strain yourself."

"Oh, Georgia, I'm fine. I am feeling stronger every day, and besides, he is my last little baby, and I'm not going to be denied the privilege of caring for him myself."

"Miz Lizabeth, you go on and give him here now. I ain't gone let you go against the docta'. Besides, you know you my baby." Georgia furrowed her brow and put both hands on her hips. "I done took care of you since the time you waz born and I'm perfectly able to take care of yo' baby."

Elizabeth handed the sleeping child over to Georgia with a sigh. "All right, Georgia, take him. I'll be up in a minute to check on him." Richard looked like a rag doll draped over Georgia's sturdy shoulder as she effortlessly carried him out of the parlor and up the stairs to the nursery. Elizabeth settled in her chair, shaking her head and smiling. "You can see who has the last word around here."

From the rear of the house, a door slammed, followed by the vibration of footsteps clattering toward the parlor. A boy of around twelve years appeared in the doorway after narrowly avoiding a collision with the umbrella stand on the adjacent wall. A wiry lad, with the same black hair, blue eyes, and porcelain complexion as his mother and baby brother, his cheeks glowed from exertion and heat. He took three giant steps to reach the sofa across from where Hattie and Elizabeth sat and flung himself down on it. "Mother, I hate that old goat. I had him tied up to the post behind the barn like Father told me, and he ate through his harness. George and Gene helped me trap him and pin him up in the shed, and we got so hot chasing him that we thought we would melt. I am fixin' to walk down to Uncle Bailey's shop and see if he has something to make this harness fit tighter."

"Charles, darlin', come on over here and give Miss Robinson a proper greeting. She's gonna be teaching at the school this year, and you need to show her your manners."

Charles stood and wiped his sweaty palms against his pants. He strode over to Hattie and extended his hand, transformed into the perfect gentleman. "Pleased to meet you, Miss Robinson."

Before Hattie could reply, they were interrupted again by two other boys who had come in after Charles. Panting like overheated puppies, they collapsed on the sofa next to their brother.

Elizabeth introduced ten-year-old George and six-year-old Eugene to Hattie, who felt a pang of homesickness for her own brothers, so close in age and identical in behavior to the Barton boys. Hattie extended her hand to Charles. "Hello, Charles. You remind me of my brother Jamie, who is eleven. He is our resident handyman and is always fixing things. Good luck with that goat. If you are anything like Jamie, you'll find a way to outsmart him."

Charles brightened, clearly flattered by the compliment, and raised himself up to his full stature before he left to complete his errand. Elizabeth affectionately called after him, "Charles, you need to have some tea and cool off before you go back out in that heat."

Hattie turned her attention to the younger boys. "George, are you ready to go back to school? Sixth grade is big year. We have a lot of important things to learn."

George was a sturdy little boy with an open face and a broad, confident smile that stretched so widely it caused his eyes to crinkle in the corners. "Yes, ma'am. I finished the second reader and I'll be in the third when we go back. I'm pretty good at ciphering, too. Miss Ryan said I was one of her best students last term."

"That's wonderful, and I am certain that you will be one of my best students as well." Hattie turned to the younger of the two boys. "Hello, Eugene. You are a fine young man. Are you ready for your first year of school?"

"Yes, ma'am. I already know my letters and I can write my name. Charles taught me. An' I can count to one hundred, and add some."

"This will be my first year at the elementary school, too. I only hope I am as well prepared as you, Eugene."

As Eugene beamed at Hattie, he reminded her of a plump cherub she had seen on a Christmas card, with a round face and bangs cut straight across his brow line. His voice was soft and sweet. "You can call me Gene if you want to."

Elizabeth gathered the two boys in outstretched arms and swept them toward the door in one continuous balletic gesture. "Y'all go get cooled off before you go back outside. I don't want you to have heatstroke." Her voice was rich and husky. She stretched one-syllable words into two, lingered on her vowels and dropped her endings. The resulting sound was textured and sensuous.

A petite woman, several inches shorter than Hattie, Elizabeth's limbs were long and graceful, and her body was amazingly slender and supple for a woman nearing forty. Hattie had met her less than an hour ago and already she was taken by her new hostess—her gracious manner, the timbre of her voice, and her light and lyrical movement.

"Come on, Hattie. I'll show you to your room so you can get settled." Elizabeth directed Hattie, and they made their way together down the central hallway. A smaller room, a more intimate version of the parlor, sat to the right of the entrance hall. An arched staircase on the left wall of the entrance led to the second floor. Behind the small sitting room was a study and next to it a bedroom.

"This is where you'll be staying, Hattie. We call it Aunt Willie Mae's room. Aunt Willie Mae is Charles's sister who has never married."

"Oh, will she have need of it? I wouldn't want to put her out."

"No, she isn't even in town now, and anyway, she hasn't stayed there since Charles built the new addition for her. She spends most of her time at their sister Alice's home down in Columbia, especially since Alice's husband, Raymond, died. Willie Mae has never been a well person, and the children make her nervous. This is the house where Charles and his sisters grew up and they always gather here for the holidays. Alice and Willie Mae are quite the pair. I'll tell you all about them when we have more time."

"Does Mr. Barton have any brothers?"

"Yes, two, and they both live in town. Bailey owns a tack-and-hardware store, and Eugene is the local pharmacist and owns the mortuary behind the store. They are such fine men and have the most wonderful wives. You'll meet them soon enough. We are a very close family."

The walls of the large room were papered in blue toile, and the crown molding and chair railing trimmed in white, as were the two arched windows facing out on the side yard. A brass chandelier with six milky globes provided ample lighting overhead, and the floors were heart of pine and covered with oval area rugs. On the wall opposite the window, a spool bedstead and footer supported the felt mattress, covered with a white Martha Washington spread and crocheted throw pillows. A side table with a marble top held a reading lamp and a vase with a fresh cutting of hydrangeas. Hattie's chest had been placed to the left of the bookcase. A giant mahogany wardrobe sat angled into the corner on the opposite side of the room, and Hattie could smell its rich cedar lining. Across the hall and built into the well of the staircase was a bathroom with a large porcelain pedestal sink, a commode, and an oversize claw-legged bathtub.

The spacious suite overwhelmed Hattie, who was accustomed to sharing a smaller room with her sister. The idea of having it to herself thrilled her and at the same time evoked a longing for home.

"I'll leave you alone so you can rest. We will have dinner about seven o'clock. Charles should be home by that time. He will be thrilled you are here. He's been worried about who would replace Miss Ryan and was so relieved when the principal, Reverend Fitts, told him that they had hired one of the new graduates from the Female College, especially one with connections to our family."

Elizabeth squeezed Hattie affectionately, and the scent of lavender lingered in the air. "Just let Georgia know if you need anything. I'm going to check on Richard."

3

Hattie turned a pirouette and fell back on the bed, kicking off her dusty shoes and liberating her tired feet. Here she was in this fancy home, all on her own, preparing to take her place in the world, a place where she could put the past behind and begin life anew. Glancing up at the bedside table from her reclined position, she spotted the vase of hydrangeas, Will's favorite flower. Instantly, she recalled the hours that the two of them had spent together walking on the campus at the college, sitting on the grass and reading poetry to one another, sharing their hopes and dreams. The familiar ache in her chest returned and she realized it was the first time she had thought about Will since she left Greenville.

As she lay there, the excitement of the day caught up with her and she drifted off to sleep. She awoke when the tiny porcelain clock on the dresser chimed the half hour and realized she was still in her travel clothes and needed to freshen up for dinner. Hattie was anxious about meeting Mr. Barton and wondered if he would be as welcoming as Mrs. Barton and the children had been.

There was no time to luxuriate in the oversize bathtub in the bathroom across from her room, and so she filled the basin of the pedestal sink, lathered her face and underarms with the almond-scented guest soap, and splashed cool water on them to freshen up. She brushed and pinned up her hair, and chose a fresh cotton frock from her trunk. Georgia was calling the family to dinner, and Hattie made her way back to the parlor, where she found Elizabeth with Charles Barton, who was taking a glass of sherry.

"Oh, hey, Hattie. Come on in and meet Mr. Barton."

Charles Barton set the glass of sherry on the end table and rose to greet Hattie. She could feel the warmth of his skin as he grasped her extended hand, his grip firm and self-confident. When she withdrew her hand, the fresh scent of sandalwood cologne remained on her palm.

"I am pleased to meet you, Miss Robinson. My condolence on the passing of your father. I understand he was a fine man and a credit to his family and community."

"Thank you, Mr. Barton. We all miss him but we have a lot of wonderful memories." Hattie knew that Charles Barton was only making courteous small talk, as he had never met her father. However, the tone of his voice was convincingly sincere. His eyes were dark and penetrating, and there was an authenticity with which he peered directly into her eyes as he spoke, without once looking away. His gaze made her nervous, and she diverted her glance briefly before looking back at him.

"I am happy that you have agreed to take the class that Miss Ryan vacated and that you will be staying in our home during the school term. I hope your accommodations are suitable."

"Oh yes. My room is quite spacious, and I have everything I need to be comfortable. I am accustomed to sharing a room with my sisters, you see, and will probably rattle around in that huge bed. And I have more closet space than I ever dreamed of."

Hattie heard herself prattling on and stopped. She had not done that with Elizabeth, but in Charles Barton's presence, she felt like a foolish schoolgirl. There was something slightly intimidating in his demeanor. He was handsome, meticulously groomed, and the wisps of silver at his temple and deep lines in his forehead enhanced his distinguished appearance. She always had felt a bit out of place when engaged in small talk in mixed company, either having too much or nothing at all to say. Hattie envied Elizabeth's elegant but personal style, how she moved effortlessly in a social setting and drew everyone into the conversation.

"Nonsense," Charles Barton said. "As a graduate of the Female College, you have been well prepared. The local school committee would never have hired you if you were not. We only recruit the most competent graduates, and the dean told Reverend Fitts that you were one of their most promising students."

"See, Hattie. I told you how happy Mr. Barton would be to have you here." Elizabeth touched Hattie's shoulder with one hand and took Charles Barton's arm with the other. "Now, let's forget about business for a while and go in to dinner."

Charles, Gene, and George joined them in the dining room, along with Richard, seated in his high chair and entertaining himself with a honey biscuit. The crumbs clung to his fingers and mouth. Objecting to the sticky mess, he held up his hands and spread his tiny fingers wide for Georgia to wipe with a warm, damp cloth. Hattie noticed that the boys had cleaned up nicely since they had come in from the goat in-cident. They had combed their hair and put on clean shirts for dinner.

"The boys had quite a time with the goat today, Charles," said Elizabeth. "It seems he managed to eat through his harness again."

"Oh," Mr. Barton responded, turning to Charles. "I thought you had figured out a way to contain him."

"I thought so, too," Charles answered before he had swallowed a large mouthful of meat that he was chewing.

"Do not speak with your mouth full, Charles," said his father, frowning. "It is most unmannerly. And your napkin belongs in your lap, not crumpled next to your plate."

Charles reddened, gulping hard and lowering his head.

"Well, I think Charles showed quite a bit of initiative," said Elizabeth, steering the conversation in a more positive direction. "When the harness broke, he hurried right down to Bailey's shop and got a piece to repair it without having to buy a new one."

Mr. Barton retained his stern tone. "And I assume you were back in time to finish your chores and did not loiter in town with your cousin Phoebe too long?"

"Yes, Father."

Elizabeth continued. "Hattie was telling us this afternoon about her brother Jamie. You know he's almost the same age as Charles, and Hattie says he's quite the fix-it man, too."

"That's right," Hattie said. "And the similarities go even further. Jamie has a nemesis just like Charles's goat; only Jamie's nemesis is an old milk cow that Mama brought from the farm when we moved to Greenville. That cow is like a magician the way she can get out of the barn and get in the corn. And she is ill as can be whenever Jamie goes out to milk her. She acts as if she is being put upon to give milk."

Charles Jr. seemed to appreciate that the spotlight had been diverted from him and relaxed a bit. His father must have tired of the small talk about the goat and turned to Hattie. "Regarding your position at the school, which we were discussing before we came in to dinner, I have arranged for you to meet with Reverend Fitts tomorrow at eleven to take care of the administrative details of your employment and to show you the classroom so that you will be familiar with it before the students arrive Tuesday."

"Thank you, Mr. Barton. That will be quite helpful."

"Charles, as I will be engaged with a client, I will count on you to drive Miss Robinson to the appointment with Reverend Fitts and to carry any books or supplies that she would like to leave in the classroom and to help her prepare the room for instruction."

Charles brightened. "Yes, Father. You can count on me to do that."

"Oh, Hattie," said Elizabeth. "I was dreading letting Gene go off to school this year, as young as he is. He just turned six in July. But I know he is going to be in good hands with you there to keep an eye on him. We are so fortunate to have you here, aren't we, Gene?"

"Yes, ma'am."

Hattie thought Gene had his mother's smile.

"Stop fussing over Gene, Elizabeth," Mr. Barton chided. "He will be fine. It is never too early to begin an education. An early start will allow him to learn his basics and then go on to advanced studies and prepare for a profession. Our state is changing rapidly, and the key to success is the highly educated man."

"He's six, Charles," Elizabeth drawled. "I'm allowed to be protective of him for a little while longer."

Charles smiled and tipped his head toward her in concession. "Well, we both agree that he is in good hands with Miss Robinson at the school to watch out for him. If he should have any problems with his academics, she is well credentialed and can teach him everything he needs to know to progress to the next level." He folded and laid down his napkin, pushed his chair back from the table, and stood. "Now, if you will excuse me, I have a few papers to review in my study."

Hattie was a bit surprised by Mr. Barton's abrupt departure. At her house, everyone remained at the dinner table until all were finished eating and often they lingered over coffee and dessert for extended conversation. It was usually the younger children who became fidgety and eager to leave. Mama and Papa and the older girls had always sat around and talked, and many nights they would adjourn from the table directly to the parlor to gather around the piano and sing. But Hattie supposed that every family had different ways of doing things and that this was the normal routine at the Bartons'.

4

Charles hitched old Boots, the mare, to the family buggy and loaded an armful of Hattie's books, notes from her methods classes at the normal school, and teaching supplies that she had brought with her from Greenville. They were on their way to the school to meet Reverend Fitts. Boots's hooves kicked up dust on the dirt road that led into town, and driver and passenger both coughed in tandem to expel it. A fine film settled on their clothes and on the books that sat beside Hattie.

"We need rain," Hattie remarked.

"Yes, ma'am. But we can sure make a lot better time on this road when it's dry than after a rainy spell when it gets all bogged down in mud."

Charles seemed proud to be escorting Hattie to the school and began to point out the landmarks along the way. "That's Aunt Sudie and Uncle George's place over there."

"Is George your father's brother? I assume your brother George is his namesake."

"Yes, ma'am. George is named for him. But Uncle George is really our great-uncle. He was my grandfather Andrew Earl Barton's only brother. Uncle George is part owner of the cotton gin with Father." He pointed to the large home with columns that Hattie had passed on her way in the day before. "Uncle George loves farming and still keeps about a hundred acres of cotton for himself, but he's given most of it over to a tenant to raise. The last one he had ran off and left behind a whole field ready to pick. Uncle George had to get him a new tenant right in the middle of the harvest."

"How ever did he find someone?"

"Father was up tending to some of the Barton holdings over in Spartanburg County and he found out that the bank had just foreclosed on a man's farm, and the man and his family were fixin' to be evicted from their property. He told Uncle George, and Uncle George offered the farmer the little house over yonder behind the barn for his family if he would take over the cotton and get it picked."

"Oh my. I'm afraid that farm foreclosures are happening to far too many people these days. They just can't make a living off the land anymore. And it's a shame, because there is simply nothing like growing up in the country and being close to the earth. Some of my happiest memories are from life on our family's farm in Anderson County." Hattie could see the tenant house. A girl about Charles's age was hanging wash on the line outside. "Is that young girl one of their children?"

"Yes, ma'am. That is Pauline Jeter. She's George's age. She's real nice, and she's smart, too."

"Will she be one of my students?"

"Yes, ma'am. When she can come. She didn't get to school much last year because her papa had her staying home with her little brother. Her mama was sick and couldn't take care of him."

"That's a shame about her mother, but she needs to be in school on a regular basis."

"Yes, ma'am. Miss Ryan sat her next to me so I could help her catch up on her math last year when she was out so much. She was real bright and caught on real quick."

The cotton fields on either side of the road gave way to grass and pine forest as they drew nearer town, where the homes were closer together. They approached Main Street and turned right at the town square, past the courthouse and the Methodist church.

"That's our church, where Reverend Fitts preaches on Sundays," said Charles. The school was located in the next block. A tall, slim man with glasses was arriving on foot as they pulled up. Charles identified him as Reverend Fitts, who waved for them to come into the school.

"You must be Miss Robinson," said Reverend Fitts, smiling and extending his hand to Hattie. "I am James Fitts."

"Hello, Reverend Fitts. I'm pleased to put a face to the name with whom I've been corresponding for the past few months." Hattie was a bit surprised to find a man in his mid twenties, not so much older than she, and thought immediately of Will. He resembled Will in build and coloring, but Will had more hair and did not wear glasses. She pushed the image of Will from her thoughts and commented to Reverend Fitts, "This is certainly a nicely kept building. It speaks well of the community's support."

"Yes, the community is proud of the school and has been enthusiastic in its support. In fact, the building sits on property donated by the Bartons, with whom you are boarding, and Charles Barton is a trustee of the school. I might add that he has been a driving force in securing high school accreditation for Calhoun. With the passage of the Rural High School Act earlier this year, we are optimistic that the state will appropriate additional funding to allow us to move forward with our plans."

"Oh, and how is that progressing?"

"We are currently able to offer a three-year high school curriculum and ten hours of credit. We meet the criteria of having two full-time high school instructors, a thirty-week year, and a forty-minute daily recitation period." Reverend Fitts seemed a bit uncomfortable with one-to-one conversation; he looked past Hattie as he spoke, not directly at her. It was as if he was addressing a phantom congregation behind her and she was sitting in the front row. Hattie found it disconcerting.

Reverend Fitts continued, "Mr. Barton envisions the day in the not-too-distant future when we will be fully accredited by the state, and the youth of the community can complete their secondary education without parents having to send their children off to boarding school prior to college."

Charles laughed on hearing that remark. "My mother is the driving force behind that idea. She can't stand the thought of any of her babies leaving the nest. The closer I get to that age, the more she urges Father to work for accreditation."

"Your mother is a fine Christian woman, Charles. I would like to have a church full of parishioners like her. With her gracious spirit and gentle power of persuasion, it would surely hasten the coming of the kingdom of God here on earth." Hattie could tell by the admiring tone with which he referred to her that Reverend Fitts was as taken with Elizabeth Barton as she had been.

"I see you have brought Miss Robinson's books. You know your way around the building. Perhaps you can take them to her classroom while we go into the office and complete the required paperwork."

"Yes, sir. I will do that right away."

After Charles left, Reverend Fitts directed Hattie to a small office just inside the door of the school. A large oak desk covered with neat stacks of books and papers dominated the room. He gestured for her to take the straight-back chair across from the desk and he settled into the seat behind it. Shuffling through the papers, he retrieved a written contract. He adjusted his exceptionally thick glasses and he began reviewing the terms of Hattie's employment.

"The local school board is hiring you for the term of the 1907–1908 school year, for eight months, at a rate of forty dollars per month, to be paid at the end of each month. In addition to your instructional duties, you will be expected to sweep the classroom regularly and maintain cleanliness and order at all times. However, we have hired a custodian to do heavy cleaning and maintenance.

"You must hold yourself to the highest moral behavior, refraining from alcohol, tobacco products, gambling, and loitering in public places. You may not marry as long you are under contract and will be dismissed for conduct unbecoming a lady. If you can agree to these terms, I will ask that you sign here so that you can begin your classroom duties on Tuesday." He offered her one of the fountain pens from the set on his desk.

Having never before signed a legal document, Hattie paused to read it and to savor the significance of the moment. She took the pen from Reverend Fitts, wrote her name in neat, careful cursive letters, and made her employment with the State of South Carolina official.

Reverend Fitts said, "As it is your first year of teaching, I would strongly suggest that you establish firm control with the students from the first day if you wish to be successful." He continued dispensing advice, which sounded to Hattie as if it had been gathered from a list of educational clichés. She had heard them all before, and she guessed there must be some truth in them, or else they would not be repeated so often.

"New teachers are often eager to be liked by the students and tend to be quite lenient in managing student behavior. Students sometimes mistake kindness for weakness and will take advantage of such situations. It is best to establish firm control from day one and to nip any behavior problems in the bud up front. It is also best when you can handle your own discipline problems, but, of course, I will be available if things ever get out of hand and you need assistance."

"Oh, well, I certainly hope that will not be necessary." Hattie had her own ideas about how to manage children. She did not subscribe to the axiom that a teacher should not crack a smile until Christmas. She knew that old attitudes about sparing the rod and spoiling the child were prevalent among many educators and suspected that Reverend Fitts might be among those who espoused the more traditional methods. However, she agreed with Mama's philosophy that you could catch a whole lot more flies with honey than vinegar. She would not be a pushover, but felt that sometimes the subtler, more indirect approach would get better results.

"Do you have any questions, Miss Robinson?" Reverend Fitts's voice cut through her thoughts.

"Oh yes. How many students will I have in my class?"

"It appears that you have a potential of thirty-two—fifteen in fifth grade and seventeen in sixth grade. That is judging from past enrollment figures. Regrettably, attendance is not what it should be, especially during the cotton harvest, and you will rarely have all of the students at one time. However, attendance should improve after the cotton is in.

"We do encourage our teachers to make frequent contact with parents and to complete a round of home visits by the end of the first quarter of school."

"How many teachers are on staff?"

"We currently have five teachers. Miss Downey instructs the first and second graders, Miss Posey the third and fourth, and you will be with the fifth and sixth graders. Mr. Larke and I instruct the high school students. He teaches the core subjects, and I teach Latin to the advanced students, as well as act as principal. All of the elementary classes are on the first floor of the building, and the high school is on the second floor.

"When I hold the tenth-grade recitations in Latin in the afternoon and Mr. Larke instructs the ninth graders in advanced grammar, we will divide the seventh and eighth graders among the elementary teachers and send them to you during that time. They can help the younger children with their studies and assist you as needed.

"The eighth graders assigned to you include Charles Barton, who as you have no doubt already learned, is an extremely mature young man. You will also have Tom Givens, who is the antithesis of Charles and can be a bit of a bully. You will need to watch him closely. The other students are girls—Prudence White, Susanna McCall, and Virginia Long. They are all quite docile and pleasant young ladies, eager to help and not difficult to manage. As I mentioned, Tom Givens is one to watch out for."

"That is certainly good to know."

"Yes, forewarned is forearmed, I always say." Reverend Fitts straightened the edges of the contract and inserted it into a manila folder. "It is always helpful to know what to expect so that you can be in control of the situation. Now, if you have no further questions, I suppose that will be all."

Hattie left Reverend Fitts's office and went to her room, which was directly down the hall. Charles had already unloaded her books onto the teacher's desk and was straightening the student desks, arranged tombstone style—five rows, six deep, with aisles between. Hattie set down the small vase she had brought with her and made a mental note to cut a bunch of gardenias from the yard at the Bartons' estate to bring with her Tuesday to add color and a nice fragrance to the room. She remembered how stuffy a class full of the warm bodies of growing children could become, especially as the day heated up.

Charles helped her wash the blackboard mounted on the wall behind the desk and gave the three erasers on the chalk tray a good dusting. Hattie took two unused pieces of chalk from the drawer and laid them on the chalk tray. With one piece, she printed *Miss Hattie Robinson* in bold letters and wrote *Grades 5 and 6* beneath it and added *WELCOME*. To the right of her name, she posted the schedule for the first day of school. A surge of pride ran through her at seeing her name written there. It seemed to announce that she had claimed the room as her space and that she would be in charge of her small realm.

Satisfied with the appearance of the room, Hattie said to Charles, "I think we have done everything we can to prepare. I see that Miss Ryan stored the textbooks on the shelves. We will have to wait until the students arrive to determine which ones to issue. I have been thinking about the young girl you pointed out on the way to the school...Pauline, I believe you said her name was?"

"Yes, ma'am. Pauline Jeter."

"Would you mind to drive us by her house on the way home? I'd like to introduce myself to her parents and encourage them to see that she is at school on Tuesday." Charles's eyes lit up. She could tell by his eager response that he liked Pauline.

"No, ma'am. I'd be happy to. Her papa will probably be in the fields, but you can talk to her mama. She's very nice. Mr. Jeter can be kinda gruff, and I don't know as you want to be around him anyway. He doesn't much take to strangers coming around their place." Charles cleared his throat and spoke with resolve. "'Course, if he does show up, I will be there to make sure he treats you right and doesn't say anything disrespectful."

Hattie smiled. "Thank you, Charles. I feel real safe with you around to protect me. But Mr. Jeter certainly should not mind his child's teacher paying a visit."

Hattie closed the door to the classroom and saw Reverend Fitts was coming out of his office. He waved and called out, "Be sure to get some rest over the next few days. Tuesday will be a big day."

The chill of anticipation over her first day of teaching created a familiar churning sensation in Hattie's stomach. It had been a long time since these feelings were associated with something other than the memory of Will.

Charles nudged Boots out from under the shade tree and down the road that they had taken earlier. Puffs of dust rose from the horse's hooves as they pulled off the main road and onto the path that led to the Jeters' house. The late-afternoon sun had slipped behind the pines and was casting shadows over the field where three male figures were crouched, gathering the cotton fiber bulging from its pods.

Charles hitched the horse and caught up with Hattie, who was making her way across the clay yard covered in patches of crabgrass. The door to the house stood ajar to catch the faint breeze. A young, slender, barefoot girl had spotted the two outside and came onto the stoop to greet them. She brightened when she saw Charles.

"Hey, Pauline," Charles called out. "This is Miss Robinson. She's the new teacher for the fifth and sixth grade."

The girl had an eager smile and intelligent eyes. "Howdy, Miss Robinson."

"Hello, Pauline. Charles was telling me about how well you did last year and how you caught up with all your studies, even having to be out so much."

"Yes, ma'am. But I couldn't have done it if Charles hadn't of helped me so much when he came down to Miss Posey's class during tenth-grade recitation. Y'all come on in, and I'll get Mama. She will be so pleased you are here."

They stepped into the tiny front room, which was neat, clean, and sparsely furnished with wooden chairs and a rocker grouped around a rough stone fireplace. Pauline disappeared through a door leading to the bedroom and returned with an anemic-looking woman carrying a round-faced, robust baby boy. The angular face and pale lips of the mother, whose strands of graying hair escaped from a loosely knotted bun at the nape of her neck, contrasted with the pink, glowing roundness of the baby's cheeks and limbs. The scene reminded Hattie of a portrait in which the artist had lavished color on the image of the child and used up the pigment before completing that of the mother. Hattie was glad to see that the child looked healthy, as she had read that a large percentage of farmers and mill operatives in South Carolina suffered from malnutrition. This baby appeared to be thriving, though she could not say the same for the mother.

Pauline introduced her mother and Hattie extended her hand and told Mrs. Jeter the reason for the visit. "I am so pleased that Pauline will be in my class this year and I hope that she can be there on the first day."

"Yes, ma'am. I hope so, too." Mrs. Jeter struggled to talk and breathe simultaneously, her vocal cords emitting a faint wheezing sound as she sucked the air into her mouth.

"She had to miss a lot last year after I had such a hard time with little Clydie and couldn't work or care for him. I'm feeling better now and I think I can manage without her, but her papa is not so convinced about that."

"I had hoped to meet Mr. Jeter myself, but I see they are still working out in the field. I know they are trying to take advantage of every minute of daylight. Please tell him I'm sorry I missed him. Good-bye now, and Pauline, I will look forward to seeing you on Tuesday."

As they headed toward the wagon, Charles pointed out Mr. Jeter, who was coming from the field in the direction of the house. Hattie hurried to meet him at the edge of the yard. A burly man with freckled skin and yellow hair, he stood there, soaked from the heat and hard labor, carrying a hoe that doubled as a walking stick. Hattie shaded her eyes from the angle of the sun and introduced herself.

"I do so want Pauline to be in school Tuesday, Mr. Jeter. It is important that she get her books and get off to a strong start."

"Well, I reckon we will try to let her go, if she's not needed here at home. Her mama says she can handle things without her and she's been nagging me all summer to free her up to go back to school. But I'll be honest with you, Miss Robinson, if the price of cotton doesn't go any higher than it looks like it's going to, we gonna lose this house and we gonna all hafta go on at the mill—Pauline included."

Hattie was appalled. "Oh, surely not, Mr. Jeter. Pauline is way too young to take a shift at the mill."

"She just turned ten and is of a legal age to work. If her mama can't get work, she'll have to help out."

"It may be legal, but it's just not right. Besides, there is a bill before the legislature to extend the employment age from ten to twelve, as well as a strong movement across the state to make school attendance compulsory. I believe that both initiatives will eventually become law."

Instantly, Jeter's hackles went up. His jaw flexed, and he raised his index finger to within an inch of Hattie's nose. "I hope to God you're wrong about that, Miss Robinson." The sour smell of perspiration mingled with the scent of alcohol, and she could see the outline of a flask in his hip pocket. He raised his upper lip and bared his teeth like an old cur staring down a possum. Hattie stood tall and met his gaze, resisting the urge to step away.

He continued, "The state ain't got no business interfering with family matters. A man is the head of his household and he has to decide what is right for his wife and children—not some agent of the gov'ment."

Hattie could see that she was losing her case and remembered her mother's advice about attracting more flies with honey. She took a step back but did not lower her gaze.

"I apologize, Mr. Jeter, if I have overstepped my bounds. I was not in any way challenging your authority. But you see, I have heard how bright Pauline is and I do so want her to learn to read and write and be able to do basic numbers. Won't you please just let her come to school on Tuesday so I can issue her books and get her started? Then, if she must be out, I'll be happy to tutor her or have Charles work with her."

Clyde Jeter relaxed his jaw. "I'll do the best I can, Miss Robinson. I want Pauline to learn to write her name and read the Bible."

"You are a generous and fair-minded man, Mr. Jeter, just like Charles said you were." Charles gave a start. "Isn't that right, Charles?"

Charles seemed about to contradict her, but must have caught on just in time and nodded in agreement. "Yes, ma'am. I was just saying that on the ride over."

Mr. Jeter's chest puffed a bit at the compliment; however, he retained his contentious tone. "I'll send her to school on Tuesday, but mind you, I don't want anybody putting ideas in her head that she can git educated much beyond the basics. We ain't privileged like the Barton family and we got to work hard to make it."

Hattie bristled at Mr. Jeter's comment about privilege and wanted to argue that Pauline deserved an education as much as anyone. Better judgment convinced her to quit while she was ahead. "Thank you, Mr. Jeter. All I ask for now is that you let her come to school on Tuesday."

Charles helped Hattie into the wagon and climbed in on the other side. Old Boots was ready for her oats and needed little prompting to begin the short ride home. As they pulled off, Charles called out to Pauline, who was standing in the doorway.

"See ya' Tuesday, Pauline."

"Gracious! That man is going to be trouble," exclaimed Hattie. "I hope all of my parents aren't that hard to deal with."

5

Over the Labor Day weekend, Hattie met a number of the townspeople. On Sunday, while the Bartons attended the Methodist church, Hattie attended the Baptist church. Earline Greer, the pastor's wife, had already called at the Bartons' and had invited Hattie to sit with her and the children and to attend a dinner on the grounds afterward. Martha Greer, their eldest daughter, was Charles's age, and Mary Greer would be in Hattie's class. Earline had grown up in Greenville and her husband Thomas had attended Southern Seminary with Hattie's Uncle Rufus.

Labor Day marked the official end of summer vacation and the Bartons invited Hattie to celebrate with them by attending the Calhoun Labor Day parade, followed by dinner on the square, provided through the combined efforts of the three town churches. The local politicians were on hand to press the flesh and campaign. Incumbent governor Frederick Ansel, upcountry attorney from Greenville, was seeking reelection on a progressive platform supporting a strong system of public education. Hattie had learned that the Bartons were big supporters of Governor Ansel and that Charles Barton was the chairman of the Pickens County Democrats.

School would begin the next day and Hattie hardly slept for thinking about it. She wanted desperately to start the year off right. After she tossed endlessly throughout the night, dawn finally broke, and she got up, washed and dressed in her white blouse and navy skirt, and joined the Barton family for breakfast. Mr. Barton would drop them all off at school in his car before he went to work so that Hattie would be there early to greet the students and Charles Jr. could walk Gene to his class and get him situated.

Georgia, Elizabeth, and Richard followed them outside to see them off. Elizabeth doted on all of the boys and hugged Gene for an extralong time before she finally let him go. Hattie was certain that royalty would not have received a better send-off than this and she thought about Pauline Jeter and wondered how she was faring and if she would be at school.

It was a cool morning, typical of early September in Piedmont, South Carolina, and Hattie was comfortable in her long-sleeve blouse. By noon, the temperature would rise and she would likely wish she had worn something lighter.

They were among the first to arrive at the school. Hattie thanked Mr. Barton for driving her and hurried into the building to her classroom. The school yard was abuzz with children greeting one another as they returned from summer vacation.

At eight o'clock, the bell rang, and Hattie took up her post at the door to greet her students as they filed through. George was the first to enter. He was wearing a new plaid shirt, his hair neatly combed and parted in the middle. He grinned at Hattie and gave her a thumbs-up. "Hey, Miss Robinson. We got Gene to his classroom, and he was doing okay."

"That's a relief, George. You can sit in the sixth-grade rows over there on the right. I'll assign seats later on when we see how many are here." Four more sixth-grade boys arrived, and Hattie greeted them and directed them to the area where George was sitting.

Mary Greer came in with three of her fifth-grade friends, whom Hattie had met at the church. "Hey, Miss Robinson." Mary's voice was cheerful, like a small, chirping bird. "You remember Jenny Buice and Sarah Pendleton and Frannie Martin? They were at church Sunday." Hattie could already tell that Mary had her mother's outgoing personality and natural leadership abilities.

"Yes, I do. Young ladies, you may sit in the fifth-grade rows over on the left side of the classroom." Hattie stood at the door with her roll book and asked each student to identify him or herself as they entered. Four more sixth grade girls, followed by three fifth grade boys entered in rapid succession.

George had spotted Pauline Jeter through the window and was waving his arm at Hattie to alert her. Hattie gave Pauline a little hug when she came in and walked her to her seat. Pauline had on a white pinafore over a faded, threadbare pale blue frock, which she had no doubt washed and pressed herself. Pauline blushed, and Hattie could not tell if was from being singled out, from excitement, or a little bit of both.

With the students settled in their seats, Hattie let out her breath and felt the nervous tension dissipate. The eager young faces staring back at her looked for all the world like her younger siblings and cousins, whom she had minded and cared for back at home. The familiarity both comforted and empowered her.

She called the roll and marked attendance. Ten fifth graders, five boys and five girls, and seven sixth graders, four girls and three boys. The students were able to tell Hattie the whereabouts of most of the absentees. They said that Becky and Billy Jackson's mama had remarried, and the family had moved to Gaffney over the summer. Hattie marked their names off the list. Somebody reported that Julian Clinkscales had gotten a bad case of poison ivy when he went blackberry picking for his grandmother and he could not stand to wear his shoes and would not be back until he could. Penny Chambers's grandfather had died, and the family was in Columbia attending the funeral. She would be back next week. Hattie made a note to send a sympathy card. The students said they knew for a fact that all six of the Tucker children and the four Gibson children who were of school age would be helping with the cotton until it was harvested. Lula Tucker and Ben Gibson were both on the sixth-grade roll.

Mary Greer said she'd heard somebody at church say that Edward Marks's father had been hired at Calhoun Mill and that—since

Edward had turned ten—he would be working a shift over there, too. Jenny Buice came up and whispered to Hattie that Mabel Parker's mother had died during the delivery of their first baby brother. The baby had lived only a week, and Mr. Parker was so upset that Mabel's grandmother had come to get Mabel and her little sister, Peggy, to go and live with her in Greenville for a while.

Jenny grew tearful as she talked and Hattie put an arm around her in comfort, promising that the whole class would write sympathy notes to Janie as soon as they could get her address in Greenville.

Hattie marked the names of the children who were absent so that she could schedule time to do home visits. She would begin with Edward Marks. After her success with Pauline's father, she hoped she would be able to talk Edward's father into letting him come to school, too. She did not want to lose him to the mill. After reviewing the class rules, Hattie sent George to the office to report the daily enrollment to Reverend Fitts.

The remainder of the day was consumed with assessing the students in their reading and math skills and issuing their books. Hattie called each child to her desk to read a passage to determine which book to issue. When she had an idea of the students' reading proficiencies, she sent them one by one to the board to write the multiplication tables up to five. She was pleased that most of them knew their math facts and jotted down the names of the few who would need extra review. The children received a thirty-minute recess in the morning and an hour for lunch from noon to one o'clock. The day was fair, and Hattie let them go outside to eat their lunches and exercise.

In the afternoon, the high school students came down—Charles, Tom Givens, Prudence White, Susanna McCall, and Virginia Long. With almost one-third of the class out, there were plenty of desks for them. It was a good thing, too. She had hoped to form her own opinion of Tom Givens, but she had to admit that Reverend Fitts had been right to warn her about his behavior.

Right away, he began picking at the younger children and causing a stir. He seemed to have a knack for noticing the frailties of others and took pleasure in publicizing them. He saw the worn spots on Pauline's dress and began taunting her about it. "How'd you tear your dress, Pauline?" Hattie saw Pauline's humiliation and moved Tom across the room to a desk at the end of the back row.

When the bell rang at four p.m., Hattie had the children stand by their desks while she reviewed their assignments—practice spelling words and multiplication tables. She stood at the door and dismissed them for the day, calling each child's name and reminding each one to be prompt and prepared the next day.

After they had gone, she sank into the chair at her desk, limp with exhaustion from the rigor of her first day of instruction in unfamiliar surroundings with unfamiliar faces. But her spirit was light, and she basked momentarily in having met the challenge. As she gazed out the open window at the children emptying into the school yard to meet with their friends and siblings for the walk home, she heard a voice below the window that attracted her attention.

"Hey there, little Genie. Whacha doing hiding over there in the corner?"

"Nothing. I'm just waiting for George and Charles to come out."

"Well, come on out here so they can see you. Whoa. What have we here? Your crotch is all wet. Looks like little Genie may have gone and wet his pants. What's the matter, couldn't you hold it on your first day of school?"

"I did not! I was getting me a drink of water, and it spilled down my front."

"That's a likely story. But, you see, I don't buy it. I think little Genie Weenie is still a baby and he needs a diaper. Isn't that right, little Genie? You betta' get your mama to send you in a diaper tomorrow."

Hattie's heart caught in her throat. Gene's first day of school and he had been confronted already by a bully. She hurried to the window in time to see Tom Givens run off laughing as Charles and George approached. George threw a protective arm around Gene's shoulder, and Charles bent down to wipe his tears. As the brothers headed toward home, she heard Charles say, "Don't you worry, Gene. If Tom Givens ever does that again, I'll whip his ass!"

Charles's face reddened when Hattie called out to him through the window, "That won't be necessary, Charles. I will take care of Tom Givens myself. You boys go on home, and I'll see you tonight at dinner." Hattie was determined to show Tom that his bullying behavior would not be tolerated in her class. She did not know precisely what she would do, but she was already hatching a plan.

Reverend Fitts called a teachers' meeting in the library after school to review the enrollment numbers and to determine the need for additional books and supplies. The room was adjacent to his office. The collection of library books that Hattie had been told were furnished primarily through funds raised by the community, were shelved along three of the four walls. The space surrounding the bare wall at the end provided an ample area to hold school and community events and meetings.

Reverend Fitts had set up the room with a lectern facing a semicircle of chairs. It amused Hattie that, with only four other adults present, he stood erect before them as if they were a multitude and presided over the meeting like he would conduct Sunday morning worship.

"As the first item on the agenda, I am pleased to formally introduce Miss Hattie Robinson, though some of you have no doubt already met her. Miss Robinson will take over the fifth-and sixth-grade class previously taught by Miss Ryan. As you all know, Miss Ryan was married in June to Mr. Ralph Sanderson, and they are living with his parents in Dacusville until they can find a suitable home of their own. Please stand, Miss Robinson." Hattie stood self-consciously, nodded to the other three and quickly sat down.

"Miss Robinson is a recent graduate of Greenville Female College. She completed the requirements for the licentiate of instruction, with honors, and comes to us with the strong endorsement of Miss Mary Camilla Judson, the dean of the college."

In unison, the other three teachers said, "Welcome," and gave Hattie a round of applause. But Hattie noticed that Mary Posey pursed her lips and cut her eyes over at Miss Downey. It was a hateful look, and Hattie could not imagine how Mary could have formed a judgment of her, since they had only recently met.

"I am, as you know, the Reverend James Paul Fitts, pastor at Calhoun Methodist Church. I will continue to teach Latin to the advanced students as well as act as principal until such time as a replacement can be found for Mr. Jasper, who left in the middle of last session to accept a position in Georgia. To my right is Mr. Chester Larke, who will instruct the high school students in all other subjects but Latin. We two make up the high school staff."

Hattie found the formalities redundant, since she had already met Chester at church the previous Sunday and everyone else already knew him. But she supposed Reverend Fitts had no way of knowing that, since he would have been at the Methodist church and she at the Baptist. Chester, a sturdily built man in his forties, was a career teacher who had taught at Calhoun School for years. His wife, Betty, played the organ at the Baptist church and Hattie had learned that Betty was in great demand as a piano teacher. The two of them managed a small farm north of Calhoun. With the farm, his teaching, and her income from taking in students, they could patch together an adequate living to support their family.

Chester had settled back in his seat. Hattie knew that managing a farm meant Chester had to complete the farm chores before driving into town to meet his students. The long day and the heat of the afternoon sun beaming through the window must have caused him to nod off, and his head snapped forward when he heard his name called. Chester blinked his eyes and straightened up in an attempt to appear alert. Oblivious to the hour and the conditions, Reverend Fitts soldiered on.

"I am pleased to introduce Miss Susan Downey, who has returned for a third year to teach the first and second graders. She is a fine teacher and has had great success with our younger students." Miss

Downey beamed at Reverend Fitts and stood up modestly to be recognized. Susan had peeked in to Hattie's classroom before the morning tardy bell rang to wish Hattie luck on her first day.

"I'm so excited, but I have the nervous jitters," Hattie had confessed.

"I know you are anxious, but take it from me, all that will pass. My first day of teaching, I had so many butterflies in my stomach that I thought I was going to take flight. Once the children came in, I realized that they were just as nervous as I was, and I began to relax. You'll do fine on your own, but if you ever need any encouragement, I'm always here."

Hattie had told Susan about Gene being in her first-grade class and asked her to look out for him. Susan was a beautiful, plump, doe-eyed woman with a gentle voice and a sweet manner. Hattie was optimistic that Gene Barton would thrive under her nurturing ways.

"And Miss Mary Posey, who returns for a second year of teaching third and fourth graders. We are so fortunate to have her back after a splendid first year. Miss Posey is also a distinguished alumna of Greenville Female College, having earned her licentiate of instruction two years prior to Miss Robinson." Mary's nervous giggle in response to the compliment ended with a little snort, and she clapped her hand over her mouth to suppress it.

She was tall and willowy with auburn hair and pale blue eyes. Susan patted her on the arm and smiled. They were obviously friends, but based on first impression, Susan would be the more likely of the two with whom Hattie might form a friendship. Hattie reminded herself that she was jumping to conclusions. Sometimes in a new situation, the people you were drawn to initially did not turn out to be your best friends, and the ones whom you had doubts about did.

It would certainly be nice if she and Mary could get along. After all, they had the most in common. Both had graduated from Greenville Female College, both were relatively new to teaching, and both would be working with the older elementary students. Well, it was only the first day of school. "Let it be and give the dough time to rise" had been Mama's advice when Hattie had tried to rush things. Still, Hattie was bothered by Mary's reaction.

With the introductions complete, Reverend Fitts moved to the next item, which was attendance. He reminded them that their funding depended on the number of students present and encouraged them to begin making home visits and to do whatever they could to increase enrollment.

It was after five thirty when Reverend Fitts finally adjourned the meeting, postponing discussion of the fall festival, the last item on the agenda. It had been a full day, and Hattie was anxious to close her room and get back to the Bartons'. She was gathering up her things when Susan walked by and tapped her on the shoulder. "See you tomorrow."

Mary Posey rose abruptly and made a beeline for Reverend Fitts. "If I could just speak with you alone for a moment..." Reverend Fitts disregarded her and broke away to say good-bye to Hattie and to remind Mr. Larke of an appointment they had with a trustee of the high school. Only then did he turn to see what Miss Posey wanted. Mary raised her eyebrows and sighed in annoyance. She pressed her lips together and glared in Hattie's direction. Mary's look was even more withering than the one she had directed toward Susan Downey earlier. Their eyes met, and Mary's expression changed to embarrassment at having been caught. *Did she think I was blind and would not notice that dreadful grimace?* Hattie thought. She responded with an embarrassed smile and a nervous wave before she turned and left the library. She was stung by Mary's actions and clueless as to what had prompted them.

Hattie had encountered one new situation after the other, and the events of the day had piled up like jackstraws, ready to tumble. An overwhelming sense of melancholy and loss overcame her. She was only twenty miles from Greenville, but it might as well have been halfway around the world, she felt so far from home. Suddenly she longed for the familiar and the known. She missed Mama and her aunts and her sisters and brothers. And, oh, she missed Papa. And Will. For the past two years, she had grown accustomed to sharing every detail of her life with him. Will had listened intently to everything she told him, empathizing with her troubles and rejoicing in her successes. He would have loved to hear about her first day of school and would have known just what to suggest to help her deal with Tom Givens and with her hurt over Mary Posey.

Fighting back tears, she hurried out of the building and walked briskly back toward the Bartons'. She could always call Mama, even if it would be long-distance and she would have to reverse the charges. But in the state she was in, she might fall apart when she heard Mama's voice. She was determined to wait until she got over her homesickness and could talk to everyone without breaking down. She hoped that her first day was not typical of what was to come. If it were, she would never make it through the year.

6

T he exertion from the brisk walk soothed Hattie's nerves, and
by the time she reached the Bartons', she had calmed down
and was feeling better.

Now that school was back in session, Georgia served dinner to the
children early so that they could finish their studies and get plenty of
rest for the next day. Elizabeth planned to eat with Mr. Barton when
he got home later on and she invited Hattie to join them. She was eager to know how Hattie had fared on her first day and was especially
anxious to glean whatever information she could about Gene.

Hattie filled in Elizabeth on the incident with Tom Givens and
assured her that she would handle it.

"Bless his precious little heart! His first day and he encounters the
school bully. Oh, Hattie, do I need to get Charles to have a word with
Reverend Fitts? We simply must nip this in the bud. I won't have my
darling child harassed in such a way.

"I know Tom Givens's mother, Lila, quite well. She and Judge
Givens attend our church and I've served on a number of committees with her. You know, the Givenses already had children who were
grown and married when Tom came along. I expect it was quite a
shock for them to have one in the nursery again after so many years
of just the two of them in that big house. I'm not sure how involved
the judge is with Tom's rearing, as busy as he is. But Lila is a lovely

person, and I am sure she has no idea her son has been unkind to Gene. I could pay her a visit and talk with her—mother to mother."

"No, Mrs. Barton, I really do not think that would be best. In fact, it might make things worse for Gene if you did and it got back to Tom. Tom needs a dose of his own medicine, and I think I know how to ensure that he gets it. Just give me a day or two to take care of it before you or Mr. Barton intervene."

"All right then. I'll trust you to handle it. In the meantime, I'm not going to discuss it with Charles for fear that I would not be able to dissuade him from taking things into his own hands. He may be a bit hard on the children, but he can be fiercely protective of them, especially if the threat comes from outside the family circle."

"I met Gene's teacher, Susan Downey, and I don't think you could wish for anyone more perfect to work with young children. I will let her know what happened to Gene today. I am certain that she will look out for him."

"Oh, Hattie. I knew it was our lucky day when you came to live with us. But, honey, you look exhausted. Do you want Georgia to fix you a plate with the boys so you can get to bed early? She'll be serving them in a few minutes."

"Yes, ma'am. I hate to admit it, but I think that would be a good idea. I wouldn't be very good company for you and Mr. Barton tonight."

The surge of homesickness that had come on her earlier receded as she ate with the Barton boys and talked about the first day of school. As they finished the meal, Georgia brought in dishes of blackberry cobbler, hot from the oven.

"Will we have science tomorrow, Miss Robinson?" asked George, his teeth already purple from cobbler. "That's my very favorite subject."

"Yes," Hattie said. "We will finish reviewing the rules and complete the reading and math assessments in the morning. We will definitely make time for science after lunch."

"What will we be studying?"

"Well, I have a little experiment in mind that I think will interest you."

"Can't you tell us what it is?"

"No. If you knew ahead of time, it would compromise the validity of the data."

"Huh? I don't understand."

"Don't worry, George. When you observe with your own eyes, everything will be much clearer. That is why experiments can be so helpful."

"I guess Miss Robinson means a picture is worth a thousand words," added Charles.

"Something like that," responded Hattie. "Now if y'all will excuse me, I am going to gather up a few things and get ready for tomorrow." Once in her room, Hattie closed the door and threw off her clothes. She collapsed into bed and slept soundly until morning.

A brand-new day brought renewed perspective, and Hattie woke up refreshed and ready to start again. She left early for school, lugging a bag of materials she had gathered from the flower shed to use in the fifth-grade science lesson—two mason jars filled with dirt and pebbles, an old metal pitcher, and several jonquil bulbs. When she arrived at school, she filled the pitcher with water and stored it, along with the other materials, in the cabinet in the cloakroom. Afterward, she dropped by Susan Downey's room to give her a heads up about Gene and the incident with Tom Givens.

"Oh, that boy!" exclaimed Susan. "He can be so mean. Nothing seems to faze him."

"Mrs. Barton says she has served with his mother on several committees at the church and could talk with her, but I told her I'd handle it."

"Well, you told her right, Hattie. Mrs. Givens is an amazing woman. She has helped to raise the money for over half the books in our collection. But she has a blind spot when it comes to that child of hers and makes excuses every time he gets into trouble. It would do no good to talk to her. I'll keep my eye on Gene and make sure Tom stays away from him. Please tell Mrs. Barton that she has nothing to worry about. He is safe with me."

"Thanks, Susan." Hattie was dying to ask Susan about Mary Posey. She dismissed the thought and started for the door, where she stopped and reconsidered. Turning back around, she said, "Susan, I may be overly sensitive, but I got the distinct impression at the faculty meeting yesterday that Mary Posey does not approve of me one bit. She has been very standoffish, and I hate it, because we have so much in common. I'm teaching the children she had last year, and I'd love to have her advice about them."

Susan shook her head and smiled. "Oh, Hattie. Can't you see it?"

"See what?"

"Mary is jealous of you."

"Jealous? What in the world for?"

"Well, I shouldn't tell you, but it is just so obvious. Mary has a terrible crush on Reverend Fitts and she regards you as an interloper."

Hattie was incredulous. "Reverend Fitts? Oh heavens. He's not at all my type. He's so straitlaced and serious. Besides, I assumed that he was already married."

"Oh no. It is not for want of trying, though. The word is that he is infatuated with a woman who teaches up in Durham. He holds out hope that she will marry him; however, she is dedicated to her teaching and simply won't consider pulling up and following him around the Methodist circuit. Meanwhile, every eligible woman in the church has her cap set for him and would gladly follow him anywhere. Mary is chief among his suitors and she guards him like a watchdog from any perceived competition. She did that with Rita Ryan until she found out that Ralph Sanderson was in the picture, and then the two of them became the best of friends."

"Well, my goodness. She certainly does not have any competition from me." Hattie blinked back tears and her voice came out like that of a defensive child. She had been determined not to speak publicly of her past with Will, at least until she could put her grief to rest in private. But Mary's assumption that she was after Reverend Fitts brought all of those feelings to the surface. "I haven't told anybody this, but the reason I am even here in Calhoun is that I am getting over a broken engagement. The last thing I am thinking about right now is a man, especially Reverend Fitts."

"Hattie! I had no idea." Susan stretched out her arms to gather Hattie in, but Hattie straightened and backed away.

"Oh, Susan, I did not tell you that to drum up sympathy, only to make the point that I am no threat to Mary. But what about you? You are single and you are simply beautiful. Mary does not seem to be threatened by you."

Susan smiled wistfully. "Oh, she knows I'm not looking to marry. There is so much baggage that comes with me that it would be a very special type of man who would want to take me on."

"What do you mean?"

"Well, I have a sister, Marie, who is now a grown woman, but she has the mind of a little child. Mama was very ill during her pregnancy. Marie was born prematurely and there were complications at her birth. In fact, both Mama and Marie almost died. Although they both survived, Marie did not develop as a normal child, and Mama never fully regained her health and stamina. Marie was late walking and talking, and as her peers grew, she trailed farther and farther behind them. She will always need help in dressing, feeding, and caring for herself."

"Oh, Susan, I did not know." Hattie looked at her with empathy, but it was clear from her expression that Susan did not desire Hattie's pity any more than Hattie had wanted hers. She smiled, gently waved Hattie off, and continued.

"I suppose Marie is the reason I became interested in teaching young elementary children. They remind me so much of her. Except they grow up and move on, and Marie stays the same. Lord knows I have already had years of experience with children from having cared for her. My brothers and sisters were nearly grown when she came along, and it fell to me to help Mama with her.

"Neither Mama nor Papa is in good health, and after I graduated from Columbia Female College three years ago, I moved back home to be with them and help out. That's when I took this job. I have accepted that I will be the one to care for Marie when they are gone. Besides, I love her dearly and could never think about being separated from her. I don't suppose there are many men who would want to walk into that situation."

Hattie was struggling for the right words with which to respond when Susan said, "Enough about me. Hattie, I think your problem with Mary can be solved if a little bird tips her off that you don't have designs on Reverend Fitts."

The first bell rang, signaling for the children to go to class. "My goodness, look at the time," Susan said. "Now you go figure out how to deal with Tom Givens in a way that will not arouse Mama Bear Givens. I will keep Gene out of his path until you do. And I'll be a little bird and tweet a message to Mary. Be sure to tell Mrs. Barton that she does not have anything to worry about with Gene."

Hattie felt a surge of affection for this woman, whose inner beauty shone even more brightly than her outer beauty. Wanting to express her feelings, she squeezed Susan tightly before she hurried off to class, calling out, "Don't underestimate yourself, Susan. Any man would be lucky to have a woman like you."

Oh goodness! Hattie thought. *Did that sound patronizing? It certainly was not meant that way.*

Penny Chambers had come in from attending her grandfather's funeral, which increased the attendance in the sixth grade from ten to eleven. Fifth-grade enrollment remained at seven.

By the end of the morning, Hattie had finished reviewing the class rules and procedures, and she had gained a basic idea of each student's mastery of skills in reading and math. From that point on, they were ready to begin the daily schedule that they would follow for the remainder of the year:

8:00: Roll call and housekeeping details, Pledge of Allegiance
8:30–10:00: Reading and spelling

10:00–10:30: Recess
10:30–12:00: Math
12:00–1:00: Lunch
1:00–2:30: Social studies
2:30–3:45: Science
3:45–4:00: Copy assignments and dismissal

The morning sped by, and before Hattie realized it, time had come to dismiss the children for lunch. As much as they needed rain, she hoped that the dark clouds gathering in the distance would not bring moisture for a little while longer. Fortunately, the bad weather held off until they were back inside. They were finishing the social studies lesson when the high school children entered. On Tuesday, she had instructed them not to interrupt but to go directly to their seats and work on their assignments if she was in the middle of a lesson.

With the exception of Tom Givens, who took a detour by Mary Greer's desk to knock her book on the floor and noisily pick it up in mock gallantry, the others had followed her directions. Hattie made no comment but regarded Tom sternly and pointed to the desk she had assigned him. He dawdled for almost a minute before he followed her cue and sat.

Hattie instructed the fifth graders to copy and answer the science questions and the sixth graders to copy and answer the social studies questions, all of which she had posted on the board.

Turning to Tom, she said, "Tom Givens, I need you to come with me and help carry some materials back to the classroom for the science experiment." Tom gave a start at hearing his name and removed his feet from the seat of the empty desk on the row beside him. He stood up, stretched, and with an expression of superiority mixed with nonchalance, took his sweet time following Hattie to the cloakroom, rolling his eyes and sauntering behind her. He seemed to be calibrating the reaction of the other students, who laughed nervously at his insubordinate behavior. Hattie ignored the snickers and acted oblivious to Tom's antics.

She pulled open the cloakroom door and indicated for Tom to enter. "I've brought some bulbs from the Bartons' garden and I'm going to start a project with the fifth graders to plant them and force them to bloom. We need to carry these mason jars and the bulbs into the classroom. Tom, would you please gather the bulbs, the mason jars, and that large pitcher of water off the bottom shelf?"

Tom bent over and craned his neck slightly. "I see the bulbs and the mason jars, but I don't see the pitcher."

"It's there. Just have a closer look."

Tom let out a long sigh before he lowered himself lethargically to the floor with as much enthusiasm as if he had been given a pick and shovel and sent into a West Virginia coal mine to extract ore. There he paused to rest himself, his descent to the floor seemingly straining every muscle in his body. *What a thespian,* thought Hattie. *He should go on the stage with that act.*

Tom crossed his legs Indian-style, tilted his head parallel to the floor, and looked to see whether the pitcher had been pushed toward the back of the shelf.

"I still don't see it."

Tom was unwittingly playing into Hattie's plan and she could see that he had not the slightest clue what would come next. For a fleeting moment, as she looked down at the boy at her feet, she saw beyond the mask of the bully, and caught a glimpse of the insecure adolescent residing underneath. She felt guilty for taking advantage of Tom's vulnerability, but it was too late to turn back now. "Oh, I'm sorry. I was mistaken. It wasn't there at all. It is here on the top shelf."

Before Tom could get up, Hattie reached over him with her right arm and grasped the pitcher by its handle. Turning back toward Tom, still seated on the floor, she began lowering the pitcher to him. Before she could steady it with her left hand, it tipped, sending a stream of water from the spout directly into Tom's lap, soaking him to the skin and leaving a large, wet triangle over the crotch of his pants.

"Oh my goodness. How clumsy of me! Tom, here, let me help you up."

Tom sputtered in anger and turned crimson. "Why did you do that? You got me all wet! It looks like I wet my pants."

"Oh, no. It's barely noticeable. I am sorry, but you know that accidents do happen. That is, I don't mean that you had an accident. I mean I did. Go on back to the classroom, and I will clean up in here. Please put the mason jars and bulbs on my desk, and if anyone is off task, write his name on the board."

"I can't go back in there now!" he began to argue, but Hattie was equally adept at playing the role and was having none of it.

"Nonsense. You go ahead. You don't need to help me. The least I can do is clean up the mess I made. I would not want anyone to trip in this puddle of water and fall. Go on, Tom, and tell the class I will be back in just a minute."

Tom must have realized that it was futile to protest. He tried his best to cover himself with the bulbs and mason jars before he left the cloakroom. Hattie cleaned up the puddle of water and procrastinated a few minutes more, until she heard peals of laughter coming from the classroom.

Hattie felt another twinge of guilt for embarrassing Tom and rationalized that he really did need a dose of his own medicine. Besides, It would all be worth the effort if it taught him a bit of empathy for his classmates.

The news spread through Calhoun School like a match struck to fat kindling. The story of how Tom received his comeuppance was told and retold on the playground and the walk home from school and was a hot topic at the Barton dinner table that night. George and Charles, who were both firsthand witnesses in Hattie's classroom, seemed to revel in the opportunity to recount the incident to Elizabeth and Georgia down to the last detail.

"And he came back in the room, and his pants were dripping wet," began George, his face lit with excitement. "He tried to cover it up with the sack of bulbs and the mason jars, but his face was all red and gave him away. And…and…and everybody started laughing and pointing to his pants until he ducked back behind Miss Robinson's desk and hid. And…and…and Miss Robinson, she stayed back in the cloakroom for the longest time. It was like she knew what was going on."

Charles broke in. "You should have seen Miss Robinson. She finally came back in and tried to act serious, but you could tell she was tickled—weren't you, now, Miss Robinson? Be honest. You had to turn your head away and start writing on the board to keep from laughing. But I could see your shoulders just shaking."

Hattie laughed and confessed, "You got my number, Charles."

"You can see that my children have selective memory, Hattie," said Elizabeth, who seemed to thoroughly enjoy the story. "When I ask them about school, most days they can't remember a thing. But let something exciting like this happen, and they can recount every iota of it."

Gene was the one who must have savored the story the most. He had been avenged. "Tell it again, Charles. Tell how that mean old bully Tom got his come-upon-us."

Charles laughed. "You mean *comeuppance*."

George had the look of one who had just experienced an epiphany. "Miss Robinson, I think I understand now why you wouldn't tell me what the experiment was going to be about, why it would—what was it you said?"

"Compromise the validity of the data?"

"Yeah, that."

Hattie's stock with the Barton children had clearly risen because of the Tom Givens incident. From that point on, they treated her not so much as a boarder, but as a member of the family. She was amazed to discover that she had somehow managed to impress her fellow teachers as well.

On her way into the faculty meeting the next day, Chester Larke came up from behind. "Well, I am impressed, Miss Robinson! You handled Tom Givens like an old pro. That little shit—I mean, dickens—has been lectured, punished, and even beaten for his picking and bullying by every teacher in this school, to no avail. I declare I believe you have finally gotten his attention. When he came to class this morning, I did not have a minute's trouble out of him. Usually he manages to make at least one of the girls in the room cry before morning recess."

Susan Downey heard them talking and chimed in. "Hattie, you are the talk of the school. Your handling of Tom Givens was pure genius."

Mary Posey came in after the others were seated. Her mood had shifted from that of the last meeting. She grinned at Hattie and remarked playfully, "I wish you had been around last year when I had Tom Givens in my room and he was worrying the bejesus out of me. We need to get together and talk. I think we might make a good team. Let's start taking our classes outside together at lunch and we can plan while we watch them. I always take mine out around the big oak tree in the side yard. The girls like to huddle there, and the boys use the field beside it to play ball. I'll meet you out there tomorrow."

"Sure...okay..." Hattie stammered, incredulous, and then looked at Susan. Susan shrugged and made little fluttering gestures with her fingers.

"I've been a little birdie," she whispered in a high, tweeting voice.

Hattie's elation over her celebrated status came to an abrupt end when Reverend Fitts called for her to meet with him immediately after school the next day. When she arrived in his office, Lila Givens was seated across from his desk, her arms folded. She was wearing an annoyed expression. An extra chair had been pulled in from the library, and Reverend Fitts indicated for Hattie to take it.

"Miss Robinson, Mrs. Givens is here over a concern about an incident in your class two days ago that involved her son Tom."

Mrs. Givens, a stylishly dressed woman, had on a green crepe dress with complementing hat, gloves, and scarf. She had dropped by the school on her way home from a woman's club luncheon. "Tom says that he was humiliated before the class after you spilled water on his pants in the cloakroom and insisted that he return to the room. He is convinced that you spilled the water intentionally, although you told him it was an accident. Is it true? Did you spill it intentionally?"

Hattie gulped as Mrs. Givens's eyes bored into her on one side and Reverend Fitts's eyes bored into her on the other. She had never been so tempted to deny something in her life. But what kind of teacher would she be if she took the easy option and lied her way out of a difficult situation? Better to tell the truth.

"Yes, ma'am."

Reverend Fitts's eyes widened, and Mrs. Givens gasped. "Why on earth would you do such a thing? That's no way for a teacher to behave. You are supposed to encourage children, not humiliate them. My poor Tom was distraught when he came home. Why, the child could not even eat his dinner."

"I am sorry, Mrs. Givens. I was trying to teach Tom an object lesson about bullying. Tom often ridicules other students, and I felt he needed a dose of his own medicine to get the point about his behavior."

"Well, I don't believe my Tom would act that way, and even if he did, I do not approve of the way you handled things. Miss Ryan would never have done such a thing. I know this is your first year of teaching, and if this is some newfangled tactic you learned over at the Female College, I say you'd better go back to the old ways. I will not allow you to test out your new methods on my son."

Revered Fitts cleared his throat nervously. "Mrs. Givens, I must say that I am also a bit surprised that Miss Robinson chose to discipline Tom in such a manner. However, he can be difficult to manage even for our more experienced teachers. Why, Mr. Larke mentioned just the other day that when he handed a paper to Prudence White, marked with a C, Tom snatched it from her and began taunting her with it. Prudence, who is accustomed to receiving all As, cried inconsolably and interrupted instructional time for thirty minutes while Mr. Larke attempted to comfort her in the hallway."

"Well, Prudence White is far too sensitive and tends toward melodrama, but that is beside the point. The point is, Reverend Fitts, I am a dedicated parent who has spent untold hours raising money for this school to ensure that we have one of the best printed collections in the state. Unless this young woman is formally reprimanded and held accountable for any further breach of teaching ethics, my resignation as chair of the Calhoun School library committee will be on your desk in the morning and the judge and I will begin enrollment procedures for our son to attend the Easley Academy. Now, good day to both of you." Lila Givens clasped her silk purse in one hand and threw her scarf over her shoulder with the other before she stood and paraded out of the office, her scarf fluttering in the breeze generated from her departure.

Reverend Fitts had removed his glasses and was rubbing his eyes. "Oh my. It seems I have a challenge ahead in mending this relationship."

Hattie was indignant. "Reverend Fitts, did you hear her refer to this incident as a breach of teaching ethics? Why, I am nothing if not ethical. I could have lied to her and said that it was all an accident, but it was due to my strong sense of morals that I told the truth. And then she had the nerve to call me unethical anyway. Well, I won't have my reputation spoiled by a woman who makes excuses for her son, who is the biggest bully in school."

"Calm down, Miss Robinson, and give me a moment to sort this out."

Hattie immediately regretted lashing out, as it dawned on her that she might be about to receive a formal reprimand. She had no idea what that meant, but it sounded awful. She had never been reprimanded for anything in her life where school was concerned. In grade school she had always been the teacher's pet, the serious one, the one who always did the right thing. And in college it was the same. After all, she was the youngest one in her class to graduate, five months before her eighteenth birthday, with honors, no less, and she had been one of Dean Judson's most promising students. Now here she was in her first week of teaching, and she had already received a mark beside her name because some woman was in denial that her son was a bully. "Do you consider me unethical, Reverend Fitts?" she asked in a humbler tone than before.

Reverend Fitts sighed. "No, Miss Robinson. Unconventional, but not unethical. However, your approach with Tom created a real dilemma for me. Normally, I would support any teacher in providing a consequence for a student's infraction of the school behavior code. Clearly, Tom broke that code by harassing a younger student, and you were well within your authority to correct him. Although you achieved the intended result, which was to demonstrate to Tom how it feels to be bullied, you behaved a bit like a bully yourself in order to carry out the lesson. I do not believe that the end justifies the means, and thus, could not defend your actions to Mrs. Givens as much as I was tempted to, based on Tom's history."

Hattie's anger turned to contrition. "I didn't think about it like that. Do you want me to apologize to her or to Tom? I can even do that in front of the class, if you want me to."

"No, that would only reinforce Tom's behavior as well as Mrs. Givens's conviction that he can do no wrong."

"Do you expect me to ignore Tom's behavior?"

"Certainly not. I simply want you to use conventional consequences so that I can defend your actions in the future."

"What did Mrs. Givens mean by a formal reprimand?"

Reverend Fitts shook his head. "I don't know, Miss Robinson." Hattie could see that he was distracted and did not care to pursue her line of questioning. "I will need to pay a personal visit to Mrs. Givens and attempt to placate her. When she has a chance to cool off, she will probably reconsider her position. At least, I hope she will. It would be a huge financial loss for the school if she and the judge were to withdraw their support."

Checking his watch, he said, "If I leave now, I can get by her house before I have to be at church for the midweek service." He pushed back his chair and stood to leave, seemingly almost forgetting about

Hattie. "Oh yes, Miss Robinson. Would you be so kind as to pull the door shut and return the chair to the library so that I can get on my way? And we will need to meet again tomorrow morning to discuss the outcome."

"Yes, Reverend Fitts," she responded as he snatched up his briefcase and bolted out of the office.

Hattie sat there for a moment, feeling like a dethroned monarch. Just yesterday, she had soared among the heights, basking in the glow of approval from the Barton family and her fellow teachers. Now she was facing a formal reprimand and possible public rebuke. Dejectedly, she picked up the chair, closed the office door and headed for the library.

Too mortified to even consider discussing the day's events with the Bartons, she made her excuses at dinner and retired early to her room. When she finally dropped off to sleep that night, she dreamed that she was still sitting in the library chair in Reverend Fitts's office. Mrs. Givens, scarf fluttering behind her, followed by Reverend Fitts and the entire staff at Calhoun School, filed by her one by one. Each held a grading pencil and stopped to mark a giant red X on her forehead.

Hattie awoke, already dreading the day ahead, but pulled herself together in time to stop by Reverend Fitts's office before class. To her surprise, he welcomed her in, looking rested and much less agitated than when he had left her the day before. She was too nervous for small talk and began to question him at once.

"I'm afraid to ask, but how did things go with Mrs. Givens? Were you able to persuade her to change her mind?"

Reverend Fitts sat back in his chair, rubbed his hands together and looked at Hattie with a pleased expression. "As a matter of fact, things went quite well. I had very little persuading to do, as young Tom had already done the work for me before I arrived."

"Tom Givens?"

"Yes. It seems that as Mrs. Givens was leaving the building yesterday, she heard raucous laughter coming from behind the oak tree in the school yard. Recognizing at once that it was Tom's voice, she stopped to listen. Tom was bragging to Virginia Long that he had tricked his mother into thinking he had lost his appetite over being embarrassed in front of the class.

"He told Virginia, and I quote, 'I have her wrapped around my little finger and now she's coming up to the school to set that reverend-principal straight and she's probably gonna get Miss Robinson fired.'

"When I arrived at her home, Mrs. Givens met me at the door and told me at once how much she regretted her display in my office. She assured me that she would stay on as chair of the library committee and that she and her husband had no intention of moving Tom to another school. She added, 'The judge is emphatic about requiring Tom to face the consequences here at Calhoun School.'

"I did not have to use any of the arguments that I had prepared on my way over and was able to visit briefly and get to church in time to review my remarks for the midweek service."

"Oh, I'm so relieved to hear that. Now that she has seen Tom in action, does that mean she supports the way I corrected his behavior?"

"Well, I would not go that far, Miss Robinson. She still disapproves of your intentional humiliation of her son, but does not feel that your behavior requires a formal reprimand." The first tardy bell rang, and Reverend Fitts stood up. "Another day begins, Miss Robinson. Let's go out and see what new opportunities it will bring."

7

Hattie began her required visits to the homes of the students who had not yet shown up at school. Her first visit was to Edward Marks's parents. She hoped to dissuade them from allowing Edward to work at the mill. The Markses lived in town, in one of the frame houses bought up by the mill down on Banks Street, which turned directly off the square. She would stop by Julian Clinkscales's next to check on the progress of his poison ivy, as his home was only a few blocks away from Edward's and was on her way home as well.

She anticipated that she might meet with the same defensive attitude from Mr. Marks as she had from Clyde Jeter, and had carefully prepared her argument on the short walk over from school to their home.

A large, bearded man with a bulbous nose and wide-set eyes met her at the door and introduced himself as Edward Marks Sr. Hattie got right to the point of her visit. "School has been in session for over a week now, and I do so need for Edward to be in his place so that he will not get behind."

"Oh?" Edward's father cocked one bushy eyebrow in puzzlement. "I thought that Eddie was attending school."

"No," said Hattie. "He has not yet shown up. The children said that you had hired him out at the mill and that he was working a shift during school hours." Mr. Marks indicated for Hattie to come into the living room, which was simply furnished but colorfully decorated with chintz curtains and matching throw pillows.

"Well, I reckon that is partly true. We did allow Eddie to work as a doffer this summer to earn a little bit of his own spending money and to keep him busy. The boy gets into mischief when he is idle, you know. Now that I am a supervisor in the weaving room and my wife is working in the spinning room, we are both away from the house a lot. We don't object to him working over there after school and on holidays, near where we are to keep an eye on him. But we told him he had to stop at the end of the summer and go back to school. Mrs. Marks and I were only able to make it through the fourth grade and we want more for Eddie.

"The wife's been packing him a lunch, and he's been leaving the house about the same time the other kids in town come by on their way to school. He talked like he was joining them so they could all walk together. But I s'pose from what you say that the little dickens is playing hooky. I don't know where he is hanging out during school hours, because Mrs. Marks is down in her back and has been out of work for the past week and she has been right here."

Hattie had a thought. "Is Edward friends with Julian Clinkscales?"

"Yes, they are the best of friends. Why do you ask?"

"Well, Julian has not been to school yet either. The children reported that he has a bad case of poison ivy, but it has been over a week now, and he still has not come in."

Mr. Marks looked up, studied the ceiling and pulled at his beard. "Hmm. That's either one terrible case of poison ivy or one big excuse for laying out of school, and likely it's the latter," he said. "Julian lives with his grandmother, and she helps out at her nephew's dry goods store most days and wouldn't be there to check up on him. He spends a lot of time over here at our house, but, come to think of it, I have seen neither hide nor hair of him lately. My hunch is that there are two boys taking advantage of an ideal situation to hang out and play hooky over at Julian's."

"Well, I would not want to jump to conclusions, not knowing either of the boys, but it is something that bears looking into. I had planned to drop by Julian's house on the way home to see how he was doing and to meet his grandmother. I'll go ahead and do that now."

"That would be a good idea. I will wait right here for Eddie. He usually gets home about this time. And please tell Mrs. Clinkscales that if things are like I suspect, Eddie and I will be in touch with her. My son will have some explaining to do."

He shrugged apologetically and saw Hattie to the door. "Thank you for coming by, Miss Robinson. And don't you worry, Eddie Marks will be in school tomorrow, and if he is not there every day afterward, I want you to let me know."

"Thank you, Mr. Marks. It is refreshing to talk to a parent who values education as you do. And please feel free to come by my class and visit anytime you can. May I keep Edward after school a few days next week to help him catch up on what he has missed?"

"Oh yes, ma'am." Mr. Marks nodded emphatically. "You may have him anytime you like and keep him as long as you like. You take care now, Miss Robinson, and let us know if there is anything we can do to help."

Well, that was a pleasant surprise, thought Hattie. *I suppose it will teach me not to jump to conclusions about one parent based on my experience with another. And it seems that I will need to check my facts before I believe everything my students tell me.*

Hattie walked the short distance to the Clinkscales home, where she spotted a haggard-looking little woman with a wiry frame and a determined expression coming the other way. Hattie concluded that this was Mrs. Clinkscales returning from work, because the woman headed up the walkway and up the stairs to the porch, her eyes drilled to the ground in front of her. Hattie introduced herself to Mrs. Clinkscales before she entered the house and, right there on the stoop, told Mrs. Clinkscales of her suspicions.

"A Lord!" exclaimed Mrs. Clinkscales, throwing up her arms in exasperation. "That child has certainly taken me for the fool. I felt terrible when he broke out with all that poison ivy on his feet after I sent him out to pick blackberries. His toes swelled up like sausages, don't you know, and it itched him so. I let him stay out a day or two until it started to dry up and he could get his shoes on. Then, when it did, he commenced to complaining that he had got a host of chigger bites on his private parts—said they were driving him crazy they itched so bad—and he needed to stay out awhile longer."

Mrs. Clinkscales shook her head, continuing to talk nonstop even as she inhaled. "I should have had him drop his pants right then and let me see it with my own eyes, but you know how sensitive these growing boys are about their privates. I just took him at his word and let it go. You see if I ever do that again! And now I'm finding out that he has been playing hooky with that Edward Marks all this time, right here in this house.

"Juuuul-yun!" she yelled as she opened the front door. "You come here this minute and meet your teacher. Step on inside, Miss Robinson. Honestly, I do not need this. I raised four children on my own after the good Lord called my husband to glory when I was but a young thing myself. And then, when they was all finally grown and out of the house, my wayward daughter, who was living in Georgia with her husband, got saved by one of them snake-handling evangelists. She took Julian and left her husband to be with that so-called holy man. Don't you know that preacher wouldn't have anything to do with her boy, and she couldn't manage him, so you know what she did?"

"No," said Hattie. "What?"

Mrs. Clinkscales was talking as fast as a freight train running late and trying to make up lost time. "She bought a one-way ticket from Atlanta to Calhoun for that four-year-old child, pinned my name and address to his little jacket and left him on the train all by himself. Just shipped him to me like a piece of freight—only he traveled in the passenger car and not the baggage car." Mrs. Clinkscales closed her eyes and vigorously shook her head back and forth, as if to will away the memory of it.

What a bizarre story, thought Hattie. *I'm sure it must be true, because she could never have thought up anything that strange. But why is she telling me all of this?*

Mrs. Clinkscales pressed on. "They called me from the Calhoun depot and told me to come get him. What else could I do but take him in? I have raised him ever since."

Hattie was struggling to think of the right thing to say and re-membered Dean Judson's words: *"Some parents will unburden the most personal and outlandish family stories, simply because you are their child's teacher. You must develop built-in shock absorbers so as to accept what is told you without surprise. Your job is to be supportive and helpful, never to be judgmental."*

Hattie decided there was no time like the present to practice Dean Judson's advice. She reached out and touched Mrs. Clinkscales's arm sympathetically. "Well, thank heavens you *were* there to take him in. My goodness, if it were not for you, Julian might be an orphan." The comment seemed to appease Mrs. Clinkscales, who finally stopped talking to take a breath.

A small boy with unruly auburn hair entered the room, and Mrs. Clinkscales got revved up again. "There you are, Julian Clinkscales. I'm so mad at you right now, I can't see straight!"

"Wha'd I do, Granny?" Julian responded innocently, smoothing down the rooster tail sticking up on top of his head.

Mrs. Clinkscales stepped behind Julian and fastened a hand atop each of his shoulders. As she spoke, she pumped her arms downward as if she were trying to drive him into the floor. She was just enough taller than he to gain sufficient leverage to give Julian a good jarring.

"We'll get to that directly." *Pump, pump, pump, pump, pump.* "But first"—*pump, pump*—"you come over here and meet your teacher." *Pump, pump, pump, pump, pump, pump, pump.* She released Julian's shoulders and stepped away, leaving the poor boy as disoriented as a drunk who had just stumbled off a curb. Hattie's eyes widened, and her jaw dropped in amazement. She had not yet developed those shock absorbers mentioned by Dean Judson.

"Miss Robinson, you talk to him for a minute while I go compose myself. Honestly, I'm just too old and worn-out to deal with this."

Hattie closed her gaping mouth. "Take your time, Mrs. Clinkscales. Julian and I will chat until you come back." Mrs. Clinkscales left the parlor and made her way to her bedroom, where she closed the door, still mumbling to herself. Hattie was glad she was gone. She would rather deal with Julian alone. She might be at a loss for what to say to a parent, but she prided herself on being able to talk to children.

Julian appeared to have recovered his equilibrium and he was staring up at Hattie with an innocent smile.

"Hello, Julian. I don't think we have been properly introduced. I am Miss Robinson, your teacher. We have been missing you at school. The children ask about you every day, and we have all been hoping your poison ivy would improve enough for you to be able to join us."

"Yes, ma'am. It's getting better, but I also got bit by chiggers in my private parts." Julian reflexively folded his hands over his groin.

"That's what your grandmother said. I have been blackberry picking many times myself and I know about those chiggers! But here is the thing, Julian. You have not been staying home because of the chiggers, have you? You have been playing hooky with Edward Marks right here in this house."

Julian's eyes widened, confirming Hattie's suspicion. "Uh, well, Eddie did come over once," he admitted.

"He came over a lot more than once, didn't he? We are almost two weeks into school and neither you nor Edward has attended a single day. Edward has let everyone believe that he is working at the mill, everyone except for his father and mother, who believed he was at school. You have used your bout with poison ivy and then the chiggers to stay home. Both of you are guilty of deception and truancy. I should warn you, Julian, that Edward's father and your grandmother have put two and two together and they are both very upset about this."

Julian began to cry. "Oh, Miss Robinson, I'm so sorry. I'm in so much trouble. How am I ever going to get out of this?" He was a cute little rascal, and now that Hattie knew about his sad history of abandonment by his mother, she felt more like hugging him than scolding. However, she could not let him get by with truancy, and so she stifled a smile, put on her serious teacher face, and answered in her most serious teacher voice.

"First, you will dry your eyes and then you will do the only honorable thing there is to do. You will come clean with your grandmother and tell her how sorry you are for deceiving her. Then you will apologize to Mr. and Mrs. Marks for helping Edward deceive them."

Julian stared up at Hattie and nodded, his head keeping time to the beat of Hattie's words.

"You will show up bright and early at school tomorrow and you will be there every day afterward, unless you are ill, in which case you will bring me a note from your grandmother stating the nature of your illness. Furthermore, you and Edward will stay after school every day next week so that I can catch you up with the rest of the class. Can you promise to do that?"

"Yes…but the kids will all laugh and make fun of us when they find out we got caught playing hooky."

"They won't have to know, Julian. As long as you keep your promise and attend school regularly, it will be our little secret."

"You don't have to worry, Miss Robinson. I will keep my promise." Julian stopped crying and straightened up his shoulders like a man reprieved.

"Good, now go call your granny so that I can say good-bye to her. And Julian, you will learn that I am not one to hold a grudge. When this is over, we won't speak of it again, as long as you hold up your end of the bargain."

When Mrs. Clinkscales returned, Hattie smiled at her and said, "Julian has something important to discuss with you. I am going to leave now so the two of you can talk. I will look forward to seeing him in school tomorrow, as he tells me that his chigger bites are much improved."

Hattie saw herself out of the door. "Mercy," she said to herself, "I feel as exhausted as I would if I had just picked a whole field of cotton."

The next day, fifth-grade enrollment was up by two. With Julian and Edward in their places, Hattie arranged to visit the Tuckers and the Gibsons, whose farms were less than a mile apart, north of town, near Chester Larke's. Chester gave her a ride, and then he and Betty picked her up on their way back into town to attend Wednesday night prayer meeting. Both the Tuckers and the Gibsons were well on their way to getting their cotton in and they assured Hattie that Lula and Ben would begin attending school regularly in the next week or so.

By the end of September, the enrollment had stabilized at twenty-two, with nine fifth graders and thirteen sixth graders. Several of the farm kids were erratic in attendance, as they were needed to watch younger children or help with the harvest. Most of the children from town were more regular. After the home visits, Edward Marks and Julian Clinkscales never missed.

Hattie was surprised at how rapidly she settled into a rhythm with her students, and before she knew it, the first frost was on the ground, and they were wearing sweaters and wraps to school. In the early weeks, she had left school at the end of the day exhausted and hoarse from projecting her voice. Now she had developed the stamina of a plow horse and could talk all day without feeling fatigued.

Managing a classroom of students involved so much more than Hattie had ever imagined. Just when she felt she had figured everything out, she would learn something new that would cause her to reevaluate and change her procedures. Between school and church and time with the Bartons, her life was busy, allowing less and less time to brood over Will Kendrick. Mostly she was able to forget about him, but at the strangest times, and especially at night, his memory would invade her mind and produce an ache in her very soul. Even after all these months, the meaning of that one phrase remained a mystery: "I have become entangled in certain affairs that must be resolved before I can commit further to our relationship." The words still haunted her. In the late hours of her insomnia, Hattie longed for resolution. She could accept the fact that he had changed his mind about her. After all, she had been amazed that he had been attracted to her in the first place. Will could have had his pick among any of the young women in the church and around Greenville Female College, where he taught Latin to the upperclassmen during his senior year at Furman.

Although tall, gangly, and not handsome in the traditional sense, he possessed a self-assurance that lacked pretense and pride, a charisma, a personal magnetism that drew people to him. At the same time, his strength of character and singularity of purpose set him off and made him seem unattainable and thus, all the more desirable.

On a subliminal level, she had expected that he would ultimately cast her off. She had chastised herself for believing that she was worthy of him, for being gullible enough to think that he could possibly love her with the depth that she loved him. No one had before and she'd been foolish to assume that Will would be the exception.

Why couldn't he have told her the reason behind the letter? He had trusted her with his deepest feelings and aspirations—his passion for foreign missions and his desire to join Lottie Moon in spreading the good news of God's love to the people of China. He had even confessed to her that his greatest dread was not in leaving his family, living halfway around the world, or even learning a complex new language and culture. His greatest dread was the passage across the vast ocean, as Will suffered from motion sickness.

Finally, just before the first light of dawn, Hattie would exhaust herself from the labor of mentally exhuming the bones of their relationship, and she would fall asleep. What seemed like only moments later, Georgia would be knocking on her door with a reminder to get up and get dressed for school.

8

The students' favorite part of the day was from twelve to one, when they received a full hour to eat their lunches and socialize. In fair weather, they would go outside on the school grounds and join the girls and boys from other classes. In bad weather, they would eat inside at their desks. Georgia always packed Hattie's pail with something tasty and substantial, like biscuits filled with pork sausage or a large sweet potato stuffed with butter and sorghum molasses. They filled their tin cups with fresh water dipped from the well behind the school, a duty reserved for the older boys.

Lunchtime was more relaxed and required less supervision when they could eat outside. Hattie would take her students to join Mary Posey's class. The boys would start up a game of baseball while the girls jumped rope or played jackstones. The two teachers enjoyed visiting and having a few minutes to converse with another adult. They would stand or sit, always facing one another, so that one could keep watch over the girls under the tree and the other over the boys playing on the field. They had both been trained that a cardinal rule for a good teacher was never to leave students unsupervised.

When they ate inside, Hattie led the students in calisthenics and had them to do deep-breathing exercises, allowing them to work off some of their pent-up energy. Those days when they could not go outside were the most trying. Fortunately, the weather held out and was fair through early fall.

Hattie noticed that Pauline Jeter remained shy and interacted very little with the other children during the lunch-and-social hour. Pauline often wandered off to the far side of the field by herself while the other girls ate their lunches. On the first day the weather forced them inside, the children waited at their desks while two of the students passed out the lunch pails. Pauline's was conspicuously missing, and it hit Hattie like the acorn falling on Chicken Little's head that Pauline had nothing to eat.

Why didn't I think of that? she chided herself. *Her father is out in the field early, and her mother is sick, and there is probably very little left over from breakfast for making a lunch. She is such a proud child. She prefers to suffer in silence than to call attention to herself. We'll just have to fix that!* She asked Georgia to begin packing an extra portion in her lunch pail. The next day, she called Pauline aside first thing in the morning.

"Pauline, please come with me to the cloakroom. I have something I need you to help me do." Pauline obediently left her seat and walked to the cloakroom. Hattie followed with her lunch pail in hand.

"Pauline, I am in such a quandary. I am boarding with the Bartons, and dear, sweet Georgia, their cook, keeps packing my lunch with more food than I can possibly say grace over. Would you be so kind as to help me finish some of it?"

"Thank you, ma'am. That would be real nice. I plum forgot my lunch today."

"Well, that's just it. I am not talking about only today. I need help every day. Do you think you could manage to keep on forgetting it?"

Pauline smiled shyly. "Yes, ma'am. I reckon I could."

"I found an extra pail right here in the cloakroom that Billy Jackson left when he moved away. We can divide up this food and have a gracious plenty for both of us. Why, there is enough here to feed the five thousand. You'll be doing me a real favor."

"That's mighty kind of you, Miss Robinson."

"We'll mark through Billy's name and put your name on the pail. Every morning when I bring in my lunch, I will set it right next to your pail. I don't want George Barton to get wind of this because he might tell Georgia, and she will fuss if she thinks I am not eating everything she sends.

"Once I get the class started on the morning exercises, I will think of an errand that will send you to the cloakroom, and you can come in here and divide out the food. That way, it will not go to waste and we will both have plenty. Are you sure you don't mind helping me?"

"No, ma'am. It won't be a bother at all. I appreciate your thinking of me." Her mouth twitched at the corners to suppress a smile; however, Pauline's sparkling eyes gave her away, and Hattie could tell that the gesture had pleased the young girl beyond measure.

"Okay, it's settled then. We'll start today. I need to get back to the students. You stay here, divide out the portions and come on back when you are done. That way, everything will be ready when we dismiss for lunch at noon, and no one will be the wiser." Pauline stayed behind and did as Hattie instructed, slipping back into her seat in the classroom unnoticed.

Hattie was delighted to observe an immediate transformation in her young student. Pauline proudly carried her lunch pail out to the field and began to socialize with the other girls. She even started to join them in jump rope and impressed the girls with how quick and nimble she was.

Mary Posey remarked at how much Pauline had come out from last year. "I am so glad to see her making friends. She is such a sweet, smart girl. What in the world did you do?"

"Just helped her preserve her dignity. That's all."

"No, really. What did you do?"

"I'll tell you, but you have to promise never to repeat a word of it. If you do, I'll tell Reverend Fitts you're sweet on somebody else."

Mary's face grew as red as her hair. "*Hattie,* don't tease about that. He doesn't give me the time of day anyway. I do not know why I keep on caring. What is wrong with that woman up in Durham? She must be crazy to choose her work over him. And this is ugly to say, but she's a mousy-looking little thing who pulls her hair straight back and hardly speaks beyond a whisper. There is not a single woman in the church would not follow Reverend Fitts to the ends of the earth if he showed the slightest interest, me included. But Reverend Fitts only has eyes for *her*."

"I don't know what you see in him. He is handsome—almost pretty. But my goodness, he is set in his ways. He takes himself so seriously. He hardly ever cracks a smile."

"Oh no, Hattie. Reverend Fitts has a wonderful sense of humor and he can be warm and quite clever."

"Well, I'll take your word for it, Mary, but he has certainly hidden that side from me."

Mary sighed. "It's probably hopeless, but I can't get him out of my system."

"You have one advantage over that woman in Durham. You are here and available, and she is not. At some point Reverend Fitts is bound to come to his senses and realize how lucky he would be to have you. And unlike the woman in Durham, you are anything but mousy, Mary."

"Oh, Hattie, I hope to goodness you are right about all that. Do you still think much about Will?"

"Sometimes I do, but it gets better as time passes."

"Would you ever consider marrying anyone else?"

"I'm not sure I ever would. I still have so many questions about why it ended."

Hattie realized that this was the first time she had openly talked about Will. The admission brought her to a new level of acceptance. It did not resolve everything; however, Hattie had begun to accept the probability that she might never receive the answers to all of her questions and that she would still have to move on anyway, with or without resolution.

9

As the holiday season approached, Elizabeth and Georgia began the ritual preparations for the gathering of the family and the hosting of events that would take place at the Barton estate. Hattie came in from school one day to find them opening and airing out the wing of the house they all referred to as Aunt Willie Mae's quarters, a spacious addition that Hattie had learned was built for Charles Barton's spinster sister. Elizabeth was removing the muslin slipcovers from two matching chairs, revealing the flowered upholstery underneath, as she explained the impending arrival of the sisters.

"Aunt Alice and Aunt Willie Mae have always come for Christmas, but since Aunt Alice's husband died of tuberculosis three years ago, they have started arriving before Thanksgiving and staying over to help with the preparations for the family gathering on Christmas Day."

Elizabeth was in high spirits and was eager to tell Hattie in great detail about the Barton holiday traditions, which were similar to, albeit far more elaborate than, those of the Robinson family. Hattie could tell by her animated expression that she delighted in hosting Charles's extended family, and Hattie supposed it was because Elizabeth had so little family of her own still living. She spoke as lovingly of Uncle George and Aunt Sudie as if they were her own parents and showed a genuine affection for Charles's brothers, Bailey and Eugene, and their wives. Elizabeth Barton's excitement over the arrival of the sisters was palpable.

"Aunt Willie Mae can do wonders with flowers and always creates the most beautiful wreaths and seasonal arrangements for every room, but she is far too frail to gather the greenery. Alice sees to that."

Elizabeth continued to fill Hattie in on the sequence of holiday events, which would begin with the men rising before dawn on Thanksgiving morning for the annual deer hunt. Alice always rose at the same time, and with the aid of Uncle George's handyman, Lonnie, conducted a foray to every corner of the Barton estate to cut branches of magnolia, pine, boxwood, and cedar, which they brought back and soaked in giant tin washtubs filled with water to keep them fresh for the season.

The greens would be used in the making of wreaths for the doors and garlands for the banisters and mantels throughout the house. Aunt Sudie would always bring her long time cook and housekeeper Ossie, and together with Elizabeth, Georgia, Alice, and Willie Mae, they would spend the better part of the week, beginning the Monday after Thanksgiving, out in the flower shed putting everything together.

Ossie would help Aunt Sudie make her famous fruitcakes the first week of December to allow three full weeks for them to soak in rum before they were ready to serve. The children would gather pecans for Ossie and Georgia to shell for the pecan pies that they would bake closer to Christmas.

Mr. Barton and the three older boys always took off into the woods in search of a giant cedar to serve as the Christmas tree while Elizabeth and Georgia unpacked the ornaments. They would go to Uncle Bailey's in town for Christmas Eve dinner and then on to the service at the church. On Christmas Day, everyone would gather for a sumptuous meal at the Barton home place.

"So you see why we start so early, Hattie. The Barton Christmas is a real production." Elizabeth smiled and pushed back a strand of hair that had become unpinned.

The sisters had arrived and had settled in when Hattie returned from Thanksgiving with her family in Greenville. In the short time she was around them, Hattie found Alice's overbearing nature to be suffocating. The woman seemed to expand into every space she occupied and breathe up the air, leaving little for anyone else. She could not be happy sitting still and was in perpetual motion, directing, planning, instigating activity, expressing an opinion at every turn. Hattie remembered Aunt Harriet's remark that "poor Alice never mastered the subtleties of navigating as a woman in a man's world."

Hattie was not without sympathy for women like Alice, who lacked the softness and finesse of Elizabeth or Mama or even a younger woman like Earline Greer and either refused to learn or did not understand how to use the politics of womanly charm and persuasion to her advantage. She admitted reluctantly to herself that she probably shared a few of those traits with Alice, such as her tendency to want to fix things that were not always her concern, and her strong opinions, which she had difficulty keeping to herself. Hattie quickly assured herself that the traits they shared were much less extreme in her than in Alice. *At least it seems to me that way.*

Willie Mae, on the other hand, was quiet and passive and rarely entered into conversation. Even when she did, she never uttered an original thought but would attach herself to the last opinion expressed. If it were Alice's, she would respond, "That's right, sister." But if the last opinion were contrary to Alice's, she would stammer, "Now—now—now, I don't know, sister. I hadn't thought of that point."

She was a tiny wisp of a woman, a few years younger than Mr. Barton, but in many ways she seemed like a simple child. At times she reminded Hattie of a wood nymph, the way she would glide about the house in pink silk slippers, popping in and out with her basket of floral clippings, which she brought along to freshen up the arrangements or create new ones when the old ones were beyond saving. You never knew when or where she would show up. She seemed to materialize out of thin air as though she had been sprinkled with fairy dust. One minute the room was vacant, and the next she was there tending her flowers.

Hattie had been startled by her presence on more than one occasion. But she appeared to be the only one who was bothered by it. Elizabeth Barton had explained that Willie Mae was frail and had suffered from headaches all of her life, and everyone seemed to accept that as the cause of her unconventional behavior.

Nevertheless, Hattie was grateful when the time finally arrived to board the train for Greenville and equally grateful to find that the sisters had departed for Columbia the day before she returned to begin the second term at Calhoun School on January 6. She did not share Elizabeth's fondness for the sisters, and she gathered by Georgia's body language that Georgia didn't either. Hattie hoped she would not ever have to spend extended time with them in the future.

Though her Christmas had been a joyous one, there was still an undertone of sadness in the Robinson home. James Robinson had been gone for almost three years, but it was only their second Christmas without him. And it was Hattie's first Christmas since she and Will had parted. She was happy to return to the Bartons' home, where everyone was in good spirits. She had missed her class and her fellow teachers and looked forward to the New Year.

On a bitter-cold January afternoon, only a week into the second term, Hattie was hurrying back inside the school building. She had rushed out without a coat after she dismissed the children for the day to catch Julian Clinkscales and remind him to bring a note for his two-day absence. She wanted to make sure he was not backsliding and playing hooky again.

Fingers and cheeks stinging from exposure to the icy wind, she hugged herself and shivered. Mary Posey met her coming from the other direction. "Hattie, Reverend Fitts says there is a gentleman here to see you. He's waiting in your room." Hattie recalled that Thomas Greer had said he would drop by to bring the music for the duet he had asked her to sing at the service on Sunday and she assumed it was he.

As she entered the warm classroom, she saw him standing there, gazing out of the window, his tall, slender frame silhouetted by the late-afternoon light that filtered through. His dark hair had grown and was curling over his starched white collar. His jacket hung on his frame. Her heart quickened, and she could feel her already reddened cheeks blaze.

"Will, is that you? What on earth are you doing here?"

Will Kendrick turned and faced her. "Hattie, I had to see you. I need to explain what happened, why I sent the letter." He reached out to embrace her. "You look wonderful."

Hattie recoiled as a surge of anger rose. She had almost conquered her feelings for Will, and now they had come back and were throbbing like an open wound. "No, Will. We do not have anything else to say to each other. Your letter and the fact that you have not made contact in over eight months have made things clear."

"Hattie, please. I know how deeply I have hurt you, but I assure you it was for reasons beyond my control. I only ask that you hear me out before you judge me. I have come all this way. Before I leave, won't you please give me a chance to explain?"

Hattie had never been able to deny Will anything. Even now, she acquiesced, gesturing for him to take a seat, pointing to the row of desks in front of her. He folded his long legs into a front-row seat, and Hattie took the seat in the row across from him. As she struggled to compose herself, he began his story.

"I was in the midst of reviewing for finals last May and received an urgent message from my mother that I must come home at once. I took the first eastbound train from Louisville and began the journey to Hendersonville. When I arrived home, I found my mother alone in her room, shades drawn. She sat in her favorite rocker, the one in which she had held me as a child, weeping inconsolably. It was the first time I had ever seen her cry.

"'Will,' she moaned. 'We are ruined. Your father has disgraced our family, and things will never be the same.'

"'Father? Where is he? What has he done?'

"'Oliver has taken his belongings and left. He had an affair with Reverend Jamison's wife, Melody, who is bearing his child. The two of them have run away together and have taken money from the church treasury to fund their new lives. Not only has your father committed adultery, he is also a thief.'"

Will grew pale in the telling of the story, and Hattie could see that the ordeal had taken a huge toll. Temporarily, her anger and resentment abated as she was drawn into his narrative.

"Oh, Will. Your poor, dear mother. And that sounds so unlike your father. You always spoke so fondly of him and held him in highest regard. Wasn't he a deacon?"

"Yes, Mother and Father were pillars of Ebenezer Church. They gave generously of their time and means to the church and would have done anything to ensure that it thrived. Mother was active in missions. In fact, it was she who encouraged me to consider a calling to the mission field. When she was president of the women's mission group in the association, our church raised more for the Christmas offering than any other."

Will continued, "And you know, Hattie, the irony is that Reverend Jamison was ready to forgive his wife, seek a pastorate in a new church, and raise the child as his own. And my mother was willing to forgive my father if the two of them would end the affair and keep away from one another until the Jamisons could move.

"And did they?" asked Hattie.

"They pretended to agree, but it was all a ruse. Father emptied out the petty cash from the store on Saturday for deposit at the bank on Monday. On Sunday, she sang a moving solo while he counted the money from the collection plate and made it ready for deposit on Monday as well. That night, they left notes for their respective spouses and sneaked away to begin a life together, with the petty cash and the offering as a start-up."

"He is the last person I would have suspected to do such a thing," said Hattie.

"Yes, it was completely unlike him, and I even refused to believe what Mother was saying until she showed me the note. I guess I had lost touch with my father, as I had not been home for any length of time in almost seven years. While I was at Furman, as you know, I stayed in Greenville and worked at the YMCA during the summers, and then when I went off to Louisville, it was much too far and too expensive to go home. I was so looking forward to our wedding when you would meet my family and get to know them. I knew that my mother and father would love you instantly as I did, and still do."

Hattie could feel herself coming unglued at his mention of love and struggled once again to keep her composure and focus on his story.

"I was trying to make sense out of all that Mother was telling me and asked her if she had noticed any indications that things were going wrong.

"'Yes,' she said. 'I had noticed a change in Oliver, but I attributed it to the ruined crops due to the flooding in the area, and to lean times at the store, with people not having much to spend. And I guess it is always sad when you reach the stage in life for your children to leave the nest. We knew you were destined for the ministry, but your father was counting on your sister to help him with the store. Margaret has such a good head for business.

"'We thought she would marry Lem Hanes and settle down on his family farm down the road. She could have still helped out at the store even when she started raising her children. Oliver would have made a little place for them, and I could have kept them while she worked. But then she up and met Jasper Gentry the summer he came to stay at the Echo Inn with his aunt from Jacksonville, and she never had eyes for anyone else again. He married her and took her off to Florida, and your father and I have had the house and the store all to ourselves ever since.

"'After she left, I did notice that he drew off to himself when he was at home and he started spending more time at the church. He got real friendly with Melody Jamison, but I thought it was due to their common love of music. She has a pure soprano voice that, honestly, she could get paid to sing with. And you know what a beautiful tenor voice he has. You got that from him. I cannot carry a tune in a bucket. She is half his age—could have been his daughter. In fact, I think she reminded him of Margaret, and I was happy that she met that need for him. Never in my wildest dreams did I suspect that anything was going on between them.

"'When he told me, I almost laughed in his face at the thought of anything so ridiculous. And even when I realized it was true, I remained strong and told him I was willing to forgive him and offer him another chance to do right. But when I found out that he had lied, deceived, and stolen money to be with her, not only our hard-earned money but money from the church—the Christmas missions offering at that—I broke down and could not go on. That is when I had to call you to come home. I just cannot fix this by myself.'"

Will lowered his head and began rubbing his temples. "Humiliation and shame for what my father had done washed over me, and I felt nothing but despair. I had never seen my mother broken like that and I knew it was on my shoulders to make it right before I could resume my studies at Louisville or even proceed with our plans to marry. It was the most wrenching decision I have ever made, but I could not face anyone again, especially you, until restitution had been made.

"I promised my mother that before I returned to Louisville, I would work night and day to get the business back on a solid footing and to pay back every cent of the money that my father had taken from the church." Will raised his chin and looked directly into Hattie's eyes. "I contacted my professors at seminary and requested a leave of absence and then I sat down to write the most difficult letter imaginable—the one I wrote to you, breaking off our engagement."

Gazing up at him in bewilderment, Hattie responded with a deflated whisper. "Will, you could have told me all of that. You know that I would have understood. Your letter devastated me, and I have spent the last eight months agonizing over what I might have done to drive you away. Now I am even more devastated that you did not feel you could trust me."

Will's voice was pleading as he leaned forward and stretched his open palms toward her. "That is just it. I knew if I told you, you would have tried to convince me not to break it off. You are much too loyal. But Hattie, it would not have been fair to you. I had nothing to give you. I was in deep debt, and my family was in disgrace. To recover from that would require me to work night and day. I could offer you neither honor nor money nor time. What else could I do for you but to set you free? Sometimes the best way to love somebody is to let them go."

Will paused, smiled and took both of Hattie's hands in his. They were strong, warm hands, and she allowed her own to remain nestled between them while he continued. "Besides, I knew you would make it on your own. I have always known that. That is one of the things that drew me to you from the start. And it seems you did just that. You found a job and a new place to live and you are almost finished with your first year as a teacher. I would say you have done well for yourself."

Reluctantly, Hattie agreed. "Well, it is a far cry from our dream to marry and go into the mission field together. But I must admit, I love my students and I have found a kind of mission field right here in Calhoun. The Bartons have been so good to me. I am devoted to the boys, and Mrs. Barton has been like a second mother. I believe that I have found a real place here." Hattie paused and held his gaze before she continued. "But Will, you know I never would have chosen any of that over you."

"I know. But perhaps the dream to go into foreign missions was more mine than yours. You are so close to your family; I always felt that it would be difficult for you to be separated from them by a vast ocean. In time, you may even have come to resent me for taking you away."

As if to steel himself for what he was about to say next, Will released Hattie's hands and straightened. His brow furrowed. "Hattie,

I want to be completely honest with you and I see that you are in a place where you can accept the decision I have made. I am still unable to support a wife. I have paid off my father's debts and scraped up enough money to go back to Southern for at least a semester, and I am going early to find simple lodging and work. I feel called to foreign missions and when I complete seminary, I will apply to the Foreign Mission Board for placement somewhere in China. Although I cannot ask you to wait for me, I could not leave for Louisville without setting things straight with you. I hope that you will at least allow us to remain friends."

Well, this is it, thought Hattie. *The denouement of our relationship.* She had spent the past eight months alternately blaming herself and then Will for their breakup, when the real villains in their story were fate and cruel circumstance. And Will was right: had he given her the opportunity, she would have raged against the outcome, would have used her best arguments to convince him that he was wrong and that that their love was strong enough to endure. True to his unselfish nature, he had made the decision to write the letter, not from a lack of love for Hattie but because of it. He had loved her enough to set her free from his burdens. Now she must do the same for him by accepting his decision with grace and understanding, when her nature was to respond with resistance and debate. She inhaled deeply to bolster her resolve and smiled up at him through her tears.

"Yes, Will. Of course we will remain friends."

They rose, and she embraced him as she had so many times before, her nose buried in his chest and the top of her head fitting neatly under his chin. This time she knew it was no more than a gesture of friendship between two kindred spirits. She inhaled his familiar scent as he kissed the top of her head and smiled down at her.

"Thank you, Hattie. You have no idea what it means to me to have your forgiveness." Will's voice caught, and he turned away. "I'd better go now, but I'll write you as soon as I get to Louisville."

After he left, Hattie watched him through the fogged window as he walked toward town and in the direction of the railway station, turning up the collar of his overcoat to shield himself against the wind and newly falling snow. When Will disappeared from sight, she remained for a while at her desk, trying to make sense of what had just happened. As she sat, tears welled in her eyes and began falling softly down her cheeks and onto the hard, wooden surface. She made no attempt to dry them, but let them continue until they had formed a small puddle on the top of her desk. She had not wept like this since that day in front of Mama and Aunt Harriet, when she'd let out tears of anger and betrayal. These tears were different. They were tears of acceptance and relief and regret for what might have been.

In those moments of full disclosure, Hattie had to admit that another thing Will had said was true. A foreign mission was more his dream than hers. Hattie was still not sure of her place, but she was relatively certain that it was not on some distant shore. She had not realized the burden she had carried in trying to make Will's dream her own. She would have followed him to China, but what then? Thousands of miles from home in an alien land with an alien tongue—would she have found her place? She suspected not. Still, if the chance had presented itself, she knew she would have followed Will anywhere.

The winter light was disappearing when Hattie heard a timid knock on her door, followed by the inquiring face of Mary Posey. "Hattie? Was that Will?"

"Yes, Mary, that was Will."

"Well, don't think I'm going to let you go home until you tell me everything."

"Okay, Mary. Come on in and sit down."

10

The bleak winter had finally given way to spring in the up-country, bringing with it a lengthening of the daylight hours and a warming of the earth. Signs of new life appeared as the redbud bloomed, followed by the budding of forsythia and dogwood. Crocus and daffodils pushed up from the soil and, once again, the fields were prepared for a new crop of cotton, with the more fertile tracts of land bearing signs of growth as the tiny cotyledons emerged.

Hattie was energized by the promise of the new season. She had almost completed her first year of teaching, had made new friends at school and at church, and had found a second home with the Bartons. Since Will had explained to her the mystery of his abrupt departure, she felt more at peace about it. She still thought about him, especially when she received one of his letters, as they corresponded with one another from time to time. But the pain of losing him was not so jagged around the edges now and felt more like a stone from a riverbed whose surface had been worn down and smoothed by the flow of water over the passage of time.

Pauline Jeter had continued to blossom since the day in October when Hattie initiated the secret lunch arrangement. Hattie had been amazed at how that one simple act had brought her out and how their little secret had strengthened the bond of trust and affection between teacher and student. They had perfected the routine so that

Pauline could slip out to the cloakroom just after roll call and return to her seat minutes later without being noticed.

The plan worked flawlessly until one spring morning when Reverend Fitts stopped by the class on one of his infrequent rounds. Hattie had sent Pauline to the cloakroom and was busy reviewing the spelling words for the day. Through the glass, Reverend Fitts must have seen something that raised his suspicion. It was a young Pauline Jeter. He stood in the doorway observing in silence while she plundered through a lunch pail, transferring a large ham biscuit into one marked with her name. Hattie heard Reverend Fitts's voice.

"Why, Miss Jeter, I am shocked and disappointed. I would never have taken you to be a thief unless I had seen it with my own eyes. Come with me at once, young lady, and you will remain in my office until we can get to the bottom of this."

Hattie immediately realized what was going on. "Class, I must be out of the room for a short time. While I am away, you will finish writing your spelling words. Tillie, you are the class monitor for the day. Please sit at my desk and help the fifth graders with their math if they need it. I will expect stellar behavior from everyone if you want to be allowed to have your lunch outside today."

Hattie hurried to the office, where she found Pauline in tears and Revered Fitts with his Bible opened to Exodus 20, pointing to the eighth commandment, "Thou shalt not steal."

"Come in, Miss Robinson. I am afraid that I have caught Miss Jeter breaking one of the Ten Commandments. She was stealing food from your lunch pail and putting it in her own. And she has the temerity to insist that she was helping you."

Hattie was unable to control the shrillness in her response. "Reverend Fitts, you have made a terrible mistake. Pauline is right. She was helping me. Oh, poor dear Pauline. It will be all right. We will sort all of this out right away."

Revered Fitts bristled. "She was helping herself to your lunch, Miss Robinson."

"I know, but you see, I asked her to do that..."

Reverend Fitts's features froze, masking the quiet fury in his voice. "I see. In that case, Miss Jeter, I have accused you unjustly. You may return to class and proceed with your lessons. Miss Robinson, please stay behind a moment to explain this further."

Pauline's face was engraved with humiliation as she glanced up at Hattie and then hurried out the door. After Hattie explained the situation to Reverend Fitts, he removed his glasses, closed his eyes, and pinched the bridge of his nose before he responded. "Dear me, Miss Robinson. You simply must stop using these unconventional tactics with your students. Your solution to the Tom Givens bullying problem pales in comparison to this one. In this instance, I can see that you were being charitable to Miss Jeter, but I cannot support your methods, which once again involved complicity and deceit. As I have said before, the ends do not justify the means. And may I remind you that there is no shame in accepting charity. You could have brought the extra food to school and offered it to her in the open. Miss Jeter would have done well to learn the lesson of accepting it with gratitude and humility. Besides, it is her parents' responsibility to provide her with physical nourishment, not yours. Your primary role is to foster her educational growth and the growth of her character. In the future, I advise you to concern yourself with that."

"Reverend Fitts, I can only do that if I can get her to come to school. I doubt seriously that after she has been so thoroughly humiliated she will come back at all." Hattie could hear herself whine like an adolescent in response to what she interpreted as sanctimonious lecturing on Reverend Fitts's part. It was not at all the impression she wanted to make, and she resolved to control it.

"Well, then you will have to concern yourself with the children who *do* come to school. However, the child does need to eat. I will pay a visit to the Jeters' home and remind the parents of their duty to send her to school with lunch."

Oh, she really had made a mess of things now. A visit from Reverend Fitts would simply heap more shame on Pauline, and she might never enter the door of a school again. However, there was no use to argue. Reverend Fitts would not back down. The way Hattie saw it, he was a man whose mind had little room for interpretations that varied from his own, especially if they came from the mouth of a woman.

He was so unlike Will, who would have understood. Instead of the Ten Commandments, Will would have quoted a passage like Matthew 25:40: "In as much as you have done it to the least of my brethren, you do it unto me." *Oh, Will. Am I ever going to forget about you? You really do come to mind at the most inopportune times.*

She left Reverend Fitts in his office and returned to her classroom. Tillie was enjoying her reign as monitor for the day and had dutifully copied down the names of three boys who had gotten into an eraser fight and would be denied recess for the next two days.

Hattie worried about Pauline all weekend and prayed that she would return to school on Monday, but realized that she was probably clinging to a false hope. As she suspected, Pauline was absent on Monday and again on Tuesday. On Wednesday, Hattie could stand it no longer and she decided to stop by the Jeters' on her way home to pay them a visit.

Mrs. Jeter cracked the door of the tenant farmhouse. She must have recognized Hattie from her visit early in the year and invited her into a front room that was stark but as meticulously clean as it had been the first time she saw it. Hattie noticed at once that Mrs. Jeter had a nasty gash over her left brow, which had given her a shiner and caused the eyelid to swell almost shut.

"Oh my goodness, Mrs. Jeter. Are you all right?" Mrs. Jeter nodded in the affirmative. "I came by to check on Pauline. She has been absent from school all week."

"Pauline is not here. She is working. Her papa hired her out at the mill."

A flame of indignation surged into Hattie's neck and cheeks as she shot back her reply. "What do you mean? She is only ten years old. She is a tiny thing and she is not up to working those long shifts.

Besides, she needs to be in school to get her education, as bright a child as she is."

Hattie could hear exhaustion and resignation in Mrs. Jeter's voice. "Yes, ma'am, I know all that, but her papa won't let her go back to school ever since that reverend came by and told him he wasn't doing his duty by her."

"Reverend Fitts? He is the principal. That was all a big misunderstanding and none of it was Pauline's fault. I take full responsibility for the incident and can explain it all."

"It won't do no good, Miss Robinson. Clyde is a stubborn man and he's had his pride wounded real bad. He's not likely to change his mind."

"This has nothing to do with Mr. Jeter's pride. It has to do with a young girl's future. Can't you do anything about this? Don't you care that your daughter is just barely old enough to meet the minimum age required by the child labor laws of South Carolina, which are woefully lenient?" Hattie's voice had become shrill.

There was a flash of defensive pride in the tired woman's response as she glared back at Hattie. "Yes, ma'am, I do care. Of course I do. It breaks my heart to see Pauline go off to the mill instead of sending her to school where she belongs. I would do anything if they would take me instead, but since I been sick, they won't hire me. Talking about it just gets Clyde all riled up and makes it worse for all of us around here. When we came on hard times, Clyde started back drinking, and when he gets on the bottle, his whole personality changes. He's a mean drunk."

"Did he do that to you, Mrs. Jeter? And did he make those bruises on your arms?"

"It's all right, ma'am. I can take it, long as he don't harm the children. I reckon I even deserve it, seeing as I'm not fit to work and can't pull my load."

"You deserve no such thing! That man needs to be stopped if he is hurting you."

Mrs. Jeter put her hand on Hattie's arm to calm her and spoke directly, demonstrating a depth of character that Hattie had not anticipated. "Don't judge him, Miss Robinson. Clyde is a good man at heart. He loves his children and he's as tore up about all this as he can be. He just shows it in a different way. There ain't nothing worse than for a man to be put in a position not to be able to provide for his family. It's no telling what they will do when that happens. He already lost the farm and the house and moved us down here to Calhoun to find work. Now he stands to lose it all again. We was barely able to make expenses with the cotton this year and I didn't do him no good getting sick and not able to work more than a few hours at a time. We ain't no better off than before, except maybe worse 'cause we've done left our kin and now we are all alone."

"How can you defend him when he is drinking and beating up on you? If he does this to you, what will stop him from going after the children? And how much of this can you take until he ends up seriously hurting you, or even killing you? It is not safe for you to stay here in this situation. I can't even bear thinking about it."

"What am I to do? He's my husband and the head of the family. Besides, if I ever did get up the nerve to leave him, I ain't got no kin around here that could take us in."

"Well, we'll just have to fix that. What if I could find you somebody? My pastor's wife, Mrs. Greer, may know of a church member who would take you in. Come to think of it, there is a widow woman who lives in town and has some extra rooms. She mentioned last week at circle meeting that she was taking in sewing and that she had gotten behind and needed some help. She might agree to let you stay with her for a while."

Hattie heard the resignation and futility in Mrs. Jeter's voice return. "I just don't know, Miss Robinson. I'm afraid that no matter where I go, Clyde would come after me."

"Just promise me you will keep an open mind and stay quiet about it for now. I'll get in touch with Mrs. Greer right away and see if I can arrange something for you, then I'll be back in touch." Mrs. Jeter nodded and closed the door as Hattie turned to go down the steps.

Hattie hurried back to the Bartons' to discuss the matter with Elizabeth. When she arrived, Georgia met her at the door. Hattie could tell by the way Georgia chewed at her bottom lip that she was perturbed.

"Lawd, Miz Elizabeth jus' got word that her aunt Nellie's done broke her hip up in Asheville and she determined to go up there and nurse her. She and Mr. Charles in the parlor discussing it an' I sho' hope he gonna try to talk her out of it, 'cause she don't have no business going all the way up there, as frail as she is."

"Georgia Barnes, that is not true," Elizabeth said as she entered from the hallway. Even when she scolded, Elizabeth's voice was warm and affectionate. "Hey, Hattie. I guess Georgia told you that I am going up to Asheville to see about Aunt Nellie."

"I'm sorry that she is ill. I did not realize you had relatives in Asheville."

"Oh yes. Her son, Robert, is up there managing the staff at the Grandville Hotel. She moved up to be with him when Uncle Porter died. She liked the climate and the social life and has made it her home. She was my father's only sister and has always been like a second mother to me. I'll take the train up in the morning. Robert will meet me at the station. I will stay with her for a week or two and make sure she has everything she needs before I come back. I know the children will be in good hands with Georgia, but I do hate leaving Richard. It's the first time I've gone off since he was born."

"Don't worry, Mrs. Barton. I'll help Georgia and make sure that Richard gets lots of love and attention while you are away."

Elizabeth gave Hattie a little squeeze. "Oh, honey, I know you will. You are such a godsend. Georgia, will you come up and help me get my clothes together? We'll need to get everything packed up tonight so that Charles can get me to the station by seven."

"If you sure you up to it, Miz Elizabeth. I can't believe Mr. Charles letting you go, though. Looks like he done lost his power of persuasion. That ain't a good sign for a man in his profession."

"Hush, Georgia. Charles is perfectly fine about my going. He knows how important this is to me, and that there would be no use to try to persuade me otherwise. I won't rest until I can see with my own eyes that Aunt Nellie is all right and make sure she's being taken care of properly."

"I know what you mean, Mrs. Barton. If anything were to happen to my aunt Harriet, I'd want to go to her and do whatever I could to help her through it."

"See, Georgia, Hattie understands. And Aunt Nellie is not as lucky as Harriet. With no daughters or sisters, she only has Robert, who is simply wonderful to her, but with him not being married, she doesn't even have a daughter-in-law around to help her with her personal needs. I want to be there to see to that."

Georgia would not relent. "That's what I'm 'fraid of. You'll go round lifting and carrying Miz Nellie and then you'll end up in the bed right beside her, or even worse."

"I'm not talking about lifting and carrying. Robert will find a nurse to do that, although he won't ever find anybody who could do it like you could, Georgia." Georgia straightened up, thrust out her chest, and cocked her head away from Elizabeth, as Hattie had seen her do any time she received a compliment. "I'm talking about helping her with her hair and her makeup and making sure she has some nice lace bed jackets to feel pretty while she is recuperating. She'll need some good reading material and I'll contact the women in her church circle to make sure they drop by and pay her a visit to keep her spirits up. I know Aunt Nellie, and if she doesn't have something to occupy her, she'll go absolutely batty. Once I get things in place for her, I'll feel better about leaving her and coming on home."

"Well, all right then," Georgia conceded, shaking her head. "I'll go up and get the bags out of the attic and get started packing."

Hattie desperately wanted to talk to Elizabeth about the Jeters; however, she felt it inappropriate to bring up the subject under the circumstances. She was relieved when Elizabeth gave her an entrée.

"Hattie, I didn't even ask you about your day at school. Did the little Jeter girl show up like you had hoped? I know you were worried about her."

Gratefully, Hattie began filling her in on the day's events as they left the kitchen together and entered the hallway. The acrid scent of cigar smoke wafted from the study, where Charles Barton was reading the paper and finishing a mixed drink.

He must have heard the two women's conversation and called out. "Are you talking about Clyde Jeter? I am the one who located him and brought him down from Spartanburg County for George. George says he's been a hard worker and if it had not been for him, last year's crop would have gone to seed."

Elizabeth entered the room and perched herself on the arm of her husband's chair. She motioned for Hattie to follow and take the empty seat across from them.

"Well, Hattie says he's taken to the bottle and that he is mean when he drinks. He has gone and hired out his precious little daughter at the mill. They don't have any family in this area and Hattie's going to make some contacts at the church to see if she can find a safe place for Mrs. Jeter to take the children and get out of the abusive situation."

Charles looked up at Elizabeth and then over at Hattie. "I hate to hear that, but I don't think it is wise for you to interfere in the Jeters' domestic affairs. In the eyes of the law, there is a fine line between spousal abuse and a man's authority to maintain discipline over his household, not to mention his right to hire out his children. I agree that he is not much of a man if he can't support his family, but he still has the law on his side."

"Charles, he is living on Barton property and farming Barton land. We can't turn a blind eye if he's harming his wife and children."

"I suppose I could inquire into the financial situation with Mr. Jeter. George will know something. I'll drop by there tomorrow after I get you to the station and finish seeing my clients."

Elizabeth stroked his arm and planted a kiss on his cheek. "Thank you, darling."

He added, "But I am telling you, Miss Robinson, you need to be very careful about doing anything to challenge Clyde Jeter's rights with his family."

"Yes, sir. I certainly will."

"Oh, Hattie, I'm just sick that I won't be here to help you with this, but you are in good hands with Earline Greer. If anybody can find a place for Mrs. Jeter, she can."

"It's all right, Mrs. Barton. Just talking to you about it makes me feel better. You need to be with your aunt Nellie, and you are right, Mrs. Greer seems like she will be a lot of help."

Elizabeth draped her right arm around Charles's shoulder and began tracing his hairline with the index finger of her left hand as she spoke. "Earline is such an asset to Thomas Greer. Honestly, I do wish our Reverend Fitts would find a wife. I am afraid he never will. He seems to have his heart set on Portia Graham, who is teaching up in Durham, but I do not think she is nearly as sweet on him as he is on her. He needs to pay attention to some of the eligible young women in Calhoun."

"I know one of them who would agree with that," said Hattie.

"You mean Mary Posey? She is such a cute thing, and it's so obvious she likes him."

"She may be too available," said Charles. "Reverend Fitts obviously responds more to the aloof type like Portia." Elizabeth continued tracing her finger over his temple and around his ear as he spoke, and he reached for her hand and stilled it in his own.

"Well, Portia would not be nearly the asset to Reverend Fitts that Mary would be. Honestly, there are so many nice young people in this community. You know, Charles, we haven't had a party in a long time.

When I get home I'm going to invite some of them over for Hattie to meet and socialize with. Now that she has gotten situated at school, it's time for her to step out some."

"Lord, Elizabeth. There you go matchmaking again. Miss Robinson, you had better watch out. She may have you paired up with Reverend Fitts."

Hattie laughed. "Oh no, he's not my type. Anyway, after growing up a Baptist, I don't think I could ever be married to a Methodist minister. They have to move too much."

"No, I was not even remotely considering James Fitts where Hattie is concerned. I was thinking about Sudie's nephew Marvin. He's just a little older than Hattie and has turned into such a fine, handsome young man. He's in Columbia, finishing up law school and Sudie says he's planning to be in Calhoun to celebrate his mother's birthday on May 15. Maybe I could plan something around his visit."

"Marvin is an outstanding fellow," said Charles. "I hope we can persuade him to hang out his shingle in Calhoun. He would be a real asset to the community. I agree with Elizabeth that you would find him good company, Miss Robinson."

"And he is also a good Baptist, Hattie," laughed Elizabeth.

"He sounds like a very nice person." Hattie was growing a bit uncomfortable being the object of the conversation and wanted to change the subject. "Mrs. Barton, if you don't need me to help with the boys, I think I'll try to get up to the church this evening for prayer meeting and talk to Mrs. Greer after the service."

Elizabeth freed her hand from Charles and rose to join Hattie at the door. "No, you go on, honey. The boys will be just fine. Do you need Charles Jr. to drive you over?"

"No, ma'am. It's such nice spring weather, I think I'd enjoy the walk, and with the days getting longer, I'll be back here before dark."

"Hattie, you have a heart of gold to care so much about that little girl. She has a real advocate in you. Be sure to get a bite of supper before you leave. I'm gonna go on up and help Georgia and check on the boys, but I'll see you in the morning before I leave for Asheville."

11

Earline Greer could not have been more helpful. She caught Rosa Griffin after the service and filled her in on the details, even down to Mr. Jeter's drinking problem and violent temper. Rosa, a plump, well-preserved woman in her fifties, seemed delighted to be given a purpose and said, "I would be happy to take on Mrs. Jeter to do some sewing in return for room and board, and I'd even pay a little extra to Pauline for keeping things tidy around the house. Lord, it gets so lonely around there since Mr. Griffin passed. I would welcome the help as well as the company. That poor little girl having to go off to the mill to work at her age, and you say she is such a smart little thing. We just need to fix this!"

"How can we get word to them that you are willing to take them in without Mr. Jeter knowing?" Earline asked.

"I have an idea that might work," said Hattie. "We can go over to the mill tomorrow during lunch, when Pauline has a break. We'll talk to her for a few minutes, and then she can go back and tell her mother. Since the mill is such a short distance from the school, I will ask Miss Posey to watch my children during the lunch hour and I'll go over there with you, as long as I am back by one. Pauline is shy but she knows me, and I think she trusts me."

"Oh, it would be so wonderful if they could get out from under that man's roof and stay with you, Rosa," said Earline. "Then they'd all be

safe, and Pauline could go back to school." Hattie remembered what
Elizabeth had said about Earline being an asset to Thomas, and she
agreed. "Rosa, why don't you and I meet Hattie at the school tomorrow around eleven thirty and we can walk over to the mill together?"

"That sounds like a good idea. If Pauline is not taking her lunch
on the grounds, we may have to ask directions and explain why we've
come. We'll just tell them we've come to invite Pauline to Sunday
school. And that would be mostly the truth. Mr. Griffin used to be
in Masons with Paul Godfrey, and I think he's one of the managers.
They like their folks to go to church, or at least they say they do. But,
honestly, I can't for the life of me understand why they think it's all
right to hire children so young."

"I know it, Rosa. Thomas showed me a pamphlet he received that
was circulated by that new child-labor committee to inform people
about the conditions in the mills and the young children who are
working there."

Hattie broke in. "That was Mr. Lewis Hine who took all those
pictures. I read about him. He was a teacher in New York and left his
position to work with the National Child Labor Committee. He traveled all over North and South Carolina, photographing children in
the textile mills and documenting the conditions."

"Well, those pictures would just break your heart. Some of those
children seven or eight years old, working long shifts and being
around all that dangerous machinery. The children look downright
peaked and malnourished. It's a crying shame. Just makes you want
to go in there and bring them all home with you and take care of
them properly," said Earline.

Rosa summed things up in her direct and matter-of-fact manner. "We may not be able to save 'em all, but we can sure try to save
Pauline. We'll tell her that she and her mama and little brother will
be welcome at my house."

"Thank you, Mrs. Griffin. You have taken such a load off my
mind. I guess I better be leaving now so I can get back to the Bartons'
before dark."

Mrs. Griffin gave Hattie a hug. "Just call me Rosa," she said.

Hattie made the short walk home quickly, her mind filled with plans for the next day. As she passed near Uncle George's property, she thought she saw Clyde Jeter crossing the field and heading toward the house. She shuddered and picked up her pace. The family had all gone upstairs, and so she went directly to her room.

She rose early to make certain she could say good-bye to Elizabeth and when she heard voices and the shuffling of feet on the staircase, she hurried to the front door to see them off. Mr. Barton had pulled the car around, and Elizabeth was holding Richard and saying good-bye to the older boys.

Elizabeth reminded Hattie of a fashionable Gibson girl in her lavender travel outfit—a light wool skirt with a fitted jacket and a wide-brimmed hat with a matching band. "I'll only be gone for a week or so, but oh, I'll miss you so much! You all be good and mind Georgia while I'm away, and I'll be back before you know it."

Charles stepped down to help her into the car, and she squeezed Richard and kissed him. He fingered the delicate pink silk shawl draped around Elizabeth's shoulders and it came loose as Elizabeth transferred him into Georgia's waiting arms. Richard buried his face in the soft fabric and began rubbing it against his cheek.

"Come on now, suga'. Les' give yo' mama back her shawl."

Richard protested. "No! Mine, mine."

Elizabeth laughed. "It's okay, Georgia. Let him keep it. I have my jacket on and an extra shawl in my bag. It's not worth struggling with him over it. He's going through that stage where he thinks everything is his. 'Bye, precious. Mama loves you so much."

As the car rolled away, Hattie stepped forward and held out her arms. "Richard, come on and we'll go out back and see if the chickens have laid any eggs. You can choose the one you want Georgia to scramble up for breakfast."

Richard allowed Hattie to take him from Georgia. She set him on his feet and took his hand in hers, and together they headed for the backyard, Richard still clutching the shawl and dragging it behind him, the fringe collecting twigs and tiny bits of grass as it snaked along the ground.

Shortly, Georgia came into the backyard to relieve Hattie of Richard so that she would not be late for school. They were reenacting the story of the Billy Goats Gruff. Richard marched across a make-believe bridge, and Hattie furnished the voice of the mean old troll. "Who's that crossing over my bridge?"

Richard pretended to shake with fear. "Me, Little Billy Goats Gruff."

"Well, pass on over, then."

Georgia chuckled. "Come on, baby. You can help me gather some eggs for breakfast. I'll cook 'em up for you with some biscuits and molasses."

Hattie watched while Richard followed after Georgia, dragging his newly acquired shawl behind him. She remembered how her little brother, John, had found an old rag doll of Lillie's. He'd carried it everywhere and could not fall asleep at night without it tucked under his arm. Hattie wondered if he was still as attached to it.

"'Bye, Richard. I'll see you after school," Hattie called and then added, "What does the chicken say?"

"Cluck, cluck, cluck."

"Right. And what did Chicken Little say when the acorn fell on her head?"

"Sky fallin'. Sky fallin'." Richard lifted up the shawl, making a canopy over his head for protection.

Hattie laughed and started toward the house to get the lunch Georgia had packed her and to gather her school things. In the confusion of seeing Elizabeth off, she had almost forgotten about her plan to visit Pauline at the mill. She talked aloud to herself along the familiar walk to school, listing all of the things she needed to do when she arrived.

"I'll see Mary Posey about keeping my children at lunch. Oh yes, and leave directions just in case I am detained past one. And if I go ahead and write the afternoon assignments on the board and appoint a class monitor, I won't have to take class time to do it when I get back. Oh, and I need to get permission from Reverend Fitts to go off campus. I dread that. He's such a stickler for the daily schedule and so inflexible about change. Honestly, if it's this much trouble to be out of the classroom for an hour, what would I ever do if I had to be out for a whole day? I would just have to cancel class altogether. I'd better pick up my pace if I am going to do all I've planned for today and get back in time to read to Richard."

Hattie was in such deep concentration that she was unaware of the approaching wagon until a familiar voice called out to her from behind.

"Hey there, Miss Robinson. Have you gone to talking to yourself?" It was Lonnie Jenkins, Uncle George's handyman and go-to person for anything that needed doing and doing right.

Hattie laughed. "I guess so, Mr. Jenkins. But at least I haven't started answering myself. They say that's when you know you've gone off your rocker." Lonnie chuckled, and a rich, mellow sound rolled out from deep in his giant chest, like notes from a bass trombone. "Where are you going so early this morning?"

"I have to go into town for Mr. George to see about getting this tiller fixed. Can I give you a ride? You look like you was in a big hurry."

"Oh, thank you, Mr. Jenkins." That would be a great help if I could get to school a little early. I have a ton of things I need to do." Lonnie helped her into the wagon and urged the horse on. When he moved over to make room for Hattie to sit, the wagon listed to the left from the weight of his great hulk. The view from behind must have been a comical one, with Hattie perched high up in the wagon on one side and Lonnie sunk down on the other.

"How's the planting coming?"

"Pretty good. We got the seeds in the ground, and if the weather holds out warm, we should be seeing some growth soon."

"You sound like you know a lot about these crops. How long have you been working with Mr. Barton, Lonnie?"

"Lawd, I been with Mr. George as long as I can remember. I was born right here on this plantation thirty-six years ago. My mama died when I was jes' a few months old, and Ossie took me in and raised me right there in Mr. George and Miz Sudie's house."

"I did not realize that, Lonnie."

"Yes, ma'am. Miz Sudie didn't eva' have no babies, and she was happy for me to be around. Mr. George let me tag along behind him to fetch things. An' he would talk to me and teach me all about the farm and how he like things done. I jes' grew up doing that, and one day, seem like I was running the farm for him."

Hattie was about to ask Lonnie how his mother had died when she realized they were pulling up to the town square. "You can just let me off here, Mr. Jenkins, and I'll walk on over to the school. That way you won't have to turn off and you can get to the hardware store when it opens. Thanks so much for the ride." He rose to help her but she had jumped down and was on her way in the other direction.

Lonnie called out after her, "'Bye, Miss Robinson. 'Member not to be answering yourself." She heard his rich bass chuckle again over the clopping hooves of the horse as it pulled the wagon toward the hardware store.

Hattie caught up with Mary Posey as she climbed the stairs into the school, and after Mary said she would be happy to cover for her, she went to see Reverend Fitts. She found him in his office, going over the attendance records. Rising from his desk, he motioned for her to come in.

Hattie poured out her request, clasping her hands to her waist to still her anxious nerves. "Reverend Fitts, I need to be off campus at lunchtime to go with my pastor's wife and one of the members of the ladies' circle to check on Pauline Jeter."

"Oh yes, Pauline. I spoke with her father recently about his responsibility to make certain that she is properly nourished. He said that they had fallen on hard times and that he would most likely need for Pauline to work at the mill to help the family. He told me that he feels he has no other option."

"The fact is, he has not only hired Pauline out at the mill, he has begun drowning his frustrations in the bottle, and when he is inebriated, he becomes violent and strikes his wife. It is a most un-satisfactory situation. I have talked with Mrs. Jeter. She is a humble woman who respects the authority of her husband. She even blames herself and thinks she deserves his wrath. However, if Mr. Jeter should decide to turn his anger on Pauline or her little brother, even she agrees that she would need to take the children and leave. The prob-lem is that they have moved away from their family in Spartanburg County, and she has no one to take her in. Mrs. Rosa Griffin is willing to give her shelter and work. The reason for our visit to the mill is to let Pauline know so that she can assure her mother that she will have a safe haven in the event that she must flee her home. We do not feel it wise to visit the home for fear of arousing Mr. Jeter's suspicion and possibly provoking his anger." Hattie took a breath and waited for Reverend Fitts to respond. She read in his endless pause an attempt to slow down and control the conversation.

"I am not at all sure that is wise, Miss Robinson. Your actions could be interpreted as meddling in the Jeters' domestic affairs and challenging Mr. Jeter's authority to make decisions for his family. The apostle Paul is very clear in Ephesians 5:21 and Colossians 3:18 about the husband being the head of the household, as Christ is the head of the church, and that the wife should obey her husband."

Hattie bristled at Reverend Fitts's comment and responded im-pulsively. As a good Baptist, she knew her Bible verses; surely he did not want to challenge her to an old-fashioned Bible sword drill right here at school. "That may be true, Reverend Fitts, but the apostle Paul also said in Colossians 3:19 that a husband must love his wife and not abuse her. And what does the Bible say about sending little children off to work for long hours in unsafe and deplorable conditions? Have you seen those pictures that are circulating in the brochure from the Child Labor Committee?"

Reverend Fitts predictably resented the challenge and countered defensively. "Miss Robinson, you need not become indignant. And yes, I have seen the photographs published by Mr. Hine and I agree that they are heart wrenching. I do not condone wife abuse, nor do

I support child labor. I have, in fact, addressed the latter from the pulpit, even though it is a touchy subject with the mill supervisors, several of whom attend my church regularly, and despite the fact that both of the local mills have donated generously to the building fund at my church.

"They discount Mr. Hine's work as sensationalism and quote recent articles as a more accurate depiction of the conditions in the mills. In their view, the mills should be regarded more as the savior than the source of social and economic problems. They argue that the mills have been an economic boon to our area and have provided welcome employment to the ever-growing number of small farmers and sharecroppers who can no longer sustain their families from the land."

Reverend Fitts must have realized that he was straying from his topic and stopped himself. "That is not the point. The point is that although I appreciate your zeal and your passion for the welfare of your students, I must warn you to be careful about being too outspoken and provoking controversy in matters involving the dynamics of these students' families.

"You must realize, Miss Robinson, that our community does not respond well to women who take on roles that have traditionally been reserved for men. People are quick to misinterpret your sincere efforts of good will—and I do believe you are sincere. But they will be quick to identify you with women such as the suffragists, who speak with more strident voices and behave in a most unladylike fashion. We cannot have one of our teachers associated with that. Why, if the community got word, it would be grounds for dismissal." As he spoke, his brows arched and his voice became progressively higher in pitch, a large vein in his neck pulsing.

Hattie knew that she only had herself to blame for setting him off like this. Why did she always have to argue and get in the last word? Once Reverend Fitts was challenged and started on his rebuttal, he was likely to go on forever. She simply did not have time for a sermon today.

Hattie thought of Elizabeth Barton and the gentle manner in which she asserted her will and got her way with everyone in the family, even Mr. Barton, whom anyone would consider the undisputed head of the household. Elizabeth spoke her mind, but without rancor and with no hint of condescension or accusation. She would know precisely how to respond to Reverend Fitts. And so would Mama. Hattie's mother might not be as sophisticated and polished as Elizabeth, but she did understand the power of honey over vinegar. Hattie realized that she would do well to take a lesson from these women she admired so greatly and turn this situation around. They knew how to navigate successfully in a man's world.

It should not be this way, though. The day would surely come when a woman could speak her mind plainly and make her argument in front of any man without pouring honey on her words and serving them up with a smile and curtsy. But that day had not yet dawned, and there was no use pretending it had. She waited respectfully for Reverend Fitts to take a breath before she spoke.

"Reverend Fitts, I apologize for my presumption. Thank you so much for looking out for my welfare. You have brought up a number of excellent points, which I had failed to consider. I will take your advice to heart and will make certain that I proceed with great caution regarding Pauline and her family. I am lucky to have someone of your insight and experience as a mentor.

"If you think it is best, I will contact Mrs. Greer and tell her that I cannot be available to go with her to the mill. I was only going along because I know that Pauline is timid and I assumed that she would feel more comfortable talking to us if there was someone familiar present. I had planned to let Mrs. Greer do most of the talking. As the wife of a pastor, she is experienced at dealing with these types of situations with utmost discretion."

Hattie's words had disarmed him. His response was formal, but he had lost his defensive tone. "It will not be necessary for you to cancel, Miss Robinson. You may go along as planned. Do you have someone to attend to your students?" Hattie said that she did and excused herself, relieved to have made it over a major hurdle in her plan. She was certain that the emotional energy she had just expended on Reverend Fitts to gain this simple favor was equal to the physical energy of a field worker picking a day's worth of cotton. And yet the school day had not even begun.

12

At a few minutes before noon, Hattie lined up her students and led them to Mary Posey's room, where they would be dismissed into the yard for lunch. Having deposited them with Mary, she hurried down the hallway and opened the heavy wooden door to see Earline Greer and Rosa Griffin coming up the walkway to the school.

They all hugged, and Rosa held up a wicker picnic basket. "I brought some slices of hoop cheese and homemade bread. I thought we could share them with Pauline while we talk. Food always helps the conversation, not to mention that poor little Pauline probably needs the nourishment."

They talked about the wonderful, clear weather as they walked back toward the square and turned right by the Methodist church. Turning right again on Banks Street, they could see the smokestack and water tower looming above the multistory rectangular brick mill. A large metal sign at the entrance announced: Calhoun Cotton Mills: 37,744 Spindles and 1,020 Looms.

"Mrs. Jeter told me that Pauline was hired to work in the spinning room," said Hattie. "I think that is where Edward Marks's mother works as well. Maybe we will see her and she can help us find Pauline."

The whistle blew, signaling the lunch break, and the lappers from the picker room began to exit the first floor. As a husky youth approached, Rosa Griffin called out, "Excuse me, young man, which way is the spinning room?"

The man doffed his dusty felt hat and held it with both hands at his waist. A dark ring of perspiration stain encircled the band. "How do, ladies? The spinning room is on the third floor of the main building. There's a set of stairs over yonder. Are you looking for anybody in particular? Some of 'em stays up there and eats their lunch, and some of 'em will be coming down to take their lunch at home."

"We are looking for a young girl named Pauline Jeter. She has just been hired on here at the mill. I don't expect she'll be going home for dinner, as she lives too far to do that."

"I reckon you'll find her up there, then."

The three women were winded by the time they had climbed the four steep sets of stairs that led to the third floor. Row after row of spinning frames and bobbins filled the room, and the air was thick with cotton dust. The huge ceiling fans above did little to reduce the oppressive heat, and they had to shout to be heard over the roar of the machines. Hattie mopped her forehead with the back of her hand and began looking for Pauline. A woman who appeared to be in her early twenties spotted them and came over.

Earline Greer stepped toward her, cupped her hand, and spoke into the woman's ear. "We are here from the Baptist church, looking for Pauline Jeter. We wanted to invite her to Sunday school and visit with her for a few minutes."

The woman had a friendly smile and a hearty voice that projected over the noise. "Pauline's down there at the end of the third row. Wait right here, and I'll get her. You might want to go downstairs on the lawn to visit, what with it so noisy and hot in here."

She set out down the endless rows and came back shortly with Pauline. Pauline looked so small and out of place, standing there beside the giant machines, her hair in one neat braid that fell down her back and wearing the same faded cotton frock that she had worn to school. Her skin was pale, but her eyes brightened with hope when she saw Hattie. Hattie stretched out her arms and gave Pauline a giant hug. She could feel the shoulder blades protruding through Pauline's skin. It was like holding a tiny bird in one's cupped hands and feeling its skeleton beneath the soft feathers. "I'm so glad to see you. You know Mrs. Greer, Mary's mother, and this is Mrs. Griffin from the church. They have brought some lunch. Let's go downstairs where we can talk."

They descended the brick staircase and found a grassy place on the lawn under a shade tree, away from the crowd of workers who had assembled to socialize and eat their sandwiches. Rosa spread out a cloth and began opening the contents of the basket. Carving a fat slice of cheese from the block, she laid it between two slices of homemade bread and handed it to Pauline. "Here, honey. You go ahead and get started so you'll have time to eat before you have to go back."

"Thank you, ma'am, that's mighty kind of you," she said before she bit hungrily into the sandwich.

"How can I help, Rosa?" asked Earline.

"You can pour us some lemonade. I'm so hot from being up there in that room, I could melt." Rosa finished handing out sandwiches, and Earline filled four cups of lemonade and handed one to Rosa first.

Earline turned to Pauline and got to the point of the visit. Peering directly into the young girl's face, she addressed her with affection, as she might have spoken to her own Mary or Martha. "Pauline, honey, Miss Robinson told us that your family has hit on hard times and, as a result, your father has felt it necessary for you to work at the mill."

"Yes, ma'am. That's right. He's hired me on as a spinner at four fifty a week. I won't get paid until I've finished my training, but when I do, it should help out the family."

"With all due respect to your father, you are mighty young to be taking on such long work hours in the midst of all those machines. But that is not the only thing that concerns us. Miss Robinson says that your father has become abusive of your mother and has struck her for no apparent reason on a number of occasions."

Pauline reddened and began to defend her father. "He don't mean nothing by it. It makes him crazy that he can't provide for us and when he gets like that, he turns to the bottle and that just makes it worse."

Earline remained calm and spoke in a steady but nonaccusatory voice. "Well, a home like that is no place for children to be raised, and your mama must find a safe haven for you and your brother if things don't get better right away. We wanted to talk directly to your mother, but Miss Robinson is afraid if we go to your house, your father might get wind of it and take it out on her. That's the only reason we are putting this on your shoulders."

Soothed by Earline's earnest tone, Pauline relaxed her shoulders and seemed to let down her guard.

"Mrs. Griffin here was recently widowed and she has plenty of space for you and your mother and brother. She has offered to give you room and board if you will help her with the household chores, and will give your mother a job in her alteration shop. That way, you could leave the mill and go back to school where you belong."

Pauline shook her head wistfully. "That would be so nice, but I don't think Mama would ever leave Papa. Even if she did, he would come after us and cause a stir."

"I know it won't be easy, honey, but let's just take this one step at a time. You carry this letter home to your mother and let her read it. It has Mrs. Griffin's name and address on it and directions for how to get to her house. She will be ready day or night to take you in if and when the time comes."

"That's right, Pauline. I'll leave a light on at the kitchen door, and you will know you're welcome anytime. I'd love to have the company. Since Mr. Griffin passed, it's been mighty lonely in that big house. Pshaw! You'd be doing me a favor."

Pauline fingered the letter as if it was a priceless jewel before she tucked it into her apron pocket. Her voice choked with emotion, and she could only whisper, "Thank you, ma'am. I don't know what I did to deserve this. Nobody ever cared this much for us before. I don't know if I can talk Mama into it, but I'm sure gonna try."

"That's the spirit, Pauline. And remember, you are not alone in this. The Lord in heaven is watching over you, and a whole host of people down here on earth are, too. Together we are going to keep you and your family safe."

As the one o'clock whistle blew, Pauline stood up and brushed the crumbs from her skirt. "I'd better get on back."

The three women huddled around her in a group embrace, each whispering one last word of encouragement and farewell. Rosa packed up the rest of the homemade bread and handed it to Pauline. "Here, suga', take this and share it with that nice lady who helped us find you, and eat the rest when you get hungry."

Pauline thanked her and gave a last longing look as she turned to leave. She took a deep breath, squared her shoulders, and lifted her chin as though she were bolstering herself for what lay ahead.

"That precious little brave thing," Rosa remarked as they watched her walk away. "She's carrying a mighty big burden on her shoulders."

Hattie's throat caught. "She's so proud and determined to act grown. She doesn't want anyone to pity her." Hattie wondered if her deep affection for the girl was due in large measure to the fact that she saw in Pauline a younger version of herself.

"Well, at least we have accomplished what we came here to do. It is just a matter of time before Clyde Jeter comes after one of the children. When he does, that will give her the gumption to leave him, if she is any kind of mother. I'll tell you one thing," Rosa said with conviction. "If Jack Griffin had ever laid a hand on one of my children, I'd have come after him with a butcher knife."

"Well, that's a mighty harsh way to put it, but I know what you mean about going to any lengths to protect your children," said Earline.

Hattie thought of her own father and his gentle manner. She could not remember an instance when James had raised his voice or his hand to any of his girls. And the very idea of him striking Mama was simply unthinkable.

It was Mama who was the disciplinarian in their family, and she rarely relied on force. She mostly used psychology mixed with a little honey to bring her children in line. She not only loved her children, she enjoyed them. But there was one thing that Mama would not tolerate and that was hurtful language.

Once, Mama had heard Hattie call their cook a "big fat chocolate turd." She had not said a word, but headed out the kitchen door, her compact body at an eighty-degree angle to the floor, propelled by her short legs that were clipping as fast as barber's shears. When she reached the laurel hedge concealing the clothesline from the rest of the backyard, she'd picked out a nice, long branch, stripped off the leaves, and headed back to find Hattie. Hattie would never forget how Mama had taken hold of her arm, fixed her mouth with her tongue between her teeth, and switched her bare ankles until she danced from the sting of the branch. Mama called it a dose of hickory tea.

"Now," she had said. "You go apologize to Chloe, and we will not hear any more ugly talk like that come out of your mouth again." With that, it was over and done. Mama held no grudges. But Hattie got the point, and it was the last switching she ever received.

All of her brothers and sisters knew that everything Mama and Papa did concerning their children and each other was done out of love. Their home was a safe and secure place where children could thrive. That was not at all the way it was for Pauline, and Hattie's heart broke for the inequity of the situation. She was all the more determined to see to it that Pauline got her chance at the life she deserved.

Hattie was grateful that Rosa and Earline were kindred spirits and felt as strongly as she did about helping Pauline. The three women conspired and planned their next moves as they left the mill and walked back down Banks Street toward town together. By the time they reached the split at the square where Hattie would leave them to go back to school, they had already developed a follow-up plan.

Rosa would go directly home and prepare her guest room for Mrs. Jeter and the children. She would leave the light over the door to the kitchen burning as she had promised Pauline. They would then sit back and wait for Pauline to convince her mother to leave, knowing that it may very well take another crisis with Clyde Jeter to give her the gumption, as Rosa phrased it, to agree. In the meantime, Earline would ask Thomas Greer to pay a visit to the Jeter home just to check on things. As a clergyman, Thomas could go there in a pastoral role without arousing suspicion on the part of Mr. Jeter.

Hattie would see Charles Barton that evening and find out if he had inquired into the situation as he had promised Elizabeth he would. Hattie knew she had better not get directly involved, based on her earlier conversation with Reverend Fitts. One thing she did not want was to get fired in her first year of teaching. That would be the most humiliating thing she could think of, far worse than a formal reprimand, which she had narrowly averted with Mrs. Givens.

When they reached the square at Banks and Main, Hattie embraced Rosa and then Earline. "Thank you so much for helping me with Pauline. I have been paralyzed with worry over her and did not know what to do. Reverend Fitts has warned me about interfering in the private family affairs of my students. He's afraid I'll get the reputation of being outspoken and strident like the suffragists."

"Pshaw," responded Rosa. "Isn't that just like an old sanctimonious preacher man? Sorry, Earline. I wasn't including Thomas in that."

Earline chuckled. "Rosa, you are a mess."

"Honestly—and don't tell anybody I said this—you could be called something worse than a suffragist. I know some of them are outlandish. But somebody needs to stick up for the rights of women in this state, and it's for sure not gonna be the men, especially the preacher men who go around quoting the apostle Paul on marriage."

"Rosa," contradicted Earline. "You putting all preachers in that category is just like people who say all suffragists are strident and outspoken. My Thomas doesn't go around quoting the apostle Paul, nor does he feel that way about women."

Neither did Papa, nor Will, thought Hattie. She was not sure how Charles Barton felt. It was obvious how much he respected Elizabeth and bent to her opinions. But he surely did not leave any doubt about being the lord and master of his household. Still, she could not imagine Charles Barton raising a hand to anyone in his family. He could be stern, but he was too much of a gentleman to engage in domestic violence. He was certainly aloof and withdrawn at times, a complex man. In fact, Hattie had never met a man of such complexity. All of the men she had known were uncomplicated and direct as well as affectionate and easygoing.

At every family gathering she could remember, the men embraced the women and one another in greeting and farewell and sometimes for no reason at all in between. She could not recall ever having seen Charles Barton embrace one of his children, even little Richard. It was evident that he was proud of his wife and family in the way he provided for them, but he never showed his affection publicly. He did have a warm handshake, which he proffered easily to anyone he met. But when it came to any other physical display of warmth, or any other kind of emotion, he was tightly guarded.

Hattie returned to school in time to gather her students from lunch and walk them back inside. Mary Posey assured her that they had been no trouble at all, but Hattie could tell by her forced smile and the way that she hustled them away that she was glad to be relieved of them. The remainder of the afternoon passed without incident, and Hattie was happy to get back to their established routine. The events of the day, starting with Elizabeth's departure and then her confrontation with Reverend Fitts and the trip to see Pauline, had left her drained. By the time the bell rang, she felt as tired as she had that first day of school. That seemed like a lifetime ago now, and here she was finishing up her first year.

Hattie wanted to get back to the Bartons' to see how Richard had made out the first day without his mother. As soon as she dismissed her students, she closed up her classroom and headed for home. Richard spotted her from the kitchen window as she walked up the driveway and ran out to greet her, still dragging his scarf behind him. "Sky fallin'. Sky fallin'," he called out, his delicate little arms raised.

"Hey, Chicken Little." She lifted him up and carried him the rest of the way into the kitchen, where she found Georgia preparing dinner.

"Mr. Charles called. He with a client. He say not to wait on him for supper and to let you know he gonna stop by Mr. George's before he comes home. Says you know what for."

"Lawd, I hope Miz Lizabeth don't haf' t' stay away too long. Mr. Charles liable to work hisself to death while she gone. I tole him to come on home and have dinner with his boys, but it don't do no good to get afta' him. He a driven man when it comes to his almighty work." Georgia shook her head and wiped a streak of biscuit dough from her cheek. "You jes' let me know when you ready and I'll serve you and the boys yo' supper."

"Let's eat early so Richard can sit at the table with us."

They were accustomed to dinner without Mr. Barton, but Elizabeth's absence left a significant void. Hattie tried to fill in as best she could to draw everyone out, to keep the conversation going and to facilitate a sense of normalcy.

"Where did you go at lunchtime today, when Miss Posey looked after the class?" asked George.

"I went with Mrs. Greer and Mrs. Griffin over to Calhoun Mill to check on Pauline Jeter," she answered. "Pauline's father has hired her on in the spinning room. We wanted to be sure she was all right and to see what we could do to get her back in school."

"Pauline was afraid her papa would do that and she was dreading it. Do you think you can do anything to get Mr. Jeter to change his mind?"

"I hope so, Charles. Mrs. Greer and Mrs. Griffin are doing everything they can to help. We'll just have to wait and see."

Friday passed with no word from Pauline, and Hattie reminded herself that she needed to be patient and let their plan take its natural course. Waiting was not Hattie's strong suit. She always felt compelled to do something, to take action. It was not in her nature to leave things alone. When she tried to rush things, Mama had always told her, "Give the dough time to rise, Hattie."

After she helped Georgia clear the breakfast table Saturday morning, she considered walking to town and dropping by to see Rosa under the pretense of needing something from the general store that was only a block from Rosa's house. However, Richard had a million demands for stories and games, and Hattie saw that Georgia's patience was wearing thin and she needed a break from him.

Instead Hattie passed most of the day with Richard, playing audience to his "Watch me" requests and telling him stories and acting them out. Like any toddler, he was supremely happy when he had the undivided attention of an adult to join him in a repetitive cycle, which began when he would tug at Hattie's hand, look up at her with his bright blue eyes and trusting smile, and give a one-word question. "Play?"

Oh, the power in that request! It got her every time. A simple nod of the head, and Richard would take her hand and lead her off to visit the goat for an enactment of the story of the Billy Goats Gruff, followed by a visit to the chicken coup and the telling of Chicken Little and "Sky fallin', sky fallin'." Richard never tired of the cycle. Both Rosa and Earline had promised to call if they got any news. However, the day passed without a word from either of them.

Elizabeth had made Georgia and Mr. Barton promise to see that the children got to church while she was away. Georgia starched and pressed the boys' Sunday clothes and laid them out before she called them in for their baths and bed.

A beautiful Sunday morning dawned, and Charles Jr. and Hattie left early in the wagon so that he could drop her off at the Baptist church and get to Sunday school at the Methodist church. Mr. Barton would bring the other boys in the car and meet them in time for the eleven o'clock service.

As Charles pulled the wagon around to the front of the Baptist sanctuary, they spotted Earline at the door of the parsonage, a white clapboard house situated next to the church. She waved her arm, motioning for Hattie to join her. Hattie jumped from the wagon before Charles could help her and hurried over to meet Earline.

"I'm so glad you got here early, Hattie," said Earline as she ushered her into the parlor. "You won't believe who's here and what happened last night."

Rising from the sofa, Rosa and Pauline rushed over to greet her. "*Pauline!*" Hattie exclaimed. "I've never been so happy to see anybody in my life. I've been thinking about you every minute. How are you? And you too, Rosa. What in the world?"

"Sit down, Hattie, in that wing chair...yes, that one. Pull it over close to the sofa so you can hear it all. Rosa, you tell it start to finish before we have to go over to the morning service. Do not leave out a detail. Hattie will want to know everything."

Rosa was flushed with excitement and began to fan her face with a napkin as she spoke. "I hadn't slept well at all since our visit to the mill, and there was just something that told me this might be the night. I was restless and kept sitting up and looking out the open window across from the bed. The moon was full and it looked like it was plumb hanging on the branches of the giant oak out back. Everything was quiet, and all I could hear was the clock ticking and the night sounds of the crickets and an old owl. Nothing was moving outside." Rosa stopped fanning herself and leaned forward.

"That was until I spotted the silhouettes of two people, each carrying a bundle, coming up the back walkway. It didn't take but a minute, and I said to myself, 'This is it. They are here.' I pulled on my robe and hurried downstairs to the kitchen to let them in. And there they were, coming up the back stoop, Mrs. Jeter holding that precious little towheaded Clydie in her arms, and Pauline lugging a sack of their belongings." Rosa reached out and patted Pauline's leg but kept her gaze on Hattie.

"They were exhausted, and I showed them to their room right away. Mrs. Jeter was anxious to nurse the baby and get him settled down, but Pauline was too excited to sleep and wanted to sit up for a while. I was dying to know all of the details and so I got us both some warm milk and stayed up with her to talk. She was a different child." Rosa turned to look at Pauline and then back at Hattie. "Pauline, you really were—from the one we saw at the mill. She was not a bit shy and could not stop talking until she told me everything. Now Pauline, you take over from here and tell it."

Pauline's eyes were sparkling and she was, as Rosa had said, a different child, eager to tell her story. "I was just waiting for a time when Papa was away to show Mama the letter. But it seemed like when I was at the mill, Papa was gone, and when I was home, Papa was back. Finally, on Saturday evening, Papa set off for town—said he was going to Jakes Grocery to pass some time with the menfolk there. He had his flask and had already taken a few swigs from it.

"When he was gone, I sat Mama down and gave her the letter. And I said, 'Now, Mama, you need to read this. It's from a nice lady at the Baptist church named Mrs. Griffin. She and the pastor's wife and Miss Robinson came over to the mill on Thursday and gave it to me to give to you. They would have come to see you but they were afraid Papa would take it out on us if he learned about it.'

"She took forever to read the letter, like she couldn't quite believe the words, and then she read it again. When she finally finished, she looked up at me with big tears in her eyes. I could tell she was as touched as I was when I first found out. She couldn't talk. She just sat there and shook her head. Finally, she said, 'Bring me my Bible. I'm gonna hafta study and pray about this for a while.' I handed her the Bible and went on to bed because I knew there was no use trying to rush Mama until she was through talking to the Lord. She wouldn't answer anybody when she was praying anyhow." Hattie started to tell Pauline that her mama was like that, too, when she was praying, but Pauline was so excited, she did not want to interrupt her.

"I woke up about midnight to Papa coming home in a terrible drunk state. He had tripped on the stoop and fallen off the front porch. Now he was banging on the window, which he must have mistaken for the front door. It would have been funny if it hadn't of been so scary. I left the bedroom and went out to help Mama with him. We each got up under one of his arms and tried to drag him up the steps. He kept swatting at us and telling us to get away—he could walk into his own goddamn home without the help of any woman. When we let loose of him, he would only stagger and fall down again.

"We finally got him through the door and into the front room. And then is when it all happened. He started rambling and confessed to Mama that he had just gambled away the rent money and that he was pretty sure we were going to get evicted from the house. He told her that some of the menfolk at Jakes Grocery said he could get hired on at the mill, and with him and me working there, we could qualify for a mill house with two bedrooms. Mama couldn't believe her ears. She knew about the drinking, but this was the first time she had heard about the gambling.

"'Why, Clyde Jeter,' she said. 'I didn't say nothing when you sent our little ten-year-old girl off to the mill to work, because I knew you felt awful about it and I thought it was the only thing there was to do. Now you tell me you have gambled away what little bit of money we have saved and have lost the house? And you figure to make it right by leaving the farm and going full-time at the mill? I have been a faithful wife to you. I never said a word when you lost the farm up in Spartanburg County 'cause I knew it wadn't your fault. You worked as hard as you could—we all did—but the cotton wadn't selling, and there was not anything you could do about it. I left my kin and fol-lowed you down here to Pickens County and did the best I could to be a good helpmate. Now we are about to lose our home again and this time it is of your own making.' Mama was riled up like I never saw her.

"'You shut up your mouth, woman,' Papa told her. He hauled off and backhanded her, and the blow split her bottom lip. Papa's strong as an ox, and the force of the swing knocked her back against the fireplace. It also caused him to lose his balance again, and he fell on top of her. The corner of the mantel caught him at the temple and tore the skin before they both hit the hearth. His temple was bleed-ing and he rolled off Mama and grabbed his head, moaning."

Hattie clapped her hands on either side of her face. "Have mercy! I can't believe you had to witness a scene like that. You are just a child."

"Let her finish, Hattie. It gets better."

"Holding her lip, Mama went over to him and started daubing the cut with the bottom of her petticoat to stop the bleeding. He swiped at her again, then fell back on the floor and passed out. Both of us knew there was no use in trying to move him then, so Mama rolled up her shawl and propped up his head with it and then got a blanket and covered him up right there on the floor.

"Something must have just snapped in Mama then," Pauline said. "She looked right at me, her eyes blazin' like a wild woman, but her voice was calm and steady."

"'Pauline,' she said. 'He's gone too far. We have crossed over the river and we can't go back. But we have to act quick while he sleeps it off. Go get that croaker sack I been storing the 'taters in, and we will fill it with just a few things to get by on what we can carry. We won't wake up Clydie till we're ready to leave.'

"So we sneaked around real quiet and got a few things together. At the last minute, Mama picked up Clydie from his crib and wrapped his blanket around him, and he never even woke up until we got to Miz Griffin's porch. We tiptoed out of the house with Papa snoring away, closed the door and started toward town.

"We were both so scared. What if Miz Griffin had forgot or had a change of heart?" Rosa patted her again and put her arm around her shoulder for support, but Pauline was eager to continue. "Where would we go and what would we do? That walk of a little over a mile to town seemed like a trek across the desert. We were leaving everything behind. At the same time, we had this feeling like we were free as the breeze. Mama said she knew just how the Israelites felt leaving Egypt and following Moses toward the Promised Land—terrified but full of hope.

"The night was cool and the sky was bright with the full moon. As we got close to Miz Griffin's house, I saw Mama take the letter out and hold it real close to her heart. But she didn't need to worry. Miz Griffin was true to her word. The porch light was on, just like she promised it would be. Mama took hold of my hand and squeezed it, and we hurried on. We didn't even have to knock on the door. Miz Griffin was there to meet us, looking for all the world like a guardian angel."

"Why, Pauline, after all that happened, I can't believe you are here today," exclaimed Hattie.

"She wouldn't hear of anything else," said Rosa, patting Pauline with affection. "Besides, I think she is still running on adrenaline from last night. Mrs. Jeter—Velma—wanted to come too, but was embarrassed about her swollen lip. We convinced her to stay at home and let it heal. Besides, she did not need to uproot little Clydie. It is best for him to get used to his new quarters. Although I do not think he ever knew what was going on. He slept all through the trip over in his mother's arms and settled right down once Velma nursed him and put him in his new bed. That bed belonged to my Janie, who is now a grown woman with children of her own, though Lord knows I never see any of them now that that their father moved them all the way to Atlanta with the railroad. Anyhow, it's best that Velma rest up and get her strength for what's to come."

Hattie dismissed the question that was undoubtedly on everyone's mind: What would happen when Clyde Jeter sobered up and found his family gone? He would have no idea where they were, but it was a small community, and he was sure to find out soon enough. For now, she was happy that Pauline, Velma, and little Clydie were beyond his reach and safely tucked into Rosa Griffin's guest bedroom.

"We'd better get over to the morning service," interrupted Earline. "Betty Larke is out with a sick child today, and Thomas asked me to fill in for her."

Rosa patted Pauline again. "Yes, let's don't be late. We have so much to thank God for today, don't we, Pauline?"

"Yes, ma'am, we sure do."

13

auline was one of the first students to arrive in class on Monday. Mary and Frannie spotted her and ran toward the door to greet her. Pauline grinned at Hattie as she proudly held up her own lunch, which Rosa had packed for her. Earline had sent her home on Sunday with two dresses that Martha had outgrown, one of which she was wearing today. Mary was already larger than her older sister and would never have fit into them. In less than forty-eight hours, Pauline had already taken on the look of a child who was cared for and loved. She seemed to be responding to the attention like a thirsty daffodil lifting its petals to receive the rain.

Hattie ended the morning reading-and-math session early and took a few minutes to talk to the students about the end-of-year production scheduled for the last Friday night in May, before promotion. It would be a night for parents to gather and for the students to display what they had learned during the year.

The lower grades would entertain with skits and songs; the students in the upper grades were writing essays and memorizing poetry related to the curriculum that they had studied. Reverend Fitts would choose the most accomplished pieces to be performed for the parents. Hattie had promised to help with the musical section of the program.

"Fifth graders will participate in a choral reading, which you will be expected to learn by heart. Sixth graders will choose either a poem that you will commit to memory and present or an original essay or poem. You may select your poems from the reader, or if you would like, you may borrow a book from the library and work on that. We will reserve some school time to prepare for the production, but extra effort will be required. I will be available after school on Monday, Tuesday, and Thursday for help sessions." It was a warm, clear day, and the children had spring fever. Hattie dismissed them to lunch a few minutes early.

She watched to make certain that Pauline was adjusting to her first day back and was delighted to see that she and Mary Greer had formed a bond over their church connection. All the girls from the church met and went outside together. Hattie was grateful that Pauline was occupied. Hattie needed to see Mary Posey about the plans for the production and knew that she could do that at lunch. The two teachers had developed a real affection for one another. They took up their regular positions so that Hattie faced the grove of trees where the girls were gathered, and Mary faced the field where the boys were playing ball. As they kept watch over their classes while eating their lunches and conducting business, they laughed about teachers needing eyes in the backs of their heads.

All of a sudden, Hattie noticed the girls had converged around Pauline. She got up to investigate. As she approached the little covey, she saw that Pauline was shaking, the color completely drained from her face. Pauline pointed in the direction of School Street. "Oh, Miss Robinson, yonder comes Papa."

Hattie's blood ran cold. She knew Clyde Jeter would come looking for his family, but had not guessed he would show up at school. If he saw Pauline, he would demand to take her with him, and as Charles Barton had reminded her, he had every legal right as her father to do so. *But not if he can't find her,* Hattie thought.

She knew she must act quickly. "Mary, I want you to take Pauline back to our classroom. Go in the cloakroom and close the door. Stay there until I come for you. Can you be brave and do that?" Wide-eyed, Mary nodded. "Go around behind the trees and through the back entrance to the school before Mr. Jeter spots her."

KATHERINE P. STILLERMAN

"Yes, ma'am." Mary grabbed Pauline's hand, and the two ran off toward the school.

"Sarah, you and Frannie go find Reverend Fitts. Tell him to come out here—that we may have some trouble. Now everybody else just act normal, and I'll handle the rest."

"What are you gonna tell him, Hattie?" asked Mary Posey.

"I'm going to say—"

"Hush, here he comes. He's spotted us out here on the grounds."

Empowered by her determination to protect Pauline, Hattie inhaled deeply, lifted her shoulders and chin, and walked deliberately toward Mr. Jeter. "Hello, Mr. Jeter. What brings you here today?"

Mr. Jeter planted his feet wide, resting his hands on his hips. "I come looking for Pauline. Where is she?"

Hattie was not sure if he had already begun drinking or if what she smelled was the alcohol that remained in his system. Either way, the odor almost knocked her over, and she could see the children back away.

"Why, Mr. Jeter, I thought you had hired her out at the mill."

"Don't you act all innocent with me, Miss Robinson. You know she's not at the mill. I just been up there, and her supervisor told me she did not show up today. I got to asking questions, and she told me Pauline had visitors from some women at the church last week. She said one of them was Pauline's teacher."

Hattie intentionally maintained her formal teacher voice, which she hoped would intimidate him and give her the edge. "That's correct, Mr. Jeter. We did pay a visit to Pauline at the mill last week. And, yes, Pauline did come to school today, but she is inside the building and is unavailable right now. Perhaps you can see her after school hours when she gets home."

"There you go again, acting all high and mighty. You know Pauline ain't coming home. You know her and her mama and little Clydie ain't been home since Saturday. But I come to git her and take her back where she belongs." He jabbed his index finger upward toward Hattie's chin and brought his face within an inch of her nose.

The cut on his temple had scabbed over and his eyes were bulging and bloodshot. Hattie could see the enlarged vessels radiating out from his pupils like newly hatched tadpoles swimming for shore. His breath reeked of stale tobacco and alcohol, and it was all Hattie could do to keep from turning her head. "I don't need you telling me she's not available. I'm her papa and I have a right to get her whenever I decide to, an' there ain't no agent of the state gonna stand in my way."

He removed his finger from Hattie's face and, in a grand gesture, swung his arm around in an arc behind him, pointing to the circle of students who had gathered and were staring in shocked amazement at this unruly and disheveled man speaking in utter disrespect to their teacher. His speech was slurred, but he punctuated each of the following words. "Now-you-send-one-of-them-kids-in-there-to-git-Pauline-so-I can-take-her-home."

"Mr. Jeter! Please back away from Miss Robinson and come with me." The circle of students had blocked Hattie's view of Reverend Fitts, who must have received Sarah and Frannie's message. Hattie had never been so glad to see anyone.

"I ain't trying to cause no trouble, Reverend. I jes' come here to git my daughter. Miss Robinson's trying to tell me she is unavailable. En' I was jes' telling her, ain't no such thing as a child being unavailable to her papa. I got a right to take her, and ain't no agent of the state can stand in the way."

"Mr. Jeter, you are in no condition to be here with these children, and I will not have you speak to one of my teachers with such disrespect. Miss Robinson, Miss Posey, take the students inside while I escort Mr. Jeter from school grounds."

Reverend Fitts leaned toward Mr. Jeter and grasped him by the arm in an effort to urge him off the grounds in the direction of School Street. Mr. Jeter jerked away his arm, and his elbow hit Reverend Fitts squarely in his spectacled eye, making a distinct thwacking sound and jarring the lens so that it bent the wire rim and snapped off from the earpiece. An audible gasp came from the children who were watching with a mix of horror and fascination.

"You four-eyed son of a bitch. I ain't going nowhere till you bring me my daughter."

Visibly shaken but undeterred, Reverend Fitts took a moment to remove what remained of his glasses and tuck them into his jacket pocket. Hattie recovered her composure and clapped her hands to get her students' attention. Her voice cut through the air like that of a drill sergeant. "Students, proceed immediately to the steps and wait. My class will form a straight line on the left side of the staircase, and Miss Posey's class on the right." The students snapped to like little soldiers and did as their teacher directed.

Mary Posey hurried toward the steps with the children. "I'll go ahead, and you stay back to see if Reverend Fitts needs any help."

"Mr. Jeter, I will not release Pauline to you in your condition," reasoned Reverend Fitts. "You are inebriated and disorderly. I will ask you to leave the premises on your own volition before I take further action to have you removed."

"I'm not taking my volition anywhere until you hand over my daughter," mocked Clyde Jeter.

"Very well, Mr. Jeter. You give me no other option but to contact the sheriff and take out a warrant to have you arrested for disorderly conduct on school grounds."

This comment got his attention and Clyde Jeter threw up his arms and lumbered off toward the street like an old circus bear performing on his hind legs. "Hold your horses, Reverend. I'm leaving. But this ain't the end of it. Clyde Jeter ain't gonna stand for nobody coming between him and his family. No sir. A man's got a right to be the head of his household and to keep his wife and his children in line. You ought to know that, Reverend. That's straight from the apostle Paul in the Bible."

Reverend Fitts, who followed him to the edge of school grounds, restrained himself from having the last word. After all, he had accomplished his goal of getting Mr. Jeter to leave, and it would serve no purpose other than to delay his departure. Hattie heard him remind himself, "Do not speak in the hearing of a fool, for he will despise the wisdom of your words." She recognized Proverbs 23:9.

Hattie rushed toward him. "Are you all right?"

"Yes, I am unharmed. Although I cannot say the same thing for my glasses. And I must admit that I can't see much without them." Reverend Fitts was squinting like an old mole that had come from his tunnel into the blinding sunlight. However, Hattie could tell by the way he squared his shoulders and puffed out his chest that he was proud to have played the role of the hero.

"Oh, Reverend Fitts, thank you so much for not letting him take Pauline. She is doing so well over at Mrs. Griffin's now that she's out from under him."

Reverend Fitts suppressed a smile and tried to regain his dignity. It was a bit difficult looking as he did, blinking and straining to bring focus to the world around him. "Well, I can keep him off school grounds, but I have no jurisdiction over what he does outside of that. It would probably be wise to make a plan for someone to escort Pauline to and from school.

"I am going now to the courthouse to report the incident and file a restraining order against Mr. Jeter to keep him from returning. I will stop by Dr. Jones's to have him replace the lens on my glasses so that I will be able to see to sign the papers. More importantly, I'll need them to read the sermon I have prepared from the words of the apostle Paul on marriage and family."

Hattie smiled and shook her head. Mary Posey had told her that Reverend Fitts had a sense of humor. Maybe she was right.

"Miss Robinson, if you would, please stop by Mr. Larke's room and ask him to keep an eye on things while I am off campus. I should be back before end-of-day dismissal."

When Hattie returned to her classroom, she found Mary and some of the other girls in the cloakroom huddled around Pauline. Pauline saw Hattie, broke away from them, and clung to her teacher in terror.

"Does Pauline have to go with him, Miss Robinson?" asked Mary. "She shouldn't have to. It's not fair how he treats her."

"No, dear. Pauline is not going anywhere." She squeezed Pauline for reassurance but could feel Pauline's body quaking. "It is all over now, and Mr. Jeter is gone. Reverend Fitts is on his way to see the sheriff to make certain he can never come back on school grounds in that condition. Everyone is safe. Let's go back to the classroom and we will talk about it. Pauline, do you feel up to going with us or do you want me to find a safe place for you to rest until school is out? I could send Mary with you if you like."

Pauline was emphatic. "No, I want to go with you and the others."

They found the boys crowded around the window, straining to catch a glimpse of what was going on outside. "Julian Clinkscales," Hattie called out, "if you lean out any farther, we'll have to catch you by your heels to keep you from falling into the bushes below." Julian turned red and he and all the boys scrambled back to their seats.

God bless Tillie Chapman. After the ruckus, Miss Posey had brought the students as far as the classroom and put Tillie in charge so that she could get her younger children settled down. They had been somewhat traumatized by the event and some of them were crying for their mothers. Tillie had assured Miss Posey that she could handle things and had gotten all of the children in their places by threatening them with a week of detention at recess. The students were compliant until they saw their teacher, and at that point Tillie's reign was over.

Hattie did not even attempt to begin the lesson until the children had an opportunity to settle down and make sense of the incident. The questions came like rain pelting on a tin roof.

"Is Reverend Fitts all right?"

"Did you hear how he talked to you?"

"Was he drunk?"

"Will Pauline have to go back to the mill?"

"One at a time, please. You will use your manners and raise your hands to be recognized." The high school students appeared at the door and Hattie motioned for them to come in. She could tell by their eagerness to find their seats that they had already learned of Mr. Jeter's appearance and were interested in hearing the gossip first-hand. "I am sorry that you had to witness such a disturbing scene, especially here at school. But let me assure you that all is well. Reverend Fitts is unharmed, Pauline is safe, and Mr. Jeter will not be allowed to come back on school property."

Charles raised his hand. "I heard he was cursing and was disrespectful to you, too, Miss Robinson, and you stood up to him just like you did that day when we made the home visit."

"Yes, well, everyone involved responded professionally. And I am especially proud of the way this class followed instructions and came back to the room. I am also proud of you for supporting Pauline during this difficult time. It shows me that you have learned to be self-disciplined and compassionate, and that you have taken to heart our lessons about doing unto others as you would have them do unto you.

"Now, I need to call on this class to go a step farther. We must make certain that Pauline does not ever have to walk to or from school by herself, and that others accompany her. Pauline and her mother are now living in town with Mrs. Rosa Griffin, on Main Street. Can I count on some of you older town folks to see her safely to and from school?"

Charles's hand shot up. "I can get up early and go into town with Mr. Jenkins and then go over and get Pauline."

"That's a nice offer, Charles. But I think you'd better let someone who lives a bit closer do that."

Pauline ducked her head, and Hattie could see her tremble. "Oh, Pauline. I'm afraid this is too hard on you. Let's walk outside for a few minutes."

"No, I want to stay here. It's just that I am so ashamed about Papa showing up. Now everybody knows about our problems. Nobody else has a papa who acts like that." Hattie moved closer to Pauline and Mary closed in and took her hand.

Jimmy Hicks stood up and came toward her. "That's not true, Pauline. My papa is awful mean when he's drinking and takes it out on my mama and me. But I've learned to take up for myself and I'll take up for you, too, if your papa ever tries to lay a hand on you while I'm around. Why, one night, my papa came home roaring drunk, cussing at Mama and shoving her around. I yelled at him to stop, and he backhanded me and said, 'Don't you tell me what to do. I wear the pants in this family, boy.' He stumbled off to the bedroom, stripped off his clothes, and passed out on the bed. I was so mad, I snuck in and got his overalls hanging on the bedpost and I went and got every pair of pants he owned, right down to his Sunday go-to-meeting trousers and his long johns, and took 'em out back and set fire to them.

"When he came to next morning, he got to looking for something to pull on over his shorts and couldn't find a thing. He was charging like a bull all over the place but there wasn't anything he could do. He had to stay in the house until Mama could go to the hardware and get him a new pair of dungarees. He suspected it was me, but he never could prove it. I guess I showed him a thing or two that day about who wore the pants in the family."

Hattie heard chuckles from the class and suppressed her own urge to laugh. Jimmy's anecdote had shifted the focus away from Pauline and served to break the tension. Pauline relaxed a little and responded, "Thank you for saying that, Jimmy. That is real nice. It's good to know I'm not the only one who has problems. Not that I would wish them on you."

Tom Givens piped up. "Shucks, I just live a few blocks from where you are staying and I'll walk you to school every day. I can walk you home, too."

Will wonders never cease, thought Hattie. *Even the bully has a heart.*

Charles cut in. "Never mind, Tom. I'll take care of her in the afternoon. Now that Gene can walk home with George, I usually go by Uncle Bailey's shop before I go home, and it's right behind Mrs. Griffin's."

"Don't forget about us," called out Mary, who was the tallest and most mature of the fifth-grade girls, as well as the spokesman for her group. "We girls always walk to school together, and we will go by and pick up Pauline. We're not that big, but we aren't afraid of Mr. Jeter."

Pauline brightened from all the attention. Hattie's challenge to protect one of their own had empowered the children into action. They began to chatter like starlings about how to carry out the plans. Hattie did not interrupt. This was the best teachable moment on empathy and kindness she could have wished for.

Mary took the lead. "Okay. Mama always gets us up by six and has our breakfast by seven. We will leave a few minutes early and go by Mrs. Griffin's. Tom, you can meet us there, and we'll all walk to school together. We'll all gather at the steps after school and walk back together."

"And don't forget, I'll be there to walk her home," put in Charles. "Don't you worry, Pauline. Everything's gonna be all right."

He's right, thought Hattie. *Everything will be all right.*

14

Mr. Barton came home in time to have dinner with Hattie and the children that night. The table was abuzz with the news of Mr. Jeter's appearance at school earlier in the day. Mr. Barton had seen Reverend Fitts at the courthouse and had helped him file the papers to have Mr. Jeter served. He had also stopped by to see Mrs. Jeter and offered her legal assistance.

"I talked with George, and he has given Clyde Jeter notice of eviction. He told Lonnie Jenkins to make sure Clyde and all his belongings were out by the end of the month and to start getting the house ready for a new tenant. George was willing to work with Clyde until he discovered that Clyde was gambling and had lost his rent money in a bet. George was surprised at the change of behavior, in that he had known Clyde to be a good and honest worker until recently. He has told Clyde that if he will sober up and stay off the bottle, as well as quit his gambling, he will help him get hired on at the mill as a carder or a loom fixer. That way, he would be eligible for mill housing and have a place to live. When he puts his life back together, he can think about getting his family back."

Charles looked at his father with surprised indignation. "But what if his family does not want to go back to him, Father? Pauline is scared to death of him and she is happy where she is."

Mr. Barton's tone was calm and unemotional. "Mrs. Jeter cannot be forced to go back to him but, in the end, the law will be on the side of the father regarding the custody of the children."

"That's not fair," Charles objected.

"It may not be fair, Charles. But it's the law. At this point, it would be best not to get the court involved, but to do everything we can to help Mr. Jeter regain his dignity and his livelihood so that he will be more likely to behave responsibly toward his family. A man who cannot support his family is likely to lose hope and feel he has nothing to work for. Pauline and her mother and brother are safe at Mrs. Griffin's while he has a chance to get back on his feet. He will be banned from school grounds, which will preclude any more incidents like the one that happened today. I think that's about the best solution we can ask for right now. But you need to realize that the law is on the father's side when it comes to his children."

Hattie could tell that Charles was unconvinced. However, it would obviously be futile to continue the conversation, as Mr. Barton had already put down his napkin and slid back his chair to leave. When his father was safely out of hearing distance, Charles remarked, "Well, if it came down to a choice between helping Pauline and breaking the law, I know what I would do."

Little Gene had apparently been soaking in the conversation and was staring blankly at his plate. *Poor thing*, Hattie thought. *With his mother away and all this commotion over Clyde Jeter showing up at school and scaring everybody to death, he must be awfully confused.*

"Come on, Gene. Let's go upstairs and read Richard a story before he goes down. Then I will listen to you read for a while and help you learn your part for the recitation."

"Okay." Gene brightened and then looked quizzically at Hattie before he said what was on his mind. "Miss Robinson, Father never would treat us like Mr. Jeter treats Pauline, would he?"

"No, Gene, he's much too fine a man and loves you too much for that."

"I know. And besides, Mother would never stand for it."

Hattie chuckled. "Yes, that's also true."

Pauline returned to school on Monday, accompanied by her fifth-and-sixth grade escorts, with Tom and Charles tripping over themselves in competition to protect her. As a sense of normalcy returned to the classroom, Hattie began to focus the students' attention on the end of year performance, using every spare moment to rehearse them on their various parts. The day passed without incident.

Clyde Jeter's inebriated appearance at school turned into old news that was quickly replaced with talk about the swollen black clouds that had gathered in the western sky, threatening to bring a drastic change in the weather. Hattie hoped the front would stall at least until they could all get home from school that day.

As April had come to an end in Calhoun, the gentle rains had given way to cool dry winds that dusted the atmosphere with pollen, as thoroughly as a young bride might dust talcum powder on her freshly bathed skin. The dry spell ended abruptly on Tuesday, with a sudden downpour that washed the sticky yellow spores from the trees and onto the earth. The running water saturated the cracks in the red clay banks, forming little rivulets that carried the pollen and collected additional detritus as it moved in search of level ground.

Despite the downpour, school had remained open. However, some of the students who lived in lower lying areas near the river where the roads had been washed out, remained at home; and, attendance toward the end of the week was down. The teachers and students who did make it to school, were damp and thoroughly covered in mud when they arrived. By the end of the day on Friday, Hattie felt like a soggy mess, and thought she would scream if she couldn't get home and into some dry, clean clothes. The rain continued relentlessly over the weekend, causing the creeks to swell and the river to rise within inches of the old covered bridge down by the mill.

On Sunday evening, Georgia was serving dinner to the family, when Elizabeth Barton called to say that Aunt Nellie was much improved and that she would be returning to Calhoun the next Friday. Charles Barton had left the table briefly to take the call and when he returned, Hattie could tell that he was genuinely elated as he relayed the information to everyone at the table.

"Robert told Elizabeth when he picked her up at the station last Thursday, that when Aunt Nellie learned of Elizabeth's visit, she perked up and became more like her old self than she had been since before her fall."

"Mother has that effect on people," said Charles, Junior. His father smiled and nodded his head before he said, "I'll be leaving on business tomorrow, but will be back by Thursday evening."

"Where are you going, Father?" asked George.

"I'm driving up north of Caesar's Head to survey a tract of land adjacent to the family hunting lodge that Uncle George and I have been trying to purchase. I'll spend the next few nights up at the lodge while I'm closing out the deal, and be back in Calhoun in plenty of time to pick up your mother on Friday."

"Won't it be awful messy up there with all the rain?"

"A man can't let a little bit of water stop him, George. Besides, the plot of land we're buying will have the same dimensions whether it is wet or dry. That reminds me, though, I need to ask Georgia to find my rain gear and a good pair of boots so I can pack them." Charles Barton excused himself from the table and headed toward his study.

"Did you hear Father say that Mother's coming home on Friday?" Gene asked Hattie.

"Yes, I heard that and I could not be happier. You have missed her, haven't you, Gene?"

"Yes, ma'am. But I'm glad she could be there to help Aunt Nellie. Aunt Nellie is all alone and sick and she needed Mother to nurse her. But I sure am happy she is better so Mother can come home to us."

Hattie was touched by Gene's words. These Barton boys were remarkable children. One rarely saw that degree of empathy expressed by the very young.

"Gene, you have your mother's sweet temperament. I am sure that right now she is thinking about you and counting the hours until she can see you again."

"I'm going upstairs to make her a big welcome home card," said Gene. "Will you help me spell all the words right, Miss Robinson?"

When Hattie came down the stairs from helping Gene, she heard Georgia talking to Mr. Barton in the kitchen. Georgia sounded agitated. Hattie had heard her use the same scolding tone with Elizabeth before she left for Asheville. She paused for a moment on the bottom step to listen.

"Mista' Charles, you know you ain't driving yo' car up to that mountain in this pouring rain. That road up to Barton Ridge is bad enough in good weather, but after all this wata', it'll be plum washed out by now. You gonna' mess around and get yo' car mired up to the top of the wheels and you'll be stuck up there all by yo' self. "

Charles Barton laughed and Hattie heard in his voice a deep affection for the woman who was admonishing him. "Don't fuss, Georgia. I'll be alright. Tom Snyder is going to open up the lodge and start a fire before I get there. I know every inch of that mountain from having hunted up there since I was a boy. I feel completely safe; but If I should get stuck, you know Tom's cabin is only a quarter of a mile down the mountain. Besides, I have no doubt that if I weren't back home in plenty of time to pick up Elizabeth, you'd send Lonnie Jenkins up there with a mule and wagon to find me and bring me back."

"Well, I spec' you right about that, but it don't make no sense to me why you have to go off in this rain in the first place. That land sho' ain't going nowhere before the sun comes out again."

Hattie shook her head and thought, *Georgia is the only one in the world who could get away with talking to Charles Barton like that.*

In the end, Georgia capitulated to Charles Barton's wishes, as she had with Elizabeth, and Hattie heard her say, "But since yo' mind's made up, I guess the least I can do is to go find something to keep yo' head and feet dry so you won't catch yo' death of cold."

Hattie was afraid Georgia may be right about Mr. Barton needing to postpone his trip. However, by Monday morning, the rain tapered off to a drizzle, the clouds began to part, and Mr. Barton drove Hattie and the children to school before he left for his trip.

On Thursday afternoon, Hattie was talking to the class about a dangerous incident that Reverend Fitts had learned about from Paul Godfrey, at the mill, and had asked the teachers to address with their students. Her shoes were still damp from the wet spell and she kicked them off as she sat at her desk, where her stocking feet would not be visible.

"We are all happy that the rain has ended and the fair weather has returned. However, there is still a good deal of standing water that we need to watch out for. The river has swollen over its banks and the water is very swift, especially down by the mill. Mr. Godfrey reported that he saw a group of students from Calhoun School climbing out on the branches of the river birch trees and daring one another to swing out over the water. He said that one boy swung out and got caught hanging from a branch."

"I bet it was Julian," said Tom Givens.

"It was not!" said Julian. "My granny's got me grounded and I can't go anywhere but school and church for two weeks."

"I don't need to know who it was, Tom. I simply want to stress to all of you how dangerous the rivers and creeks can be when there is flooding. The water is swift and deep in spots, and there are all kinds of debris being pulled along by the currents. Some of you can't even swim, and if you fell in you could be dragged down before someone could rescue you."

"I wasn't one of the ones down there either, but I'm a good swimmer," said Jimmy Hicks. "I can beat anybody in a race to swim to the other side."

"Even a good swimmer must respect the water under flooding conditions, Jimmy."

"I bet I can beat you, Jimmy," said Edward Marks. "'Course I wadn't down there either."

Tillie Chapman piped up. "You boys are such liars. Why don't you just go on and admit it. Every one of you has been down to that river since it flooded. You're drawn to it like a bunch of rats to cheese."

"Tillie, it is not ladylike to call anyone a liar. Besides, I just told you I am not interested in casting blame on anyone. I only want to warn you of the danger and make certain no one returns there until the water recedes."

"Well, I just think they all ought to be kept in from recess for it."

"You would," said Tom Givens. "Why don't you mind your own business and stop being such a tattle tale?"

"That's enough, Tom," said Hattie. "Thank you for your opinion, Tillie, but since I am in charge of the class we will do it my way. I don't intend to punish anyone for what happened in the past, but from this point on, if I hear of anyone going down by the river before the water recedes, I will report it to Reverend Fitts as well as to your parents. I could not bear it if any harm came to one of my students, especially harm that is completely preventable." Hattie thrust her feet back into her damp shoes and stood. "Now, we will consider this subject closed. Please get out your social studies homework and place it on your desks for me to check."

As Hattie circulated around the room, she spotted something through the window that aroused her curiosity. She watched as Uncle George pulled his yellow Packard roadster to the front of the school. Charles and George had noticed it as well. In their triangulated glances, they appeared to be asking one another, *What in the world is he doing here?*

George parked the car and hurried up the concrete steps, disappearing from view. Hattie refocused her attention on the class and continued checking homework, trying to dismiss the strange sense of foreboding that she was feeling and not wanting to alarm Charles and George. It appeared to work with George; however, the more perceptive Charles continued to glance around distractedly, biting at the end of his pen and shifting in his seat.

Several moments passed before the classroom door opened and Reverend Fitts entered, appearing rather solemn and ministerial. It was the same look he always wore whenever an important community member visited the school. "Miss Robinson, please have George and Charles Barton gather their things. Their uncle George is in my office with their brother Gene, waiting to take the three of them home. And as soon as you have dismissed your students, please come to my office as well." George and Charles had already put away their books and were scrambling to the door, happy to be released early but seemingly clueless as to the reason.

Hattie's pulse quickened. Something unexpected had clearly happened, but what on earth could it be? She knew that Charles Barton had been at the family lodge and was due to return by the end of the day so that he could pick up Mrs. Barton on Friday. Had the roads washed out or had his car gotten bogged down in the mud as Georgia warned? Would Georgia have contacted Lonnie Jenkins to drive the mule and wagon up to bring him back? And maybe Uncle George was going with Lonnie and had come for the children and Hattie before he left? Or, could Elizabeth have called to say that Aunt Nellie had taken a turn for the worst, and summoned the family to Asheville? That did not seem likely in light of the rosy prognosis that Elizabeth had given during her recent call. *Well, I am sure there is a logical explanation for all of this,* thought Hattie, attempting to refocus on her class.

The other students began to murmur and get off task. Tom Givens took advantage of the interruption to leave his seat and stare out the window as Uncle George, followed by the three Barton boys, got in the car and drove away from the school.

"Sit down this minute, Tom." Hattie's voice was sharp and strident. She could not deal with his shenanigans right now. "Class, please finish your seatwork as I write the assignments on the board." She put up the assignments and reviewed them with the students, willing herself to remain on task until, blessedly, four o'clock arrived. She had the students straighten their rows and line up at the door for dismissal.

After they were gone, she rushed to tidy up her desk and hurried to Reverend Fitts's office. Reverend Fitts stood and ushered her in, waiting for her to be seated. She could tell by his somber expression that the news he was about to deliver was of grave consequence. His speech was measured and slow.

"Miss, Robinson, the Bartons have just received word of a tragic loss in their family. As you know, Mrs. Barton was in Asheville where she had gone to care for her aunt, Mrs. Nellie Simpson."

"Oh, it's poor aunt Nellie. And Mrs. Barton had sent word that her leg was healing nicely. What happened? How did she die?"

Reverend Fitts cleared his throat. "No, it's not Mrs. Simpson. She survived. But there was a fire in the hotel, and Mrs. Barton...well, I am afraid Mrs. Barton did not survive it."

"You mean Elizabeth Barton?" Hattie recoiled in horror.

"Yes, the same. And true to her unselfish nature, she perished trying to save her aunt. The fire broke out in the wee hours this morning and burned the hotel to the ground. It seems that Mrs. Barton was in the room next to Mrs. Simpson and went in to see about her when she heard the fire alarm and smelled the smoke. The woman who attended Mrs. Simpson had left for the night, and there was no one to help Mrs. Barton get her aunt to safety.

"Mrs. Barton lifted her all alone and carried her halfway down the hallway until Mrs. Simpson's son arrived from his quarters to help them. Everyone got out safely before the building burned to the ground. However, the exertion of carrying her aunt combined with the inhalation of the smoke proved an overwhelming burden on her already frail heart, and she died of heart failure less than an hour later. I understand that as soon as Mr. Barton received the call about his wife, he left for Asheville to bring back her remains."

The words crashed in on Hattie like tidal waves. Their roar was deafening as they echoed and reverberated in her ears. *Fire...did not survive...heart failure...bringing back her remains....Elizabeth Barton...*

"Miss Robinson? Are you going to be all right?" Reverend Fitts was bending over, gazing at her with concerned eyes. He laid a hand gently on her shoulder. His tone was humble and honest, lacking the pretense and affectation it normally carried.

"It is difficult to understand why God would call home one so pure in heart just when her presence is needed so much here on earth. Still, we must trust in him and have faith that she is in his hands. Come, I will drive you home to the Bartons'. You are in no condition to walk. And I need to pay a call and check on the family."

"Thank you," she whispered and allowed him to lead her out of the office and into his car.

As she struggled to regain her composure, she remembered Richard and reeled at the thought of what this loss would mean to him. The image of Elizabeth as Hattie had last seen her, blowing kisses to him from the car, made her swoon. How would their lives go on without her?

Georgia met them at the door, grief-stricken eyes flooded and overflowing. Reverend Fitts made his way into the parlor where the rest of the family had gathered in dazed disbelief. The two women embraced in unspoken sorrow, clinging to one another for dear life and swaying gently back and forth. Hattie, a good head shorter than Georgia, buried her face in Georgia's ample bosom. Intermittently, Georgia moaned, "My baby, my baby…she was my baby. I tol' her not to go. I tol' her not to go." Her tears rolled down and bathed Hattie's cheeks and neck in cleansing grief.

The immediate hours and days unfolded against a backdrop of con-fusion and disarray. Time lost meaning. Hattie experienced a replay of her own father's death when she'd felt like an observer, watching herself in scene after scene of grief through a smoky glass, muddling through the formalities, the death rituals and customs, aware of little else but the ache deep inside. The pang would subside briefly when she was distracted from the reality of the moment, only to return when Charles or George or Gene would enter the room to greet a guest or when Georgia would pass by with another dish sent in by one of the church ladies.

It broke her heart to see the boys dressed in black mourning clothes, circulating among the guests, with their impeccable manners ingrained from birth, second nature and automatic. But their flat voices and empty, haunting stares through wide eyes betrayed their confusion and grief.

For the present, Richard was immune to news of his mother's death. He was aware that something was not as it should be and he continued to cling to Elizabeth's scarf and carry it with him everywhere. Basking in the hugs and adoring looks that he received from community members and family who filed into the house in droves to pay their respects, he would point his index finger and make jabbing motions upward, explaining, "Mama up dere. Mama in hebben."

When Mr. Barton was not attending to his duties as host, he withdrew to his study and was somber and melancholy. Without Elizabeth, the Barton home was empty. Where before, her presence had filled each room with energy and warmth like a fireplace that heats the air and dispels the cold, now each space echoed like a medieval castle, and the place rattled as though every piece of furniture had been removed.

Hattie attended the funeral at the Calhoun Methodist Church at eleven a.m. on May 11, followed by interment in the church cemetery. The sanctuary was packed with family and community members who gathered to pay their respects to the dearly departed. The *Calhoun Sentinel* published a lengthy obituary that described Elizabeth as "one of the town's most beloved residents; a gracious woman, kind to all she met and with whom she came in contact."

With the obsequies concluded, the period of mourning officially began. Everyone in the household resumed their daily regimes. School would be out on May 29, and Hattie struggled to regain her focus on preparing the students for their final exams and for the end-of-year performance. She was glad to have a reason to leave the melancholic atmosphere at the Barton house and discovered that the boys felt the same way. They all welcomed the distraction of school and found themselves looking for reasons to linger later and later before returning home.

Mary Posey was deeply concerned for her friend and hovered around Hattie like a mother bird guarding a nest of fledglings. During the day, she darted in and out with numerous reasons to interrupt and check on Hattie, on the pretense of needing to know something about the end-of-year performance. At the end of each day, she would gather up a stack of papers and head directly to Hattie's room. Mary had become a good friend, and Hattie was glad for the company and for the attention. She felt she could tell Mary anything. Who would have predicted from their rocky start that they would end up being this companionable?

Usually when Mary came through the door, she found Hattie busy tidying up the room or planning for the next day. Today she found her sitting at her desk, staring out the window.

"Hey, Hattie. How are things going over at the Bartons', really?"

"Honestly, Mary, we are all back in a routine, but I don't think anything will ever seem normal again at that house without Elizabeth Barton. We are all just going through the motions."

"How is Mr. Barton faring?"

"He has pretty much buried himself in work. He has had Mrs. Barton's room closed off and won't allow anyone to go in there or move anything. He only goes upstairs to dress and he spends the rest of the time, precious little that he is home, in his study, which is not too different from before, but before she was always there to round things out and make things feel normal."

"How do you think the boys are doing?"

"They seem to be fine at school when they are with their friends and busy, but I can tell they dread going home. If Charles didn't feel like he needed to spend time with Richard, he would probably stay over at his uncle Bailey's shop until dinnertime. He feels such a responsibility for his brothers now that his mother is gone. It's all so sad."

"Charles is a fine boy. You can tell he was raised right. An absolute gentleman, and so responsible. What are you going to do about next year, Hattie?"

"I already signed my contract to come back, but I have such mixed feelings about the future. I love the Barton children and Georgia and my heart just breaks for Mr. Barton. I feel guilty leaving them for the summer, but a part of me wants to walk away and forget everything here in Calhoun. I'm just so tired, Mary."

Mary smiled sympathetically. "I felt that way at the end of my first year of teaching, too. And I didn't have to go through a terrible tragedy like you have, with Mrs. Barton's death. I went back home to Walhalla for the summer and it did me a world of good. I plan to do the same thing this year. I think a change of scenery will do that for you, too."

Hattie sighed. "Who would have dreamed that things would end this way? I came here to Calhoun because the world as I knew it had fallen down around me and I needed a new start. I found my place here, and now the world seems to be crumbling again."

"I know, Hattie, and you have every right to be down."

"Well, as Mama always said, you either rise above it or sink down in it."

"Hattie, you're pure cream. You will always rise to the top. You have proved that. Now you go on and take the summer off back in Greenville, and don't you feel a bit guilty about it. Those Barton boys have Georgia and a host of family in Calhoun to keep an eye on them. They will be just fine."

"You're right, Mary. I'm certainly not indispensable to them."

"It's not that, Hattie. I just think you need to look out for yourself more. I probably shouldn't mention this, but you don't know how things will change in that house now that Mr. Barton has been widowed. He's likely to remarry some time down the road and you may not be as fond of his new wife as you were of Elizabeth Barton."

"That's true. He's a very attractive man and I'm sure he will be sought after by all of the eligible widows in town as soon as a respectable mourning period has passed. I doubt there would be a place for me in the house under those circumstances."

"Well, who knows? You could be the one to meet someone first. You'll probably find a handsome fellow back in Greenville this summer and he may convince you not to return to Calhoun at all."

Hattie smiled and shook her head. "I don't think that's very likely."

15

Hattie decided to take Mary's advice about making a clean break from Calhoun for the summer. On the day after school ended, she packed her bags and said a tearful good-bye to Georgia and the Barton boys before Lonnie Jenkins drove her to the depot. With a lump in her throat, she hugged each one and promised to write at least once a week as well as call at least once or twice just so she could hear their voices. On the way to the station, she asked Lonnie to take her by Rosa Griffin's house to say goodbye to Pauline.

"She's at the church," said Rosa when she came to the door. "Earline is organizing a young girls' mission group and Pauline is thrilled that she has been invited to join. Don't you worry about her now, Hattie. Earline and Velma and I will look after her and make sure she's busy every minute."

"Oh, I know you will. But, what about Mr. Jeter? What does Velma hear from him?"

"She hadn't seen him since he got banned from the school, and then he came around here a few days ago, all contrite, begging Velma to take him back. He told her they were taking him on as a carder at Calhoun Mill. Velma showed a lot of gumption. She stood right up to him and said she wouldn't consider uprooting the children again until he could prove he could quit gambling, stay sober, keep a job, and find a place for them to live.

"He started to argue and tell her he could take the children any time he wanted to, with or without her, and she fired right back and said, 'Where are you gonna take 'em Clyde? You don't even have a place to live. An' how are you gonna provide for 'em when you can't hardly provide for yourself?' He couldn't much argue with that, and he tucked his tail and went on off. He hadn't been back around since."

"Well, good for Velma taking up for herself like that! Oh dear. Look at the time. I wish I could stay until Pauline gets back, but my train is about to leave and I need to get on to the station. Please give her a big hug for me and tell her to have a wonderful summer."

As Hattie's train pulled out of Calhoun station, she allowed the rocking motion of the car and the redundant clacking of the giant metal wheels to lull her into a contemplative state. The engine picked up speed and events of the past year flashed by in her mind, much like the scenery from the large picture window through which she peered from her seat. The distance from Calhoun grew and the memories of the past year receded and were replaced by thoughts of home as the train crossed into Greenville County and neared the Greenville depot.

Spending the summer at Mama's provided a wonderful respite for Hattie. The first week she was home, Hattie, Minnie, Lottie, and Mama talked nonstop, catching one another up on everything that had happened. Aunt Harriet dropped by almost every day, and they would all sit around the table and enjoy Mama's rolls and lots of coffee with cream and sugar. Harriet had been stunned by the news of her dear friend Elizabeth's death and wanted to know all about the family and how they were faring.

Hattie signed up for a summer teachers' institute at the college, which gave her the chance to reconnect with her former professors as well as the opportunity to be around other teachers and to share their common experiences. She ran into Dean Judson, who urged Hattie to consider returning to the college to do postgraduate work now that she had a year of teaching under her belt. The idea appealed to her and Hattie promised the dean that she would give careful thought to the suggestion.

She enjoyed Sundays back at First Baptist and even agreed to join Lottie in performing a duet at one of the Wednesday night prayer meetings. Hattie always thought about Will when she was there, but her memories of their time together were growing sweeter and less painful as time passed.

When the teachers' institute ended, she and Mama decided on the spur of the moment to squeeze in a trip to Atlanta to see Maudie and the new grandbaby before Hattie had to return to Calhoun. Maudie had not been home since Easter, and her husband, Frank, would not get time off from his work to bring them up again until Christmas.

"That baby will be half-grown before we see him again. We just can't let that happen," declared Mama. "Besides, I'm so hungry to see Maudie I don't know what to do. I've missed her so much since she and Frank moved to Atlanta."

Mama was reluctant to leave the boys behind, as they could sometimes be a handful, especially now that they were out of school for the summer. Minnie assured her that she and Lottie could handle things with the help of their trusted cook, Chloe, and with Aunt Harriet dropping by daily to check on things.

"Don't you worry one bit, Mama. They will do whatever I tell them now that we have the car. All I have to do is threaten to take away their privilege to drive it and they will snap right back into line."

Minnie had received a raise and had recently purchased a 1908 Model T Ford for $850. It was the first automobile the family had ever owned, and the two older boys were mesmerized by the handles and gears and all of the inner workings of the shiny contraption. Jamie had learned to drive it and he was teaching Henry.

Mama laughed and concurred that the car held almost magic sway over them. In the end, she agreed to make the trip but decided that they would have little John stay over at Aunt Harriet's and leave Minnie and Lottie with only the older boys to supervise.

They got along fine while Mama and Hattie were away, with only one minor mishap with the car, when Jamie was driving and spotted a group of his friends walking along. He started waving and craned his neck back to make sure they saw him at the wheel and he ran the car off the road and right into a telephone pole. Fortunately, no one was hurt, and the car suffered little damage, other than a broken headlight. The incident gave Minnie even more leverage over the boys' behavior. She grounded both of them from the car and required Jamie to work off the cost of the headlight in return for not mentioning it to Mama, although she did confide it to Hattie.

It was true that Mama did want to see the new grandbaby; however, she had not been altogether forthcoming about her reason for making the trip. Shortly after they arrived, Maudie let it slip that she had conspired with Mama and Minnie and Lottie to get Hattie to Atlanta to set her up with one of Frank's coworkers from the railroad.

"His name is Phillip Jordan and he is the nicest young man, Hattie." Maudie mixed up a bowl of cereal for little Frankie's dinner and handed it over to Mama, who was dying to feed him. "He just moved up here from Birmingham to manage the ticket office at the Atlanta depot. He told Frank confidentially that his sweetheart had recently ended their long-term relationship and that he needed to get away and make a fresh start. We both thought of you and were determined the two of you should meet." Maudie put her hands on her hips. "Now don't go making that irked expression you always put on when you think someone has meddled in your business."

"Honestly, Maudie, you *could* have consulted me first. Did it ever occur to you that I might not want to meet Phillip? You should have at least given me a choice in the matter." Maudie always did assume to know what was best for everybody, and it seemed like she could talk Mama into taking her side every time. It would have been easier to stop a freight train than to stop Maudie once she hatched a scheme.

"Oh, Hattie. Don't be such an old schoolmarm. After all you've been through this last year, you deserve to get out and kick up your heels a bit. Isn't that right, Mama?" Mama nodded, but she didn't seem to be paying much attention to the conversation. She was too busy feeding and cooing at little Frankie.

Maudie added with finality, "I have already invited Phillip over for dinner. You'd better go get freshened up so you'll look nice for him. He and Frank will be here around six thirty."

Hattie *was* irked. She had begun thinking about getting out socially again, but she wanted to do it in her own time and at her own speed. She knew her sister meant well and she loved her for it. But honestly, Maudie could be so presumptuous!

As much as she hated to admit it, she enjoyed meeting Phillip and spending time with him. They talked easily at dinner and Phillip asked if he could call on her the next day. Frank and Maudie lived in a cozy bungalow a few blocks from Grant Park, and Phillip asked if Hattie would like to walk over there to see the zoo and the cyclorama of the Battle of Atlanta. She agreed and offered to fix a picnic lunch for the two of them.

Hattie and Phillip were only two years apart in age and had both graduated college in 1907. Phillip had attended the University of Alabama. He had been new to his job with the railroad, just as Hattie had been new to her position as a teacher. They discovered a number of commonalities between Phillip's experience working with passengers in the ticket office and Hattie's experience working with students and their parents in school. Hattie told him about Julian Clinkscales and his grandmother and Phillip told her a humorous story about a passenger who demanded to buy tickets for her two dogs to travel first-class and receive service in the diner.

"It was the darnedest thing. The woman had dressed them in little knit vests and the porter said they sat straight up in their seats like regular passengers without making a sound. And he said that when she took them to the diner, she ordered from the menu for them and had the waiter bring them bowls of soup, which they lapped up without spilling a drop." Phillip had a quick wit and an easy laugh and Hattie found him to be good company.

The last night she was in town, Phillip took her to dinner at the fashionable Piedmont Hotel. Hattie had to borrow a dress from Maudie because she had not brought anything fancy enough to wear. Maudie had just the right thing in her wardrobe, as she and Frank liked to take advantage of the nightlife in Atlanta.

At the end of the evening, Phillip walked Hattie to the door, where he paused, smiled, and reached for her hand. "I've certainly enjoyed our time together, Hattie." He hesitated and then said, "To be honest, I wasn't sure if I would ever be ready to go out with another woman again. You see, the person I have loved since I was a boy and thought I would marry and be with all of my life told me three months ago that she no longer feels the same way. I have been wandering around like a lost soul ever since. When Frank asked me if I would like to meet you and take you out, I would have declined on the spot had he and Maudie not been so kind to me since I moved to Atlanta. And I'm so glad I didn't say no. Being with you has made me realize that I will eventually be able to move on and find happiness with someone else. I am not yet ready to give my heart away completely again, but when the time comes that I am, you are just the kind of person I will be looking for. I sure hope you won't already be taken by then."

Hattie shook her head, touched his arm, and looked at him sympathetically. "You don't have to explain to me of all people, Phillip. It was only a little over a year ago that the love of my life broke off our engagement and I was forced to cancel our August wedding."

Phillip laughed at the irony of it all. "We're a pitiful pair. No wonder we get along so well. I'll get your address from Maudie and drop you a line. And next time you come to Atlanta, I'd like to take you out on the town again. As a matter of fact, I will even send you a ticket. Since I work for the railway, I can buy one from Greenville to Atlanta for next to nothing.

"You're a swell girl, Hattie and I really do hope we can see each other again." Phillip bent and kissed her lightly on the lips and Hattie felt a warmth inside.

"Me, too, Phillip," she said, squeezing his hand before he opened the door for her to go inside.

"There may be hope for you yet, Hattie Robinson," she said aloud as she leaned against the door, waiting for him to get to his car before she turned off the porch light.

The trip to Atlanta forced Hattie to delay her return to Calhoun until the day before classes resumed. She looked forward to her second year at the school but was anxious about her boarding arrangements at the Bartons'. Georgia had told her when she called to confirm her arrival that Aunt Alice and Aunt Willie Mae had come from Columbia to stay awhile. Hattie assumed that one or both of the sisters were in hearing distance of the phone, because Georgia would not go into detail about the nature and duration of their visit. However, she could tell by Georgia's tone that the aunts' departure could not come soon enough for her. Hattie dreaded to think how things would change with the sisters there and Elizabeth Barton gone.

On the night before her departure for Calhoun, Hattie lay awake questioning her decision to return. Now that she had reestablished her ties in Greenville over the summer and had met Phillip, she wasn't certain if she ever wanted to go back. She could always take the year off, move back in with Mama, and pursue postgraduate studies, as Dean Judson had encouraged her to do. She had saved most of last year's salary from living rent-free at the Bartons' and had sufficient funds to pay for her tuition, with enough left over to cover her personal needs and contribute to the household expenses. And if she stayed in Greenville, she would have time to make another trip to Atlanta and perhaps foster her relationship with Phillip. After all, he had said he would send her a ticket. Who could predict where that friendship might lead?

She knew it was late, but Reverend Fitts could probably find a replacement teacher. Why, she could even recommend one of Lottie's classmates who had completed the LI degree and would be looking for a teaching job.

Hadn't Mary Posey convinced her that she was not indispensable—that the Barton children were surrounded by family to love them and get them through the loss of their mother? And hadn't she pointed out that Mr. Barton would surely remarry at some point and that his new wife might not relish having her around? Didn't she have a right to look out for herself and her own happiness?

Exhaustion finally took hold and Hattie drifted into sleep. In her dream, she was seated in the dining car of a train. Two dogs in red knitted vests sat across the table from her. The car resembled the elegant ballroom of the Piedmont Hotel, except for the large observation windows and the sensation that the room was rolling forward on rails.

Hattie was dressed in Maudie's blue taffeta evening gown, which had not been fastened in the back. She was struggling with the buttons when she realized that one of her shoes had come off. She began feeling under the table with her bare foot in hopes of finding it when Phillip appeared and sat down beside her. Phillip ignored Hattie and began carrying on a lively conversation with the dogs. The train slowed down as it approached the station and Hattie saw a group of passengers waiting on the platform. As the wheels ground to a halt, she recognized their faces: Georgia, Richard, Gene, George, Charles, and Mr. Barton. Behind them stood Pauline Jeter and Mary Greer, along with Julian Clinkscales and Tom Givens. She smiled and waved at them as they stepped forward with their boarding passes.

From a distance, Hattie heard the conductor call, "All aboard." The train pulled out of the station, leaving the passengers standing on the platform, holding their tickets. Hattie pushed past Phillip, who was still talking to the dogs, and ran down the aisle, holding the back of her dress together with one hand and hobbling along with one shoe still off. She was trying to get the attention of the conductor, calling out, "Don't leave them, don't leave them," when she awoke and realized it was morning. She climbed out of bed, dressed, and packed her bags. She might not remain in Calhoun indefinitely; however, she would not renege on her contract or leave the Bartons just yet.

Lonnie Jenkins met her at the depot at three p.m., helped her with her trunk and drove her back to the estate in time to unpack her things and get ready for school the next day. Charles and George were delighted to see her, as was Georgia, who was in the kitchen, peeling potatoes for dinner. She laid down her paring knife, wiped her hands on her apron, and squeezed Hattie tightly. "Lawd, Hattie, ain't you a welcome sight? We so glad you back, but we a far cry from where we wuz when you came las' year this time."

"I know, Georgia. Tell me how things are going?"

Hattie could detect in the mellow voice a hint of resignation. "Well, Miz Alice, she managing the household now and she 'bout rearranged everything 'cept Miz Lizabeth's room, which Mr. Charles still forbid anybody to touch. Ooh, I betta' hush up. Here she come now."

Alice filled the room, her presence portended by the clicking of her black pumps advancing rapidly down the hallway. Moving with an efficient pace wherever she went, she never sauntered, but strode with purpose and determination from one destination to the other.

"Hello, Miss Robinson. We are happy you are back. You'll be staying in the blue room again." Even Alice's speech was clipped and efficient.

"Thank you, Miss Alice. I think Charles already carried my trunk back there."

"Well, good."

"Will you and Miss Willie Mae be staying on for a while?"

"Oh my, yes. We will be here to see Brother through his bereavement."

Oh dear, thought Hattie. *I don't believe Alice is going anywhere soon.*

"I have put everything on hold in Columbia so that I can be available to run the household for Brother now that poor, dear Elizabeth is gone." In referring to the departed, Alice raised her eyes heavenward and drew out the vowels in *poor* and *dear*, creating an almost ghostly sound. "Elizabeth never was a good organizer or delegator, bless her sweet soul, and I have had a time getting everything on schedule. But I think we understand how things need to run now, don't we, Georgia?"

"Um-hmm." Georgia's eyes narrowed, and she bit her bottom lip as she turned away from Alice and went back to peeling potatoes.

Alice must have interpreted the response as affirmation and plowed on, oblivious to the effect of her words on Georgia. "Everyone has a role and a responsibility, and it is imperative that we keep to those roles and not get them confused. That was something Elizabeth had a hard time doing, may she rest in peace." She raised her eyes again.

Hattie was uncertain of the direction of this conversation. However, based on the way Alice had just put Georgia in her place, she predicted that she was about to be put in hers. Had she made a mistake in returning to the Bartons'?

"For instance, Miss Robinson, you are here to help the children with their schooling. And I believe that in the past, you sometimes dined with Brother and Elizabeth, didn't you?"

"Yes, ma'am, I did."

Alice smiled and widened her eyes, speaking as though she were explaining something very complex to a small child. "Well, I think now, for propriety's sake, since you are an unmarried woman living under the roof of a widowed man, it is best if you *always* take your evening meals with the children and see to their needs. I have in-structed Georgia to serve them and you every evening at six so that they can get on upstairs to their studies, and so that you can help them with their homework if they need it, and of course prepare your own lessons for school the next day. Now, don't you think that will work nicely?"

Hattie hated being patronized, but as a guest in the Bartons' home, she had no right to protest.

"I suppose so," she said, controlling her urge to argue.

"Good. I'm glad we got that settled. After all, we are all here to keep things running smoothly while the family is in mourning. Poor Brother. He is not handling his loss well, and we want to shoulder his load whenever possible. One way we can do that is to establish a daily household regimen. Now, here is how it will work:

"Whenever Willie Mae is up to it and does not take her dinner in her room, she and I will dine at eight with Brother. He is usually home by then. It will give us an opportunity to discuss any issues relating to the management of the house. Now, as I said, you will eat with the children, and I've instructed Georgia to ring the dinner bell promptly at six every night to get everyone in the habit of being punctual."

Alice reached into the bosom of her navy shirtwaist dress, pulled up the gold watch suspended on the chain around her neck, and consulted the time. "Let me see...it is 5:02 p.m. You should have just enough time to get unpacked and freshened up by six, Hattie. I'm going to check on Willie Mae and see if she's feeling well enough to eat with Brother and me or if she needs a tray brought to the room." With that, she turned and left the kitchen.

The room seemed to contract as Alice disappeared into the passageway connecting the kitchen and the sisters' quarters. When the sound of her staccato footsteps grew faint, Hattie and Georgia resumed their conversation.

"Oh, I see what you mean, Georgia. I am glad I didn't come back any earlier. She is just awful. But where is Richard? I'm dying to see him."

"He down at Miz Sudie's. He spend a lot of time with her and Mista' George these days. I 'spec that's where Gene is, too. I'm going down to get him in few minutes, 'fore I rings this here dinnah bell." She rolled her eyes.

"I'll come with you. I can unpack later."

Aunt Sudie was sitting at a picnic table in the yard shucking corn and watching the children play. She was the first to spot Hattie.

"Oh, Hattie. I know two boys who will be glad to see you! They have been asking all day about when you would arrive."

Gene and Richard had apparently heard Hattie's voice and came running from behind the house. Gene was grinning from ear to ear.

Hattie gave him a big hug before she scooped up Richard in her arms and twirled around with him.

"Look at you! Why, you have grown like a weed over the summer. I can hardly lift you now." Richard threw his arms around Hattie's neck and planted a big wet kiss on her cheek.

"I miss you," he said. A lump rose in Hattie's throat as she realized she had made the right decision in returning.

"I missed you, too, Richard. I missed all of you. Now let's go back to the house for dinner, and I want to know every detail of what you have done over the summer."

Mr. Barton missed the eight o'clock dinner hour and arrived home just as the two sisters were finishing their peach cobblers. Hattie was in the hallway and heard him come in. She stuck her head in the parlor to say hello, which clearly displeased Alice, who was watching from the dining room.

Mr. Barton turned and took her hand. "Hello, Miss Robinson. We are indeed happy to have you back. The boys and Georgia have been counting the days until your return." He displayed the same well-bred manners as always, but the words were flat, and in his utterance as well as expression, she understood that he was a stranger in his own home, a man adrift in a sea of loss.

"Oh, Mr. Barton, I thought every day about all of you and said a prayer that you were doing all right. I remember how hard those months were for our family right after Papa died. We all felt like we had been unmoored."

"Thank you, Miss Robinson. We are getting along, though as you put it, feeling a bit unmoored."

"Brother, you need to come on now and eat some dinner," Alice interrupted. "Miss Robinson is busy getting unpacked and preparing for the opening of school tomorrow."

Hattie took the hint and excused herself. "I don't want to keep you from your dinner. Good night, Mr. Barton." Charles Barton nodded and made his way to the dining room almost as if sleepwalking.

Hattie went back to the kitchen to say good night to Georgia and found her perched on a stool, her elbow resting on the wooden counter and her head propped in her hand. It wasn't like Georgia to slouch. As long as Hattie had known her, she was always up and busy, her posture straight and tall. She turned her head just slightly and looked up at Hattie.

"Honestly, Georgia. How do you stand it around here? Miss Alice is so bossy and controlling. It makes me angry how she talks down to people. Why do you put up with it?"

"I'm too tired, and it ain't worth it. Seem like I done lost my starch since Miz Lizabeth was took from us. I jus' takes care of the house, fixes the food, looks after Richard, and stays out o' her way as much as possible. If it was jus' her, I'd be clear on out o' here, but I couldn't leave Miz Lizabeth's children 'lone with her. She don't care nothing 'bout them, and they don't do nothin' but get in her way and get on Miss Willie Mae's nerves.

"And Mr. Charles, he ain't hardly eva' here no more and when he is, he don't have no starch in him either. He neva' did care nothing 'bout running the house. Always lef' it to Miz Lizabeth and me. Naw, I couldn't leave these children or Mr. Charles, so I guess I'll make the best of it. But you, chile, young as you is, you don't have to stay here and put up with this. Why don't you go on and get with some of yo' young folks at the school and get on with yo' life?"

"Don't think it hasn't crossed by mind, Georgia. As a matter of fact, I got such cold feet last night, I almost decided not to come back at all. But I feel just like you do about the children. Besides, I made a promise to Mrs. Barton the day she left for Asheville that I would help you take care of Richard until she came home. That was the last time any of us saw her, and I'll never forget that picture. Now that I am back and see how Miss Alice has changed things, I could never leave you to deal with her by yourself."

Georgia's eyes filled with tears. "You are one unselfish chile. Mr. James and Miz Sallie raised you with a lot o' love. I sho' am glad you gonna stay."

16

Aunt Sudie had arranged for Lonnie Jenkins to drive Hattie and Charles and George and Gene to school in the wagon the first day, as Mr. Barton had an early-morning appointment. The boys had been somewhat quiet and reserved at dinner the night before, but once out of the house, they became more like their old selves, talkative and full of life.

Gene was looking forward to seeing Miss Downey again, and was feeling confident about moving up to second grade. George would be a seventh grader and would move upstairs to take his classes with the high schools students. The promoted class had been large enough to require the addition of a new teacher, whom Reverend Fitts had hired over the summer.

As a ninth grader, Charles would begin the high school curriculum and could earn graduation credits. He would have Latin with Reverend Fitts, who had contracted to stay on as principal for a third year and continue the efforts he had started to qualify Calhoun School for high school accreditation.

With the addition of the new teacher, there would be no need to farm out the older students to the elementary teachers during recitation. Hattie would miss having Charles come down, but she did not regret losing Tom Givens, who had matured considerably since the water incident but continued to require strict supervision.

Hattie had heard the conventional wisdom from other teachers that the second year would be easier than the first and she assumed that it was exaggeration. However, she found it to be right on the mark. It seemed paradoxical that this place, so strange and new to her last year, was now familiar and comforting.

Her classroom greeted her like an old friend as she opened the door and found everything as she had arranged it last spring: desks in rows, erasers dusted, fresh chalk in the tray, and textbooks lined up neatly on the bookshelves. The scent of lemon oil wafted from recently polished floors and mixed with the smell of lye cleaner and vinegar, which the custodian had used in scrubbing the desks and shining the glass surfaces. The windows were raised to their full height to allow the stale air to escape and the fresh fall air to replace it. Reverend Fitts had left new roll books on each of the teachers' desks and had installed metal name plaques on the doors to replace the cardboard ones. Everything looked and smelled like new beginnings.

Little else needed doing. Hattie posted the daily schedule on the chalkboard and pitched out the dried daffodils from the famous science experiment on her desk before replacing them with the vase of gardenias that Georgia had handed her along with her lunch pail. Satisfied that everything was ready, she made her way into the hallway, where she reunited with Mary Posey and Susan Downey, who were standing at their doors, ready to welcome the students. They barely had time to hug and greet one another before the first bell rang and the children began pouring into the building.

"We'll catch up at lunchtime, Mary," said Hattie. "Same time, same spot. And I'll see you at staff meeting this afternoon, Susan."

Hattie had nine students returning from last year and, remarkably, they were all present on the first day: Mary Greer, Jenny Buice, Sarah Pendleton, Frannie Martin, Ben Sauls, Bobby Riley, Timmy Turner, Julian Clinkscales, and Penny Chambers. She received ten new students who had been in Mary Posey's class last year, as well as Bye Stanton, the son of the newly hired high school teacher. Eight were present, and two would join the class as soon as the cotton had been picked.

At lunch, Mary Posey told Hattie that the situation had improved with Reverend Fitts. "The word around the church is that the woman in Durham ended the relationship and has become engaged to a professor at Trinity College."

"Oh my, what a shame," Hattie said in mock dismay. "How is he taking it?"

"Well, he actually seems to be making the best of it. He has become more involved in the Calhoun community and has started accepting more social invitations, which he never did before. I hear he has been invited to Sunday dinner by every parishioner who has an eligible daughter or niece or distant relative. And, you know, he has actually begun paying more attention to me. He commended me on the minutes I took at the church council, and at the last covered-dish dinner, he took a second helping of my apple pie and made a point to come over and visit for a few minutes at my table. Of course he was not able to stay long and had to make his rounds among the other parishioners so as not to be accused of favoritism."

"That's wonderful, Mary. I told you he would wake up and appreciate you one day."

"Well, it's not much, but at least it is something. What about you, Hattie? Did you find an interesting fellow to pass the time with?"

Hattie blushed. "As a matter of fact, I did go out with a nice man named Phillip Jordan when I was in Atlanta visiting Maudie and Frank."

"Ooh, Phillip Jordan. What a nice name. I just had a feeling you might find somebody this summer. Tell me every detail."

"Well, Maudie was the one who instigated it and I was mad about it at first. But he turned out to be a lot of fun. He took me to see the Atlanta zoo, the cyclorama, and the last night, he made us a reservation to have dinner at the Piedmont Hotel."

"How fancy! It sounds like he really knows how to treat a woman. Are you going to see him again?"

"I hope so. He said he would write and wants me to come back to Atlanta when I can. But he's getting over a broken relationship just like I am. I don't think he is ready to get serious about anyone else right now, and that suits me fine because I'm not, either. Still, it's nice to know that I may someday have another chance at love."

At the end of the day, after Hattie dismissed the students, she was gathering up her attendance book for the faculty meeting when Pauline Jeter stopped by. Her cheeks were rosy, and her hair was shining with summer highlights.

"Pauline, look at you. You look wonderful. What have you been doing all summer?"

"Well, all of us spent a lot of time with Charles, trying to cheer him up after he lost his mama. He spends all the time he can at his uncle Bailey's in town. I do not think he likes to go home so much. That old aunt of his is so bossy, and his father is never around.

"When I was not trying to cheer up Charles, I was helping Mama and Miz Rosa at the shop. Miz Rosa taught me how to cut out a pattern and sew. See, I made this dress." She twirled around to model a pretty cotton jumper with gored skirt. Hattie noticed that she had grown and filled out over the summer.

"It's beautiful, Pauline. The green matches your eyes. And just look at your tiny waist!"

Pauline blushed at the compliment and continued, "And Mary and Martha and I helped Miz Greer at the church during Bible school. They started a new group called JYWAs—or Junior Young Women's Association—which I joined and have been working on learning my Bible verses. We also learned about the missionaries, and I have even written to Miss Lottie Moon in China. I am hoping to receive a personal letter from her. I'm saving my money and I plan to put it in the Christmas offering for foreign missions."

"Well, it all agrees with you, Pauline. You know, I have a very special friend who introduced me to the work of Lottie Moon and hopes someday to join her on the mission field. Miss Moon is also one of my heroes. I am glad she is one of yours as well. Do you mind if I ask how things are going with your father? You don't have to tell me if you feel uncomfortable."

Pauline hesitated for a moment and then she touched Hattie's arm and nodded her head in assurance.

"No, it's okay. I can talk about it now." Hattie could tell that Pauline had matured since she had last seen her. She was no longer the scared little girl who had been the victim of domestic violence resulting from an alcoholic parent. "Papa dried out for a short time and got a job at the mill. He came around to ask Mama if she would go back to him, and Mama said she'd only think about it after he proved he could stay sober, keep his job, and stop gambling for six months. He barely made it a month before he started drinking again. He got into some kind of argument with one of the other operatives, and Mama thinks he must have gotten fired. After that, he left town."

"What has become of him, Pauline?"

"Last thing Mama heard, his great-uncle had taken him in over in Gaffney and got him a job picking peaches. Mama says that when the peach season is over, he'll probably be back around here looking for another job at the mill. She says they are so desperate for workers they'll probably hire him back. But I don't even want to think about that. I'm glad he's gone. We are all better off without him. Mama is so happy working for Miz Rosa. She has gotten so many orders to make dresses for the women in town, she can hardly fill them all. And you should see little Clydie. He's up walking and jabbering away."

"Oh, Pauline, I'm going to miss having you in my class so much. You are such a smart girl and you are well prepared to move on to the next level."

"Yes, ma'am. I get to be upstairs this year with the high school students. I get to be near Charles. But I'll miss you, too, Miss Robinson. I'd never be doing this if it weren't for you. I hope I can make it through high school and go on to the normal college and get a teaching degree like you did."

"Pauline, that's the nicest thing anybody could have said to me." Hattie brushed away a tear and hugged Pauline tightly. "Well, if I want to keep my job as a teacher, I'd better be on time to Reverend Fitts's faculty meeting."

When Hattie entered the library, she had an immediate sense of déjà vu. The room was arranged exactly as it had been last year, with one seat for the new teacher added to the semicircle facing the podium. Reverend Fitts covered the same agenda, beginning with welcome and formal introductions. This year he introduced Byron Stanton, whose turn it was to appear awkward at being asked to stand formally in front of the other five to receive an ovation.

Mr. Stanton had been teaching in a private academy up in Illinois when his wife died of a ruptured appendix and left him with two young children. Now in his early thirties, he had grown up in the Calhoun area and was returning to be near his family, where the children would be surrounded by grandparents, aunts, and uncles. His son, Bye, was in Hattie's class.

Reverend Fitts recognized Hattie as teacher of the fifth-and sixth-grade class, returning for her second year. In turn, he recognized the other teachers, whose credentials were unchanged, save for the additional year of tenure that each had acquired.

What Mary had said about Reverend Fitts deciding to invest himself in the community must have been true. He told the staff that he would be working toward two objectives in the coming year.

"The first is to work with the trustees to procure funding so as to add courses to the high school curriculum, increase the number of credits to fourteen units, and move toward offering a four-year program.

"The other is to offer ongoing staff development to our elementary teachers to increase the rigor of the elementary curriculum in support of the high school curriculum. We can think of it as building a ladder. We need to build higher rungs, but unless the bottom rungs are strong and stable, our students will not be supported at the top.

"To stimulate our minds and help us remain informed, we will begin setting aside one faculty meeting a month to discuss current issues in education. I am aware that both Miss Robinson and Miss Posey attended summer teaching institutes, the former in Greenville and the latter in Walhalla. Miss Posey has talked with me about an address given by Judge J. J. McSwain at the institute in Walhalla. I have asked her to share it with the entire staff next week. Miss Robinson, I will ask that you be prepared to present to us for the following session."

Hattie gave a start. It was the first she had heard of that assignment. She began racking her brain to remember where she had packed her notes from the institute.

"Miss Robinson?"

"Oh yes. Of course, Reverend Fitts, I will be happy to do that."

When the meeting ended, the elementary teachers independently made a special effort to speak to Mr. Stanton. Hattie got to him first.

"Welcome to Calhoun School, Mr. Stanton. I am happy to have Bye in my class. Please call me if you need any help getting settled. This must be a difficult time for you, raising your children without your dear departed wife."

A well-groomed man with a professorial demeanor, Byron stroked his carefully manicured mustache and nodded. "Yes, Miss Robinson. It has been a difficult two years, but we are getting our lives back in order and moving forward little by little. It feels good to be home, where the children can be near their relatives."

"You may know that one of your students, George Barton, lost his mother last May, just before school let out. I am currently boarding with the Bartons. George has two other brothers who attend school here and a little brother at home. This will be a difficult year for all of them. I am certain that George will benefit from having a teacher who understands what he is going through."

"Oh yes. His mother was Elizabeth Barton. My family were friends of the Bartons. I was still in the community when Charles and Elizabeth Barton were married. He met her while he was at law school and she was at Columbia Female College. She made a huge hit with everyone in the community when he brought her home to introduce her to his family. What a tragic loss! I seem to remember that along with all of the numerous causes and concerns she gave her time to, she was also a pillar of the Methodist church."

"Oh yes," interjected Mary Posey. "There never was a more faithful member than Mrs. Barton. We all miss her dearly."

"Speaking of church, I need to find one where the children and I will feel at home."

"Are you folks Baptist?" asked Hattie. "If so, I'd love to invite you to attend our church. We have a marvelous pastor, Thomas Greer. Mr. Larke attends that church, and his wife plays the organ almost every Sunday."

"I was raised Presbyterian, but my wife was Methodist and we always went to her church in Illinois. Now that we have moved back home, I'm not certain where we will go. My parents still attend the Reedy Fork Presbyterian Church out in the county. We have been visiting there but have not joined yet."

"Well, we would love to have you come and visit at our church," interrupted Susan Downey. "I am Presbyterian, too, but I go to the church in town. We have a wonderful congregation and our minister, Reverend Stewart, is a fine preacher."

"And of course," added Mary Posey, "you know that Reverend Fitts preaches at the Methodist church where I am a member. I never miss a Sunday and always hang on every word of his sermons. He is such a spiritual man."

Hattie grinned and winked at Susan. "Yes, Mary, we understand that you are one of his most attentive parishioners." Mary blushed. "Mr. Stanton, I think you would find a warm church home at any of the three churches in town. Reverends Greer and Stewart and Fitts maintain a cordial relationship with one another, and they encourage their congregations to work together for the common good of the community. And they are all extremely supportive of the school."

"I'll keep that in mind. Oh, and I will look forward to your presentations on the teacher institutes you attended, Miss Robinson and Miss Posey. I was impressed with Reverend Fitts's goals to improve the rigor of our curriculum and to increase the high school credits available to our students. I am also highly in favor of ongoing staff development opportunities. Since I have moved back to South Carolina, I have been surprised by the low esteem in which we teachers are held by the public in general. Many of the editorials I have read are downright negative and, in some cases, mean-spirited in their attacks on teachers. Anything we can do to add credibility to our profession is a positive step in my eyes."

"I must admit that I just about dropped my teeth at the faculty meeting when Reverend Fitts asked if I would present. I just returned to Calhoun yesterday and this is the first I've heard of it," Hattie said.

"I'll fill you in tomorrow at lunch," said Mary. "I think I understand what he wants us to do."

As Mr. Stanton turned to leave the library, Susan Downey followed him. Hattie and Mary watched her touch his arm and smile up at him sweetly. "Now, don't forget, if you and your children decide to try Calhoun Presbyterian, I'll be glad to introduce you around."

"Was she flirting with him?" whispered Mary.

"I sure hope so," responded Hattie. "Those two would make a great match."

17

At the next faculty meeting, Mary Posey was well prepared to lead the group in discussing the speech that Hon. J. J. McSwain of Greenville had delivered to the teachers' institute that she had attended in Walhalla over the summer. The speech had been printed in Mary's hometown paper, the *Keowee Courier*, to which she still subscribed. She had typed it up and made carbon copies, which she distributed to each faculty member before stepping up to the podium. Hattie noticed that Reverend Fitts was staring intently at Mary and nodding approvingly at the handouts and at the opening comments.

"You have before you a copy of the entire address on the 'High Calling of the Teacher,' delivered by the Honorable J. J. McSwain, a former teacher and practicing attorney from Greenville, whom I was privileged to hear in person at the teacher institute in Walhalla this summer. I will begin our session today by reading aloud an excerpt of the address. We will then discuss Mr. McSwain's view of the calling of the teacher vis-à-vis our own views of that calling."

Hattie recognized in Mary's bearing and her confident presentation the strong influence of Dean Judson at Greenville Female College, who challenged her students to think independently, excel academically, and speak publicly. Dean Judson's elocution students were required to join the Judson Society, which became an outlet for practicing public speaking and debate. By the time they graduated, even the most timid of her students had developed the poise and skill to speak before a group. Hattie felt a surge of pride for her fellow alumna as well as for her alma mater.

Mary drew herself up to her full stature, took a cleansing breath and began reading flawlessly and with clarity. When she finished, she laid the speech on the podium and straightened the edges of the paper. "Now the floor is open to your comments."

"I can see that Mr. McSwain views the teacher's job as molder of character," began Byron Stanton. "I consider that view to be somewhat simplistic and I take issue with his implication that children only need to be honest and hardworking to succeed. Knowledge and skill are integral to the equation of success and cannot be ignored. I believe that it is primarily the teacher's duty to develop the intellect of the child. Character is certainly important, but surely the home and the church must share equally with the school in the responsibility for nurturing the child in that area. But a teacher must strive to be much more than the paragon of virtue described in this speech. He, or she, must develop the intellect, attain a strong understanding of the content of the curriculum, and then master the art of teaching to the degree that he is able to lead the child to an understanding of that content."

"Well said, Mr. Stanton," Susan Downey replied admiringly.

"To be fair," countered Reverend Fitts, "I do not think that Mr. McSwain was discounting the importance of knowledge and skill, but merely stressing the critical nature of character and values as the foundation for learning."

"I agree, Reverend Fitts," said Mary. "It really is not an either/or thing. A teacher is called to assume many roles—a moral compass, a scholar, a critical thinker, and an instructor."

"You might as well add to that list the ability to walk on water like Jesus, because that's what you'd have to do to live up to those expectations," said Mr. Larke. "And that part about the greatest reward of the teacher being the proud fact of having 'taught the boy.' Well, that is certainly true, because there is little monetary reward in it."

"Always the skeptic, Mr. Larke." Mary laughed. "And yet you consistently go the second mile for your students, and a few of them think you *can* walk on water."

"Thank you, Miss Posey," Mr. Larke said with a wry smile. "But I want you to know that I really wasn't fishing for compliments."

"I was inspired by what Mr. McSwain said about teachers needing to look for the diamond in the rough," said Susan Downey. "When I get a new crop of first graders, I look in their little hopeful faces and I remind myself that each one is like a tiny bud that, with the proper care and nourishment, can bloom into a beautiful flower."

"That's why you teach six-year-olds," said Mr. Larke. "I look in the faces of my students and think, *What are they up to and how can I outsmart them before they outsmart me?*"

"Mr. Larke, you do not." Susan Downey laughed. "You are really an old softie at heart."

The time in conversation passed quickly, and before Hattie knew it, Mary Posey interrupted to say, "Well, this has been a good discussion. However, our time is up, and I will turn the meeting back over to Reverend Fitts for any concluding remarks."

Reverend Fitts took to the podium and, with admiring eyes, turned to address Mary. "You have done an excellent job of leading us today, Miss Posey. I have only one point to add in summation. It is that each of us may define the roles that a teacher should play in various ways, but it is evident to me that the message we need to take away from this excellent address by Mr. McSwain is that teaching is not a mere job, but a true calling. Miss Robinson will lead us in our next discussion, which we will all look forward to participating in."

Hattie walked out with Mary. "My gracious, Mary, you are going to be a hard act to follow. Dean Judson would have been so proud of you the way you led the discussion and spoke with such confidence and poise."

"Thank you, Hattie. I'm sure you'll do just fine. After all, we were taught by the best, weren't we? I'm so grateful to Dean Judson and the faculty at the college for encouraging us to be modern women and for equipping us to take our place in society. Her elocution class and all that practicing in the Judson Society nearly wore me out. However, in the end, it built my confidence and made it so much easier for me to stand before a mixed audience."

"On a different subject, somebody else was mighty impressed with your presentation," said Hattie. "Reverend Fitts never took his eyes off you. You are definitely making inroads."

Mary blushed. "Oh, I hope so. Lord knows I have done everything but stand on my head to get that man's attention. Who would have thought that this would be the thing to do it?"

"Well, we already know he likes the academic type. You may have just hit on the one thing that will make him forget that woman in Durham after all."

"What are you going to do for your presentation, Hattie?"

"I'm not sure. One of the main topics this summer at the institute I attended was on the condition of schools in our state. We read and discussed several editorials by Professor Hand in Columbia, who contends that schools in South Carolina are faltering due to lack of financial support and adequate teacher training. As you can imagine, that topic aroused some lively debate among the teachers present."

"Yes, I am sure it did, and I think that might be an interesting topic for our staff to entertain as well, since we are working toward accreditation. You should definitely do that."

"Well, I'll need to pick something that will keep everyone's attention. Four o'clock is such a ghastly hour to assemble a group of teachers and require them to engage in any kind of mental activity. After being with the students all day, it is a wonder that any of us can remember our names. And poor Mr. Larke must get up with the chickens and has done a half day's work before he even gets to school."

"Yes, I know. I do well to just take care of myself. I can't imagine what it would be like holding down two jobs and managing a family to boot. But, speaking of a topic that would keep everyone's attention, I think I may have something to fit the bill." Mary flipped through a folder she was carrying and produced an article which she handed to Hattie.

"Lord, Mary. Look at all those newspaper clippings you are lugging around!"

Mary blushed and shrugged her shoulders sheepishly. "Yes, I know. I've always loved to save articles from the paper. I suppose you could describe me as an organized hoarder. I still subscribe to my hometown newspaper, and I read the *Calhoun Sentinel* and the *Greenville News* any time I can get a hold of one. I have a whole shelf full of scrapbooks that I have filled with clippings that I've been collecting ever since I was old enough to read. They always like to make me secretary and historian any time I join a club or women's group. Just last month, they nominated me to be on the historical committee at the church."

"Well, I can see why. I never knew that about you. My goodness, I'm terrible about not keeping anything. I had to do some scurrying around just to find my notes from the teachers' institute this summer. May I take this home with me and read it? It looks pretty long."

"You sure can. I hope it helps."

"Me, too, but I think I'll get Georgia to make a batch of her pecan tassies and I'll bring them to the staff meeting as a backup. Maybe a little something sweet would give us all extra energy to get through the hour."

"Ooh, bribery. That's a great idea. I wish I'd thought of that."

"I'd better get back to the Bartons'. See you tomorrow, Mary."

Hattie worked diligently on her presentation in the coming weeks. She stayed late in the afternoon to grade her papers and set up her classroom for the next day and then arrived at the Bartons' in time to have dinner with the Barton boys promptly at six, as instituted by Alice. Afterward, she excused herself and retreated to her room to work on her presentation for the remainder of the evening.

Charles Barton was away on business for most of that first week. It seemed like he left for more and more extended periods of time and avoided being in the house almost as much as the boys did. When he was home, he sequestered himself in his study into the wee hours, the light from the study lamp escaping from the crack under the closed door.

Once when Hattie got up to use the bathroom in the middle of the night, the door was slightly ajar, and she caught a glimpse of him slumped in the leather wing chair facing the window, his papers strewn on the floor around him. In the reflection cast upon the glass pane by the desk lamp, she could see him staring blankly ahead, still nursing his nearly empty snifter of brandy.

He appeared exposed and vulnerable in that light, and watching him in his solitude made her feel like an intruder. She hurried back to her room, closed the door and slid between the covers. For some time, she lay awake contemplating the eerie feeling of being all alone in the downstairs with him, separated only by one wall, aware of the pain he must be experiencing and unable to offer even the slightest bit of comfort to a fellow human being in grief. She longed to reach out to him, to find something to say or do that would at least temporarily lift him out of his sorrowful state. For the life of her, she did not know what that something would be.

Charles Barton had obviously chosen to grieve in private. Some people were like that, although Hattie could not understand why. After Papa died, the only thing that brought her comfort was to be near Mama and her sisters and brothers. Sometimes they would gather around together and talk about him and sometimes they would sit there and draw strength from one another's presence and from the embraces that they all gave so freely to one another. It did not bring back Papa, but somehow it eased the pain to face his loss together.

In this house, with Charles Barton either away or cloistered in his study, each family member was left to face the terrible loss of Elizabeth Barton alone, and under the watchful eye of Alice. "And there is not one thing you can do about it, Hattie Robinson," she said aloud to herself. "So you may as well go on to sleep and stop fretting."

Hattie enjoyed rereading her notes from the teacher institute and found the challenge of preparing for adult learners to be stimulating and satisfying. She was still considering the notion of applying for postgraduate studies so that eventually she could teach at the college level. Perhaps she could pursue that next year, after a bit more time had lapsed since Elizabeth Barton's death.

Hattie decided to use the materials from Professor Hand's assessment of the condition of the schools as a basis for her presentation. After reading the editorial that Mary had given her, she found that it fit nicely into the topic as well. The editorial expressed opposition to Professor Hand's views and leveled the blame for failure against teachers, trustees, and parents. She would use it in juxtaposition to the materials from Professor Hand to illustrate the polarized views of the public vs. professional educators.

Hattie remarked aloud, "Now, if that doesn't spark some lively debate, I don't know what will. That and a plate of Georgia's tassies should help to compensate for the hour and the fatigue of the participants."

On Tuesday, Hattie arrived early at the library to set out the refreshments and place a handout on each of the chairs in the semicircle. The teachers brightened when they saw the sweets. Hattie began by sharing a summary of the presentation that Dr. Hand had given to the teachers at the institute.

"According to Dr. Hand's research, our schools in South Carolina are in great need of repair and reorganization. After you have had sufficient time to read over the summary I have prepared, I will welcome your comments."

Reverend Fitts was the first to speak. "We are fortunate to have a community that follows through with its commitment to support the local school. Though teacher salaries may be well below those of other professionals, as Professor Hand has pointed out, at least we have never had to wonder whether we would receive our monthly pay. That has been possible because the community has raised extra funds for building maintenance and books for our library so that we can reserve our state allotment almost exclusively for salaries.

"We can also boast of a highly professional staff. All of our teachers have completed the normal course at well-respected schools, and some, like Mr. Stanton, have pursued advanced degrees."

"And you, as well, Reverend Fitts, with both a college and seminary degree," Mr. Stanton added.

Reverend Fitts bowed modestly. "Thank you for recognizing that."

Mr. Stanton nodded and added, "With a progressive governor in the statehouse, South Carolina will surely continue to invest in education and establish a system of accredited high schools that will enable our children to receive the preparatory courses needed for college. And hopefully, with the Republicans in disarray over the departure of Theodore Roosevelt, the Democrats will easily win with William Jennings Bryan and his platform of progressive reform in this year's presidential election. Having a Democrat in the White House can only strengthen state efforts toward progressive reform."

"You know, Mr. Stanton, our current governor, Mr. Ansel, is from my hometown of Walhalla. As a matter of fact, he is a third cousin once removed of my mother," said Mary.

"You don't say. I heard that he had strongly considered challenging Senator Lattimer for his seat in this year's election, instead of serving out a second term."

"I 'm glad he didn't," said Mary. "He has been successful in passing the High School Act and ending the dispensary and the corruption associated with it. I'm afraid if he left the governor's office, some of the progressive measures he has taken would be undone, especially if Coleman Blease should be voted in."

"I understand that Mr. Blease has developed quite a following among the mill operatives and tenant farmers," said Mr. Stanton. "Many of them have broken away from supporting Ben Tillman and have organized as Bleasites. They are very loyal to Mr. Blease and could turn the tide for him in the 1910 election."

"That would be a setback," added Hattie. "I hope Governor Ansel will remain our governor. All of us in upstate South Carolina are proud to have him in office."

Hattie moved on. "Now that we have considered the points made by Dr. Hand, we are going to look at the subject from another point of view—that of the dissatisfied patron. I saved this until last because I am certain that it will stir your blood and arouse a definite response, even at this late hour."

"This editorial is entitled 'The Trouble with the Schools,' and it was sent in from a subscriber in Anderson, who takes issue with Dr. Hand's thesis and has proposed her own theory for why the schools are failing." Hattie read aloud the scathing article.

Mr. Larke summed things up in his typical tongue-in-cheek manner. "Well, that editorial certainly leaves no question as to where the blame lies for the sorry state of affairs the schools are in—lazy teachers, apathetic trustees, complacent parents, and a curriculum consisting of pabulum. There you have it. I wish I had the certainty to be able to place all of our societal problems in a nutshell like she does. We might as well go home now, friends—that is, if we are competent enough to find our way." He reached for one of the pecan tassies that Hattie had brought and popped it in his mouth.

Byron Stanton smiled and nodded in agreement. "As an educator, I have to admit that it is insulting to read something like that, especially the part about schoolwork being a secondary concern for teachers except on payday. However, I am afraid that many of our parents and community members share that view. In my opinion, the public is far too quick to place the burden on teachers for the upbringing of its collective young. They expect teachers to work miracles with a class full of children when they cannot even raise *one* successfully."

"Perhaps it is the unrealistic teacher expectations that are at the root of the problem," said Mary.

"Yes," Hattie added. "And if you combine that with a teacher who is inexperienced, lacks preparation, and has insufficient knowledge, you have the perfect setup for failure."

"When the teacher is unsure," said Mary, "the students respond with unruly behavior, and the result is either chaos in the classroom, where nobody learns, or the unruly students are expelled to preserve order."

Susan continued. "Either scenario reinforces the ill-conceived notion that teachers are unfocused and uncommitted to their jobs. Clearly, as Professor Hand has suggested, teacher preparation is one of the key elements in reforming the schools. That and adequate funding—"

Hattie interrupted. "We need to bring this discussion to an end, as it is well past our dismissal time. Reverend Fitts, I will turn the meeting back over to you."

"Thank you, Miss Robinson. This has been another robust session. It appears that we are right on target with our goal to increase our opportunities for staff development. I would remind you that teaching is truly a calling and one that requires the perpetual honing and development of skills. We will continue our sessions on a monthly basis. Mr. Stanton, perhaps you would be kind enough to lead us next time and share with us the perspective of one who has taught outside of the state."

Although Hattie received positive comments from the other teachers, she was relieved to have the presentation behind her. She had not realized how much pressure she had been under in preparing to lead the session with her peers. She was never nervous in front of her students, but adults were a different matter. Still, she had enjoyed the challenge and found the time that the staff spent together stimulating, even at the ghastly hour of four o'clock.

Hattie thought she could never become as attached to any group of students as she had been to her class last year. However, she was growing to love her new fifth graders and was amazed to discover how last year's fifth graders had matured over the summer and were ready to take their places as sixth graders.

Her friendship with Mary Posey and Susan Downey deepened, and she enjoyed the opportunity to interact with the high school teachers at their weekly staff meetings and monthly staff develop-ment sessions. Last year, Hattie's energy had been consumed with her students and with learning the ropes of being a new teacher. This year, Calhoun School was not only her place of work, but had also become a real social outlet for her, as well as a refuge from her life at the Bartons'.

Byron Stanton proved a welcome addition to the staff, and Reverend Fitts had become much more social and interactive now that he had broken his ties with Durham and was making an effort to become more invested in the Calhoun community. Chester Larke, as the one with the most seniority in both age and experience, contin-ued to be a group favorite. He always played devil's advocate during their discussions and pretended a lack of concern for his students. However, Hattie agreed with Susan Downey that Chester was, at heart, "an old softie."

At least two courtships were brewing among the staff. Reverend Fitts's interest in Mary continued to heighten, which did wonders for her self-confidence. Mary stopped hovering over him and began to relax and be herself when she was in his presence, which seemed to make her immeasurably more attractive to him. Hattie could almost see his affection for her growing, and she could not have been hap-pier for her friend.

Byron had begun attending Calhoun Presbyterian with his chil-dren. He said it was because he found Reverend Stewart's sermons to be more suitable to his theological leanings than that of the pas-tor at the country church his parents attended. However, Hattie sus-pected that the quality of the sermons was only part of the story. She had heard that Susan Downey made sure to save room for them on the pew down near the front where she and her sister Marie always sat. Marie loved Byron's four-year-old daughter, Anna, and the two of them became fast friends.

When Susan invited them home for dinner one Sunday, they dis-covered that Byron's mother and Susan's father had grown up togeth-er out in the Reedy Fork community before the Downeys married and moved into Calhoun. The next Sunday, Annie Laurie Stanton invited all of the Downeys out to their farm at Reedy Creek for a picnic on the grounds. Susan shared with Hattie that they'd had a wonderful time together. After that, the two families socialized on a regular basis, creating a natural environment for a friendship between Byron and Susan to blossom into an eventual romance.

They gathered weekly for staff meetings and continued the extended staff development sessions that sparked lively debate and discussion. They continued the tradition that Hattie had started with Georgia's pecan tassies by arranging for something sweet to be served at each meeting.

18

Life at the Bartons' would never be the same without Elizabeth, but everyone was becoming accustomed to Alice's style of home management and, although they did not like it, they were getting used to the new routine. They were all learning that her bluster was just that, and that as long as her authority was not challenged and things were running according to her protocols, she was satisfied.

Charles was still stopping off at his Uncle Bailey's after school and the other boys spent a good deal of time at Aunt Sudie and Uncle George's, but they were always home well before Georgia rang the dinner bell at six.

At least with Alice, you never had to wonder where you stood. She held firmly to the view that there must be a hierarchy for running everything from home management to the education of the young to the social order. "A place for everything and everybody; everything and everybody in its place." Life was clear and simple as long as Alice's hierarchy went unchallenged.

Willie Mae, on the other hand, was a real curiosity. Whenever she was not confined to her bed from one of her headaches, she moved about the house on cat's paws in her satin slippers, her comings and goings taking place without a sound. Her headaches caused a sensitivity to brightness, and she preferred dark rooms and avoided the sunlight. She seemed to lurk in the shadows, and it was never apparent when or where she would materialize.

One afternoon, Hattie arrived home from school with an armful of papers, which she was taking to her room to grade after dinner. The shades were drawn and the room was dark. She flipped on the overhead chandelier, gave a start and flung the papers into the air, scattering them like autumn leaves upon the carpet. There, sitting in the rocker, was Willie Mae.

"Oh sweet Jesus! Miss Willie Mae, you nearly gave me heart failure. Is there something you needed from my room? I would have been happy to get it for you." She pressed her hands over her chest to still the pounding and leaned on the bedpost.

"My goodness, Hattie. You needn't go on like that. I just brought a bunch of my roses to arrange in the vase on your side table when my head started throbbing and I had to sit down for a minute."

Hattie determined never to be taken off guard like that again. She made a mental note to switch on the light before entering any room at the Bartons' house in the event that Miss Willie might be there.

Willie Mae had another habit that drove Hattie to distraction—she could enter a room noiselessly. Hattie would be reading or grading papers in the parlor, completely unaware of the presence of anyone, until she felt a warm breath on the back of her neck and knew it was Willie Mae.

"I brought you some violets. Don't you just love violets? They remind me of spring. You know that the blue ones are symbols of love and faithfulness."

Everybody seemed to take it in stride that Willie Mae was like that, and it did not appear to bother the others as it did Hattie. Maybe there was something she didn't know about Willie Mae that, if revealed to her, would cause her eccentric behavior to make sense. She would have to get up her nerve to ask Georgia about it one day.

Willie Mae did have her good points. She was an artist when it came to working with flowers, with an eye for design and the ability to arrange greenery and buds into pleasing displays of color, which were always carefully chosen and appropriate to the occasion. Hattie knew that Willie Mae was completely harmless, but oh, she was a strange one!

Reverend Fitts announced to the teachers one afternoon at staff meeting that Lila Givens had agreed to take charge of the annual fall festival, held at the end of October. He had persuaded Lila to continue on as chair of the library committee by agreeing that fifty percent of the proceeds from the ticket sales, as well as all of the proceeds from the cakewalk, would go into the library fund. Chester Larke shook his head and remarked to Hattie that if Lila had been made a general on Monday, she could have recruited an entire army and had it geared up and marching off to battle by Tuesday.

"She's that good," he said. "Delegation and guilt: that's how she does it. Pulls that knife of shame out of her fancy silk purse, slips it right up under your ribs like a farmer getting ready to gut a pig, and she's gotcha squealing to chair any committee she wants to put you on. She's volunteered around here so often she has something on every person in this school. Now that she has taken on the fall festival, you'd do well to lie low when you see her coming."

"Oh, Mr. Larke," Hattie laughed. "I don't mind helping out. In fact, I think the fall festival sounds like lots of fun."

"Famous last words, Miss Robinson. Don't say I didn't warn you. As for me, I'm keeping a low profile."

The next morning, with clipboard in hand, Lila Givens met Hattie at the door as she was arriving to class.

"Miss Robinson, I want to talk to you about helping out with the fall festival."

"Yes, ma'am. What can I do?"

"I was remarking to Reverend Fitts the other day about how far you have progressed since last year and that unfortunate incident with Tom." Hattie could feel her face flush, partly from embarrassment and partly from irritation. Lila appeared to be oblivious to her reaction and continued.

"As a matter of fact, Reverend Fitts and I both agree that you have gained sufficient expertise to chair publicity and prize donations, one of our most important committees. And then, of course, each teacher is expected to manage one of the fun booths. I have put you on the cakewalk."

"Oh. What will that entail?"

"Your committee will see to the printing of flyers, which you will distribute to all of the shops in town. As you take the flyers around, you will collect non-cash donations from the merchants, which we will use for door prizes. Your committee will also solicit at least twenty cakes for the cakewalk. Usually, the bakery will donate five cakes and the rest will come from the ladies' circles at the churches."

"Well, I am happy to do my part, but that sounds like it will be awfully time-consuming. I am still fairly new to teaching and need sufficient time to prepare for my classes."

Lila plowed on with her agenda like a farmer driving a mule over a rocky patch of soil. "Yes, indeed it will require a number of extra hours," she replied cheerfully. "All time well spent in the effort to raise funds for school maintenance and books. What could be more important to a teacher?"

Perhaps the nurture and instruction of the children, thought Hattie. The genteel tone of Lila's voice concealed the nature of her message. She had mastered the art of making what was in actuality an order sound like a request. It dawned on Hattie that Lila Givens's stylish dress and refined manner were the perfect camouflage for her controlling personality. Beneath the surface, she was a lot like Aunt Alice. Lila had checked off *Publicity and Prize Donations* as well as *Cakewalk* before Hattie could respond.

"Miss Robinson, you're a real soldier," she said. "I knew I could count on you. Be sure to activate your committee right away. We'll need those flyers distributed by next week so that they will be up well before the festival. And feel free to recruit a cochair." Hattie assumed that Lila Givens had concluded her business, because Lila turned and glided down the hallway, ostensibly in pursuit of her next recruit, her signature scarf fluttering behind her.

Oh my. Chester Larke may have been right. What have I gotten myself into?

Hattie wasted no time in enlisting Mary Posey's help. Mary agreed, almost too readily, to cochair the publicity and prize donations committee and help with the cakewalk, and Hattie got the feeling that there would be a price attached to the deal. She was right.

"Lila Givens has a nose for publicity," said Mary. "She found out that Governor and Mrs. Ansel will be on their way home to Greenville for him to cast his vote in the general election and that they will be making several stops in upcountry South Carolina to thank the voters for their support in the primaries and to encourage everybody to vote on November third. They'll arrive in Calhoun on October twenty-ninth, and Lila has invited them to stay with her and Judge Givens. She is throwing a huge backyard dinner so that all of the party bigwigs and the town leaders can meet the Ansels."

"That's the night before the fall festival," said Hattie. "How can she have the dinner on Thursday and turn right around and get the festival up and running on Friday?"

"That's Lila! She views it as an opportunity, not an obstacle. She has talked the governor into stopping by the fall festival before he leaves Calhoun, as a gesture of his support for public education, which was a huge factor in his election."

"And she will no doubt get plenty of publicity for the library fund," said Hattie.

"Yes, and don't you know she has already recruited half of the Methodist women to bake desserts and make potato salad? She has me down for two apple pies, and I'm supposed to supervise the dessert table and make sure that Mrs. Ansel is attended to. You remember I told you that I'm a distant cousin of the governor."

"And all that on top of expecting our committee to get twenty cakes donated for the cakewalk the very next night. I don't know how she thinks all of that is going to get done."

"Like Chester Larke says, 'delegation and guilt.' If women could vote and hold office, she'd be the mayor of Calhoun."

Hattie laughed. "Unless Miz Alice Barton Rivers beat her to it."

"Hattie, we're in this together. I'll help you with publicity and prizes and you help me at the dessert table at the Givenses'."

"I guess that's the least I can do," said Hattie. "Where should we start?"

As usual, Mary was full of good ideas. "Let's kill two birds with one stone by making a class project out of the work. We'll sponsor a poster contest and judge the entries on how well the students convey the information about the fall festival. It will be a great project to evaluate them on penmanship, artistic quality, accuracy of information, and originality. We'll send the winning entry to be printed as our flyer and post the rest around the school."

To review the students' letter-writing skills, Mary suggested that they require each one to compose a note to a local merchant, asking for donations for door prizes. When the posters came back from the printer's, the classes took an outing to town so that the students could deliver their letters personally to the merchants, along with a flyer. Through involving the students, Mary and Hattie hoped to create a spirit of cooperation and anticipation for the festival that would translate into a record attendance.

One of the businesses that the class solicited was Jakes Grocery, located on the edge of town, near the mill. The owner, Perle Jakes, had been born with a cleft palate, which Hattie had learned had been improperly repaired by a surgeon of questionable skill, leaving Perle with an angry scar on his upper lip, which was red and inflamed. His unsightly appearance and impaired speech must have been detrimental to finding a wife and he remained unmarried. However, Perle was a friendly soul who never met a stranger, and Hattie had heard Uncle George say that despite his speech impediment, Perle could strike up a conversation with a stone if there were no one else around to talk to.

He was sole proprietor of the store, which also served as his residence. Perle possessed keen entrepreneurial insight that everybody said he'd inherited from his father and grandfather, both of whom had owned the establishment before him. Over the years, the Jakeses had developed a robust business by catering to the mill operatives and local tenant farmers, extending them credit on seed and staple goods and accepting noncash goods for payment. The establishment hovered on the fringe of respectability, probably due to the fact that Perle asked no questions and offered little judgment of his patrons who loitered about the store.

The well-to-do and more respectable citizens of Calhoun tended to trade at the S and L, the general store on the square. But it was common knowledge that when an item could not be had in town, it was worth taking the time to look for it at Jakes before sending off to Greenville or Spartanburg or Columbia for it. After almost fifty years in business, the Jakeses had built up an impressive and varied inventory. Whatever items had not been sold still remained somewhere among the ordered chaos in the front room of the store. Nothing had apparently ever been thrown away. Perle could root around and within minutes produce almost any item requested, from odd-sized buttons to spare parts for farm equipment or hard-to-find spices and flavorings.

With no children of his own, Perle lavished attention on his nephew, Edward, the son of his sister Theresa Marks. As Edward was in Hattie's class, he was chosen to deliver a note and flyer to his uncle. At the end of the visit, Perle told Hattie that he would donate a jar of salt brine pickles and a case of pork rinds for the food booth at the fall festival, if she could send someone over to get them.

Lila Givens had delegated so many tasks to Hattie's committee that between working on the festival and keeping up with her daily lesson preparation, she had neglected to pick up the donation. The festival was only a few days away and she thought of it as she was leaving school late one afternoon. On her way home, she stopped by Uncle George's to ask Lonnie Jenkins if he would drive her back to Jakes, load the pickles and pork rinds into the wagon, and help her get them to school.

They reached town as the sun was going down and a damp evening chill was setting in. Hattie pulled her shawl around her shoulders, grateful she had brought it along. "Fall's in the air and winter will be on its heels," remarked Hattie.

"Sho' is," Lonnie said as they neared Jakes' Grocery.

The shape of the building reminded Hattie of a railroad boxcar, with two narrow rooms stacked one behind the other. From the class visit, she remembered that in the front room, the bulk items sat in crates and barrels on the floor, filling every square inch of space. A narrow pathway had been cleared for customers to navigate through with their purchases to the large oak counter, which held a brass-plated adding machine and a set of balance scales for weighing out coffee and seed and items that had not been prepackaged. Cured hams and other merchandise that did not fit on the shelves hung on hooks from the ceiling. Several feet behind the counter, a door led to the back room, which doubled as Mr. Jakes's living quarters and gathering place for the locals with time on their hands to play poker, talk politics, and drink.

Hattie had learned from the community grapevine that a rare Saturday night passed without at least one poor fellow losing his week's wages from the mill or the egg money his wife had tucked away for safekeeping in the family Bible in a poker game played in that very room.

Lonnie pulled the wagon to the rear of the building and began hitching the horse to the iron post. He followed Hattie up the plank steps to the back entrance and the screen door creaked as she opened it and stepped inside. The fire from the potbelly stove illuminated the figures of two men gathered around it. The air smelled of smoke and hard liquor. Hattie saw that one of the men was James Hicks, Jimmy's father. The other man looked familiar, but with his back to her, she wasn't certain who he was. He turned around and she drew in her breath sharply as she recognized the face of Clyde Jeter. Clyde was the first to speak.

"Well, if it ain't Miss Robinson."

"Good evening, Mr. Jeter," she stammered. "I didn't know you were back in Calhoun."

"You *didn't*?" Clyde feigned shock. "You mean nobody didn't tell ya'?"

"No," said Hattie, scanning the room desperately for the sight of Perle Jakes. "Nobody told me."

"They didn't?" Clyde was seemingly emboldened by the alcohol and eager to show off in front of his friend.

"No," Hattie said again.

Clyde Jeter reared back in his chair and shot a glance at James Hicks, like a performer checking for the attention of his audience before delivering his punch line.

"Well, I guess that's ''cause it wadn't any of ya' *damn* business." He brayed with laughter and slapped James on the knee. James grinned and snorted acknowledgment of the insult before passing Clyde the bottle of spirits the two were sharing.

Hattie was taken off guard by the unexpected confrontation with Clyde. In past encounters she had not allowed herself to be intimidated by his gruffness and inebriated ramblings. But there was something coarser and more menacing about him now. She could see in his eyes a self-loathing that consumed him like the rotgut liquor he imbibed. It was the look of a man aboard a sinking ship whose last pleasure lay in taking all those around down with him. She remembered Velma Jeter's words to her: "There ain't nothing worse than for a man to be put in a position not to be able to provide for his family. It's no telling what they will do when that happens."

Hattie had always pitied Clyde Jeter; now, for the first time, she feared him. Why was he here? Pauline had told her he was sixty miles away picking peaches. Did she know he had returned to Calhoun? Although her mind spun with questions, she was struck dumb as she struggled for a response.

During the pause that followed, Clyde Jeter had spotted Lonnie Jenkins. He reared his chair back again and looked up.

"Well, I might have known. The high and mighty Miss Robinson has done brought along her uppity nigger."

Hattie flinched defensively at the comment, but before she could speak Lonnie stepped around in front of her, his hulking frame sheltering her from Clyde Jeter like a giant oak. Lonnie peered down at Clyde with dark, honest eyes, his speech controlled and respectful. A jaw muscle twitched, betraying the resentment that Hattie suspected had simmered there for years, from similar encounters, all part and parcel of a black man dwelling in the midst of a social order dominated by white men.

"Mr. Jeta', I know you don't care much fo' me, but there ain't no need for you to disrespec' Miss Robinson. Now, we jus' here to see Mr. Jakes. If you'll move yo' chair on over, we'll pass on through and go find him."

Clyde's jaw clinched and his lips curled in disgust, as if he had just caught the scent from a buzzard feasting on carrion. James Hicks, who had been leaning forward with his elbows resting on his thighs, reared his head. "Wha'd them two do to piss you off so, Clyde?"

"Wha'd they do? I'll tell ya'." Clyde nodded his head at Hattie. "She was the one talked Velma into leavin' me an' poisoned Pauline against me. Then, when I was 'bout as low as I could git, George Barton sent his black bastard to throw me outta my house. Why, if it wadn't for the two of them, I'd still have my fam'ly and a decent place to live."

"Well, I'll be," said James.

"Mista' Jeta', that jus' ain't true," said Lonnie. "You done brought yo' miseries on yo'self. Mista' George was mighty good to you."

Clyde ignored Lonnie and continued. "Look at 'em, James. They high and mighty now. But when we elect ole Coley Blease gov'nor, he's gonna put 'em in they place."

"How's he gone do that, Clyde? I voted for him, too, but he got beat in the primaries in August, en' that sews it up for Governor Ansel to get a second term," said James.

"Yeah, I know. But don't you count Coley out for 1910. I guarantee he'll win then. Coley don't hold to the races being equal. An' Coley don't believe in the gov'ment forcing parents to send their children to school. No, sir, ole Coley will bring down the high and mighty an' put the coloreds in their place when he sits in the governor's mansion. An' I'm gonna do everything I can do to help him. Coley Blease will—"

Before Clyde could finish his sentence, Perle Jakes pushed through the door to the back room. Hattie found her voice and called out to him, averting the confrontation that was hanging in the air like the smoke from the potbelly stove.

"Hey, Mr. Jakes. We've come to pick up the pickles and pork rinds for the fall festival."

Perle Jakes brightened, raised his arm in greeting, and began talking a mile a minute.

"Howdy, Mi' Robinson, Mista' Jenkins. Sorry I nidn't hear ya' come in. I was on da' phone wif' a custona'. Just had a line to da' store put in last week. We bringing Jakes Grocery into the twentieth century. It's been great for bid'ness. Nid'ja see how I posted ya' flyer ova' there on that wall so ever'body can read it?"

"Yes, I did. Thank you, Mr. Jakes," said Hattie. Perle Jakes turned to James Hicks and Clyde Jeter.

"You fellas been talking with Mi' Robinson? She's da' best teacher in Pickens County. My sista's boy, Eddie, he's in her class. En' ya' know, she figger'd out he was playing hooky da' first week o' school and she nidn't waste a minute taking care of it...came afta' him at da' house en' got him back in school. Why, if it wadn't for her, Eddie woulda dropped out jus' like ever'body else in the fam'ly. Now, he's likely to make it at least to the eighth grade. Shucks, he might even gradurate from high school."

Perle Jakes beamed with pride and continued talking nonstop, oblivious to the situation he had interrupted. "You come on wif' me, Mi' Robinson. I got da' pickles and pork rinds all packaged up for ya'. They heavy, though. I 'spec tha's why ya' brought Mista' Jenkins. Move on ova', Mista' Jeta', and let these folks through. They on important bid'ness for the school en' you guys ain't doing nothing but jawing and drinking." He poked Mr. Jeter's arm with his index finger. "I'm just joshing with ya', Clyde."

Clyde Jeter sneered and moved his chair so slightly that Hattie would have fallen against the stove as she passed if Lonnie had not caught her elbow and helped her through. Lonnie's stride was sufficiently long to allow him to step over the outstretched legs of Mr. Jeter, avoiding the slightest bit of physical contact.

Hattie and Lonnie followed Perle to the front of the store, where Perle pointed to a pile of wooden crates stacked against the counter and indicated the ones that were going to the school.

"I'll jus' pull the wagon round and load up through the front door," said Lonnie. "We done disturbed Mr. Jeta' and Mr. Hicks enough tonight."

"Good idea," said Hattie. She couldn't help herself from asking, "What's Mr. Jeter doing back in town? I thought he was over in Gaffney." She was sure that Perle Jakes stayed abreast of all of the local gossip.

"Says he's back lookin' for work at da' mill now 'at da' peach season's ova'.

"I thought he got fired at the mill," said Hattie.

"Naw, I don't think so. My sista's husband, Eddie, says it was 'cause he was messing around wif' Grady Johnson's wife. Grady come home afta' second shift one night an' found the two of 'em together. An' Grady said he'd blow Clyde's head off wif' his shotgun if Clyde nidn't get outta town right away. Grady tole Eddie 'at Clyde was so ready to leave 'at he dove headfirst out da' bedroom window. Hoowee! 'At musta been a sight," Perle cackled, slapping his knee. Then he shook his head and became serious. "I s'pose It ain't right to josh about a man when he's down. Pore ole Clyde, he's sho' made a mess o' things."

"Isn't he afraid that Mr. Johnson will follow through with his threat if he comes back?"

"Well, the way Eddie tells it, turns out 'at Clyde wadn't the only one womanizin'. Grady Johnson was stepping out wif' a woman ova' at Easley and afta' he kicked Clyde out, he and his wife, Lola, got into a big fight. She tole Grady she knew about the other woman and 'at what was good for da' goose was good for da' gander. Grady got mad and stormed out. Eddie says Grady's livin' with da' woman in Easley and has got him a new job at the mill ova' there.'"

Lonnie had finished loading the wagon and Hattie thanked Perle for the donation and left through the front door, relieved to avoid further contact with Clyde. She wondered how much of this gossip Pauline had heard and if she even knew that her father was back in town.

Mary Posey sat wide-eyed as Hattie told her about her trip to Jakes's store the next day. "What a tragic character he is! He's just the type to be influenced by the negative campaign that Coleman Blease always runs. He can't take responsibility for the misfortunes he brought on himself and is looking for someone else to blame. It's hard to believe he could be Pauline's father. Does she know he's back in Calhoun?"

"I don't think so. I feel like she would have told Charles if she did, and he certainly hasn't mentioned it to me. I'm going to stop by Rosa's on my way home and make sure Velma knows. I'm not sure I should repeat the gossip that Perle Jakes told me, but I don't want Velma to be in the dark about things that everybody in the community may be talking about. She may know more than she is telling Pauline, but Pauline thinks her father left Calhoun because he got in a fight, and she never mentioned anything to me about another woman."

"I agree. You should probably just tell her about seeing Mr. Jeter. The rest will come out in good time, and if it is only gossip, it doesn't need to be repeated anyway. Now don't forget your promise to help me at the dessert table at the Givenses' dinner for the Ansels tomorrow night."

"I haven't forgotten. In fact, I'm rather looking forward to being included in such an important affair. I heard Aunt Sudie say she's baking a pound cake, and Georgia is making two pecan pies."

"Won't Mr. Barton be invited, as chairman of the school trustees and former chair of the Pickens County Democrats?" asked Mary.

"Yes, and he seems surprisingly enthusiastic about it. These days he doesn't socialize much and there are very few topics that appear to interest him outside of his work, but the subject of politics and the election have proven to be an exception."

Since Elizabeth's death, it had been almost impossible to engage Charles Barton in conversation extending beyond the basic pleasantries. Hattie had watched his sisters and his children attempt to communicate with him without success, and she could see how it hurt them, especially Charles Jr., who seemed starved for his father's attention. Mr. Barton was always polite and gracious to Hattie, but she could tell that his mind was elsewhere when they spoke. He appeared restless and eager to leave whenever she observed him in the company of others.

Hattie had been heartened that Charles Jr. had finally discovered a topic to spark his father's interest, when Byron Stanton assigned his students in civics class a report on the platforms of the major candidates running for state and national office. Hattie had found the two of them in the parlor, where Charles was listening intently to his father's analysis of the gubernatorial elections.

"Based on precedent, Governor Ansel will have no difficulty being elected to a second term," Hattie heard Charles Barton explain. "Coleman Blease was little threat to him in the primary this time around. However, I predict that if Blease continues to organize the mill operatives, they may prove to be a formidable bloc that could sway future elections in his favor."

"Why will the mill operatives vote for him, Father?" Hattie could see that Charles would have listened with equal intent if his father had been reciting the Cyrillic alphabet, so happy was he to have his father's attention, if only briefly. It warmed Hattie's heart to see them there, sharing a rare moment together.

Mr. Barton answered, "Because he plays on their fears and their disappointments, and he claims to represent their interests."

"What are they afraid of?"

"Afraid of losing their livelihood, afraid of losing control, afraid of being left behind. Most of the operatives took jobs in the mills because they lost their farms and are in debt. They are looked down upon by the small farmers and shop owners and they feel isolated and left out. Politically, they have been excluded by both the conservatives and the Tillmanites in the Democratic Party. They would never side with the Republicans and don't fit in anywhere. Cole Blease recognizes that and realizes that the mill operatives are a potential minefield of support for the candidate who identifies with them."

"Do you think it's wrong for Mr. Blease to try to get the mill workers' vote?"

"No, Charles. What I object to is the way he goes about it. In my opinion, he is little more than a demagogue and a source of embarrassment to our state."

Hattie considered Charles Barton's analysis astute as she remembered what Clyde Jeter had said about Cole Blease bringing down the high and mighty and keeping "coloreds" in their places. She enjoyed listening to Mr. Barton talk about political affairs almost as much as Charles seemed to. She was impressed with his extensive knowledge of the election process and admired his ability to argue objectively, without allowing emotion to sway his judgment. Hattie wished she were more like that.

Mary's voice cut through Hattie's thoughts. "You might want to go ahead to Rosa's, Hattie, before Pauline gets there."

"You're right. I wouldn't want to upset her unnecessarily. Charles did tell me that all of the high school students are staying late today to help Chester Larke. It seems Lila Givens finally caught up with him and put him in charge of the apple bobbing."

Mary laughed. "Chester talks big, but he's as intimidated by Lila as the rest of us."

Hattie found Rosa in the alteration shop finishing up a pair of trousers that she was hemming. Velma had gone out with little Clydie to deliver a dress to a customer and to pick up more thread at the piece goods store. Hattie was glad that Rosa was alone and she could question her before she talked with Velma. She told Rosa about her chance meeting with Clyde Jeter.

"Lord, if that man is not a big old albatross hanging around Velma's neck! And yes, Velma does know he is back in town." Rosa secured the last stitch and snipped the thread. "He came over here looking for her the other night, just as drunk as a lord."

"Does Pauline know?"

"No, thank goodness she was at youth group at the church when he came by."

"What did he want, Rosa?"

Rosa hesitated as she folded the newly hemmed pants and laid them in a stack to be pressed. "Now Hattie, you have to swear on a stack of Bibles that you won't breathe one word of what I'm about to tell you."

Hattie nodded. "Of course, Rosa."

"Well, he told Velma he was going to get his old job back at the mill and asked her to move back in with him when he got a place. Said he was sure that with Velma's sewing skills, she could get a job as a weaver, and if Pauline works part-time, they could have a three-bedroom house."

"Oh, you know he did not say that! What did Velma do?"

"Velma told him that beside the fact that he was drunk and not thinking straight, she knew about him taking up with Lola Johnson and said she would not go back to him."

"So the gossip about Lola Johnson is true?"

"Yes, and he did not show a bit of remorse about it. Clyde told her that as Clydie's father, he plans to have his son with him and Velma can either help him get a mill house and reunite the family, or he'll move in with Lola and Velma can have another woman raise her child."

"Oh, Rosa. How awful. How did Velma take it?"

"Well, she was frantic at first, but then she settled down and made a plan. She has her doubts that Clyde can stay sober long enough to keep a job, and even if he does, she says she can't forgive him for shaming her by taking up with Lola Johnson. She made contact with one of her sisters up in Spartanburg County and bought railway tickets so that she can leave Calhoun with Clydie and Pauline at a moment's notice if Clyde tries to take his son."

"And Pauline doesn't know any of this?"

"No, and Velma wants to keep it that way as long as possible. She knows that Pauline will have a fit if she thinks she has to leave Calhoun. She has so many friends here and is so happy and well adjusted. Velma doesn't want to do anything to ruin that."

"What can we do about this, Rosa? We can't just let Clyde Jeter come in and mess things up again. I could talk to Mr. Barton. He was the one who offered legal advice to Velma after Clyde showed up at the school."

"Now Hattie, I know you mean well, but you promised to keep all this in confidence. Velma is determined to handle this in her own way and if you go and tell anybody, it will get back to her."

"Rosa! Surely there is something we can do."

"Hattie, don't think I haven't been staying up walking the floor the last two nights, racking my brain for some way to help. But Velma is such a private person and she is mortified enough at the thought of having her dirty laundry aired all over town. She hears the whispers and knows everybody is talking about what Clyde did."

"Well, that's no reflection on Velma."

"I know. But you remember how Velma blamed herself for the way Clyde got back on the bottle when they were about to lose the house. She feels the same way about this. She thinks somehow if she had been stronger and been able to work harder, Clyde would not have shamed her and her family in this way. It is like she thinks it is a personal cross that she must bear."

"Did she tell you that?"

"In so many words, yes. But Velma would not have mentioned it at all had I not been here when Clyde showed up that night and heard the whole thing. And I'm glad I was here, because I am really the only person she feels she can talk to—she would not even do that until I promised not to share it with anyone. So you see, Hattie, if you breathe one word of it and Velma finds out, she will know that I broke her trust. We are just going to have to sit on this and let it take its course."

"Okay, Rosa. You know I won't break my promise. But it won't be easy to just do nothing."

As the two women talked, Hattie spotted Pauline in the distance, coming toward Rosa's house with Charles Jr., who had apparently walked her home after they finished at school.

"Here comes Pauline. We'll talk later, Rosa," said Hattie, as she was leaving the shop to catch up with Charles so that they could walk home together.

On the walk home, Hattie noticed that Charles seemed distracted and restless. Several times he started to speak and paused. Finally, she took his arm and stopped him. Looking directly into his serious blue eyes, she said, "What is it, Charles? What is bothering you?"

Charles looked away. "It's nothing, really. Or, at least, nothing I can talk about without breaking a promise to someone. But what if by keeping my promise, that someone gets hurt? Then I'd feel awful for not saying something."

Hattie could see that Charles was talking more to himself than to her. He was such a thoughtful young man and whatever he was hiding was obviously causing him to wrestle with the moral dilemma of keeping his word versus the responsibility of protecting someone he cared about. Hattie was experiencing the same dilemma. She had a feeling she knew who the somebody was that Charles was worried about.

"Charles, does this have something to do with keeping Pauline safe?"

Charles's surprised look convinced Hattie that she had read his mind. "How did you know?" he said.

"It wasn't too hard to guess. You have always cared a great deal for Pauline and been protective of her. And that's a wonderful trait. But

Charles, if Pauline is in trouble, you need to tell an adult, perhaps your father or Reverend Fitts. Or you can tell me. You know how fond I am of Pauline and would go to any ends to keep her safe."

"I can't tell Father or Reverend Fitts. They would both say I was meddling in family concerns that are not my own. I guess I can tell you if you promise not to let Pauline know."

"Charles, this won't be the first secret I've been asked to keep today."

"It's just that Pauline found out that her papa is back in town. Jimmy Hicks saw him with his papa and he was sure they were up to no good. Pauline didn't say anything to her mother because of all Mrs. Jeter's been through."

Hattie wanted to tell Charles that Velma already knew that Clyde was back, but she remembered her promise to Rosa. "Well, Jimmy was right about that," she said. "I saw Mr. Jeter myself the other night, when Lonnie Jenkins drove me over to Jakes's store to pick up a donation for the fall festival. He was with Mr. Hicks and they were both inebriated and acting pretty rowdy."

Hattie knew she had to choose her words carefully. "How does Pauline feel knowing her father is in town? Is she afraid?"

"I don't' think Pauline is so much afraid now as she is mad at her papa. She hates him. He almost ruined their lives and now that they are out from under his roof, they are all better off. Pauline is determined to figure out a way to protect her mama and keep her papa away from them."

"Oh, Charles, I really think Pauline should discuss all of this with her mother and at least let Velma know she knows about her father. Please do try to talk her into it."

"I did, and she said she would, but she says she wants to wait until after the fall festival is over."

"What on earth for?"

"I don't know. She says if her mama finds out about her papa being in town, she might not let Pauline take Clydie to the fall festival as we had planned. Pauline wanted Clydie to see all the fun booths and we were gonna introduce him to Richard, since they are about the same age. If Mrs. Jeter finds out, she might not let either of them go."

"They would certainly be safe at school, because Mr. Jeter has been banned from school grounds after his appearance last spring. Does she think Velma would worry about them getting there and back safely? We could always go by and pick them up when Lonnie brings us all in to town." Hattie suspected there was more to it than that. "Is that the only reason, Charles?"

"Well, there could be more. She and Jimmy Hicks have been talking a lot lately about their papas, and I heard Jimmy tell Pauline that he had an idea about how to fix things so that Mr. Jeter couldn't come around anymore. But you know how Jimmy is. He hates his own papa and is always talking big and scheming about how to get back at him."

Hattie tried not to show surprise over Charles's comment about Jimmy's plan. After all, Charles had opened up to her and she did not want to shut down the line of communication between them by seeming shocked. She responded nonchalantly. "Yes, I remember the pants incident and how he was willing to stand up for Pauline that day her papa came to school. Jimmy can be quite inventive."

"Jimmy's really helped Pauline not to feel so self-conscious about her papa. He pokes fun with her about him and Pauline doesn't mind because she knows Jimmy understands what it's like. But Jimmy is real crafty. Maybe he *does* have an idea about how to make Mr. Jeter go away. I hope he does. I mean, as long as it's not something hurtful or against the law, I'd be all for it."

Hattie could tell that Charles was talking to himself again and that he was still trying to reconcile his loyalty to Pauline with his need to speak the truth. She had no idea what trick Jimmy might have up his sleeve, but perhaps if she didn't overreact now, Charles would continue to confide in her and she would find out more about it as the plan unfolded. At the same time, she felt a responsibility to Velma to let her know that Pauline was aware that her father had returned to town, as well as a duty to inform Mr. Barton of what Charles and his friends might be up to. If she just hadn't made that promise to Rosa!

Hattie could tell by Charles's worried look that he was afraid he had said too much. "Miss Robinson? Please don't tell Father what I just said. And please don't tell Pauline's mama anything right now."

They were approaching the house and Hattie stopped and took Charles's arm. "The fall festival is only a few days away. I guess it won't hurt to wait. But after that, Charles, if Pauline hasn't confided in Velma, I'll have to tell her. And I'll have to say something to your father and Reverend Fitts as well. If anything changes, you must promise to let me know at once."

Charles look relieved. "Okay, Miss Robinson. I'll tell you if anything changes. I'm going to feed Boots and tend to the goat. I'll see you at dinner."

Hattie rubbed her temples to release the tension. It made her nervous to be keeping all of these secrets. She tried to convince herself to relax and let things take their course. Pauline would surely talk to Rosa soon, and Jimmy Hicks couldn't possibly implement a plan of any consequence before Friday. And she had so much on her plate with getting ready for the festival and helping Mary at the dinner for the governor, she simply could not worry about all this right now. Hattie took two more cleansing breaths and decided to let it be.

The dinner on the lawn of the Givens mansion proved to be a gathering of all of the prominent business and professional leaders in Pickens County. The weather was fair, but the late-October air grew chilly and damp as the evening progressed. Before the party ended, Lila Givens invited the guests inside to hear the remarks the governor had prepared.

Hattie and Mary stood at the dessert station, cutting pies and cakes and serving them on crystal plates stacked at either end of the table. Their job was to make certain that a variety of selections were always available to the guests as they finished their barbecue and were looking for something sweet to top off their meals.

Mr. Barton had invited his sister Alice to accompany him to the dinner. Alice was eager for firsthand news from Columbia and wasted no time in seeking out Mrs. Ansel, who had become a part of her social circle there.

"Look, Hattie," said Mary. "That Emily Hutchens can't keep her eyes off Mr. Barton. She just picked up a slice of chess pie and is headed over to take it to him right now. She's been hanging around him all night."

Hattie did not know why, but she felt a twinge of resentment, maybe even jealousy. She certainly had no claim on Charles Barton. He was way out of her league socially and was much older than she. She knew that when Charles Barton completed his official time of mourning, every eligible woman in the community would pursue him. One of them would eventually turn his head and when that happened it could change everything. Still, she hadn't thought anything would transpire this soon. "Mr. Barton usually doesn't care for sweets," she said.

"He seems kind of uncomfortable with her attention, "said Mary. "Like a trapped animal looking for a way to escape. And based on the way he's picking at that pie with his fork, you're right about him not caring for sweets."

"Well, it has only been six months since Mrs. Barton passed. I'm sure he feels strange coming to a social event without her on his arm. She was such a lovely person and I'm sure he wonders if he will ever get over her."

"I declare," said Mary. "That Miz Alice Barton Rivers is completely monopolizing Mrs. Ansel. I bet Mrs. Ansel would like a break. I think I'll go over there and take her a piece of my apple pie."

While Mary went off to rescue Mrs. Ansel, Hattie continued to watch Charles Barton as he interacted with Emily Hutchens. He had that same vacant stare and restlessness that she had observed in him so often since Elizabeth died. Hattie sighed. She guessed she didn't need to worry about things changing just yet.

The news that the governor would make an appearance at the fall festival resulted in record attendance. In years past, the event had attracted mostly the students, their parents, and immediate family. This year it turned into a community affair.

From her classroom window, Hattie could see the crowd arriving. They stopped to buy their tickets from Reverend Fitts, who was stationed at the entrance to the walkway. The aroma of fried chicken and country ham biscuits lured most of the attendees to the food booths on the lawn, and only a few bypassed them and went inside first.

Hattie and Mary had stayed over after school to organize the cakes and set up the stations for the cakewalk. Byron Stanton was using Mary's room for the ring toss and Susan Downey had set up the fish booth in her room. Chester Larke had set up the apple bobbing tubs out back.

Lila Givens was determined to showcase the book collection and had arranged for the grand finale to be held in the library. "People will buy what they want for supper on the lawn, have time to visit all of the fun booths, and then gather in the library for the drawing of the prizes and a presentation. I'll call on the governor to say a few words at that time."

Hattie looked over to see Pauline coming through the door, holding the hand of her little brother, Clydie, who was sucking on one of Perle Jakes's giant pickles. Charles and Jimmy Hicks were with her.

"Hey, Miss Robinson. We brought Clydie over early so he could go to the fun booths before his bedtime. Mama and Miz Rosa are coming for him after a while so I can help out in the apple-bobbing booth and get to the presentation in the library." Pauline picked Clydie up so that he was eye level with Hattie. "Clydie, this is Miss Robinson, my favorite teacher." Clydie grinned and pickle juice ran down his chin.

"Clydie Jeter, I cannot believe you like that sour pickle," laughed Hattie. "Let me get you a cupcake. We have plenty of extras over here. I'm saving one for Richard when Aunt Sudie brings him."

Pauline laughed. "Oh no, Miss Robinson. Clydie'd rather have the pickle. He's always loved anything sour. He'll even suck on a lemon if you let him."

"Don't worry," said Charles. "That cupcake won't go to waste. Richard will eat two of them when he gets here. He likes to have something sweet in each hand."

Mary Posey came over and reached out for Clydie, who was happy to let her take him. "Let me see that boy. Honestly, he is so big! Look at those chubby cheeks. I don't believe you got those by eating pickles and lemons. Your mama's feeding you something else good." Clydie grinned again and held out the pickle for Mary to take a bite.

"No, thank you," said Mary. "I'm full. He's precious, Pauline," she said as she handed him back to his sister.

"We'd better move along," said Charles. "If you see Aunt Sudie, tell her we'll be in the fishing booth. I want to make sure Richard gets to see Clydie. They are about the same age, although Clydie would make almost two of Richard."

"I'm going to go get me one of those pickles," said Jimmy. "I'll meet up with y'all in a few minutes." Hattie recalled her conversation with Charles two days prior and wondered if Jimmy were up to something. She did not have long to entertain that thought because a sufficient number had gathered in the room to begin the first round of the cakewalk.

When Mary started *The Maple Leaf Rag* on the Victrola she had brought from home, the contestants marched around in a circle on top of the numbered squares. After several turns were completed, she stopped the music. Hattie selected a cake randomly from the shelf and looked for the number attached to the bottom of the plate. "Number nine," she called.

A squeal of delight came from Mrs. Marks, who was standing on the corresponding square. "Well, that takes care of my Sunday dessert," she said. "I have a whole houseful of kinfolks coming for dinner and now I know just what I'll serve. Ooh, and it's a seven-layer caramel cake. I'll bet it's one of Rosa Griffin's."

The cakewalk proved to be a popular station, as well as a profitable one, as three tickets were required to participate. Hattie understood why Lila Givens had wanted the proceeds from that event for her book fund.

After numerous desserts had been awarded, a chocolate pound cake was the only one that remained. It went to Susan Downey's sister Marie, who had come with Anna Stanton and her grandmother Annie Laurie.

"Let's close up and get to the library for the presentation," said Mary. "My poor feet are killing me after all this standing over the past two days."

They found two seats together in the next-to-last row of chairs. Governor Ansel was seated up front behind the podium, with Judge Givens on one side and Reverend Greer on the other. Hattie spotted Pauline, who was sitting between Charles and Jimmy several rows in front of them. She wondered if Jimmy was a bit nervous because he kept looking behind him as though he expected something to happen. But then she decided she was jumping to conclusions based on her conversation with Charles.

Lila Givens had brought in a special table to display the newest books in circulation, along with a cardboard box decorated in crepe paper with a slot in the top for contributions. With boundless energy, she directed everyone by the display and on to their seats, gliding around the room, the layers of her crepe dress swirling gracefully from side to side, obviously basking in her accomplishments at having assembled such an auspicious array of guests in support of her cause.

Reverend Greer stood to offer prayer in accordance with the program that Hattie had been handed at the door by Byron Stanton. Next, Reverend Fitts recognized Judge Givens, who would in turn introduce the governor.

As the judge was making his way to the podium, the audience was distracted by a commotion that appeared to be coming from outside. The sound of men arguing and feet shuffling gave way to the inebriated voice of Clyde Jeter demanding, "You ain't got no right to stop me! I was called here by the gov'nor hisself." Hattie could see that Byron and Chester were attempting to detain him as he struggled to move toward the front of the room.

A collective gasp escaped from the audience. Lila Givens stood, mouth agape and eyes bulging indignantly. Governor Ansel seemed to be straining to identify the intruder and to retain a dignified demeanor.

Hattie squeezed Mary's arm and looked over at her in shocked amazement. "I can't believe this is happening," she said. "Why on earth would Clyde Jeter come here after being banned from the school? He's gonna get himself arrested for this."

As she spoke those words, Hattie recalled what Charles had said: "Jimmy has an idea about how to fix things so that Mr. Jeter can't come around anymore." She looked for Jimmy and saw three empty chairs where he, Pauline, and Charles had sat.

Reverend Fitts caught the eye of Mr. Barton, who rose to his feet, motioned for Reverend Fitts to follow, and made his way toward Clyde Jeter. Reverend Fitts shot an apologetic glance at Judge Givens and before he hurried off said, "Please do proceed while we attend to this interruption."

As if presiding over his courtroom, the judge assumed a stern expression while he waited for the commotion to cease.

"Let me go, goddammit," roared Clyde Jeter as he struggled against Byron and Chester's restraints. "I was called here to see the gov'nor."

Charles Barton walked up authoritatively and spoke into Clyde's ear. Clyde continued to struggle as Mr. Barton escorted him from the building, flanked by Byron and Chester, each holding Clyde by one arm. Hattie saw the relief on Reverend Fitts's face as he turned and walked back toward the front, where Judge Givens was still standing in silence.

Reverend Fitts raised his arms as if he were about to pronounce a benediction. "Please do continue, Judge Givens. My deepest apology for the commotion. Mr. Charles Barton, who is the chairman of the trustees of the school as well as an attorney, has taken things in hand and will see to it that our intruder is dealt with. I am certain that he will give us a full report when he returns."

Judge Givens introduced Governor Ansel, who astutely read his audience and made his comments brief, albeit full of praise for the trustees in their support of high school accreditation. He ended by recognizing Lila Givens for her tireless efforts in raising funds for the library and thanked her and the judge for their gracious hospitality. He nodded at Reverend Fitts, who raised his arms again, thanked the crowd for coming, and dismissed them.

The library was abuzz with questions about Clyde Jeter's appearance as members of the audience made their way to the front, ostensibly to shake hands with the governor, but more pressingly to question Reverend Fitts about the incident.

"I see that Pauline has left," said Hattie. "I need to go find her and make sure she's all right."

"I'll come with you," said Mary. "It looks like James—I mean, Reverend Fitts—will be occupied for a while. We can come back and close up later."

They escaped from the bedlam in the library to the hallway and out into the cool night air. Pauline was nowhere to be seen and Hattie suggested that they drop by Rosa's to make sure she got home safely.

When they arrived, Rosa met them at the kitchen door and invited them into the parlor, where Pauline and her mother were sitting together on the sofa, embracing one another and talking emotionally. Rosa explained that Charles and Jimmy had walked Pauline home before they returned to school to help Mr. Larke clean up the apple-bobbing booth. She also mentioned that Mr. Barton had stopped by to check on them as well.

As soon as Pauline saw Mary and Hattie, she grew animated and began talking excitedly. "Mama knew he was back and I knew he was back and neither one of us wanted to worry the other one with it." Pauline hugged her mother and said, "Oh, Mama, I promise I won't ever keep secrets from you again. I know it wasn't right to do that."

Velma stroked Pauline's hair. "I just wanted to protect you from him, honey. Otherwise, I would have told you, too. But it's all over now and Mr. Barton says we won't have to worry about your papa bothering us for a long while."

"Rosa said he was here. What did he tell you?" asked Hattie.

Velma smiled up at Hattie. "What a fine and considerate man! You know, with all he had to do tonight, he took time to stop by here and make sure we were all right and tell us all the details. He brought us such peace of mind."

"So what did he say?" Mary asked anxiously.

"Well, you know Clyde was served papers banning him from the school, and he showed up tonight anyway, drunk and rambling on about needing to see the governor."

"Yes, we know that. We were there and saw it," said Hattie a little impatiently. "What happened after that?"

"Mr. Barton said they got Clyde outside the building and found Sheriff Bonner, who was already there at the festival. He arrested Clyde for trespassing and took him off to jail. Mr. Barton went with them to tend to the legal part."

"So, what is to become of Mr. Jeter?" asked Hattie.

"He said they'd hold Clyde over in the jail to dry out and until he goes to trial. But Mr. Barton said he hadn't seen Clyde since last May, and he was really shocked at how bad Clyde looked. Mr. Barton is afraid Clyde's going to drink hisself to death if he doesn't get some help. Mr. Barton called Dr. Wheeler over to the jail to take a look at him and Dr. Wheeler agreed. He said Clyde is already showing signs of cirrhosis of the liver. Dr. Wheeler said Clyde may have got into some bad moonshine and that would account for the way Clyde was rambling on about getting a phone call from the governor."

"Are you saying Mr. Jeter thought the governor had called him and told him to come to the school?" asked Mary.

"Yes, according to Mr. Barton, Clyde was convinced that the governor had rung him up over at Jakes Grocery and told him to come to the school right away."

"That doesn't make any sense," said Mary.

"Of course it doesn't," said Velma. "I don't know how in the world Clyde got that into his head. Unless, like Dr. Wheeler said, he drunk some bad whiskey and was hallucinatin'."

Hattie was curious why Pauline had become quiet and shifted nervously in her seat at the mention of the phone call. Did she know something she was not saying? She looked directly at Pauline. "I suppose the sheriff could send a deputy out to talk to Perle Jakes and find out if he took a call for your papa," she said, mostly to test whether she was right about Pauline's reaction. Pauline drew in her breath and her eyes widened. When she caught Hattie's glance, she looked down and coughed into her hands, as if to cover her surprise.

Hattie had a sinking feeling about the way things were adding up. First, Charles had told her about Jimmy's plan to keep Clyde Jeter away from Pauline permanently, then she'd found out that Pauline was keeping the secret from her mother until after the festival. Then Jimmy left Pauline and Charles to go outside at approximately the time Clyde had said he received the call, and then Pauline and Jimmy and Charles disappeared right before Clyde appeared. And most suspicious of all, Clyde had showed up in the first place.

Was Jimmy Hicks really that clever that he could have a pulled off a plan to lure Clyde to the school so he would get himself arrested and taken off to jail? And had sweet little Pauline and honest, upright Charles gone along with it? Surely, it was all a coincidence. But they could be in a lot of trouble if it turned out to be true. Still, she had to admit, if it was true, she admired their gumption.

Velma continued, "Mr. Barton said that the most the judge could do would be to fine Clyde for trespassing and disorderly conduct and to sentence him to jail for less than thirty days. And Dr. Wheeler told Mr. Barton that Clyde wouldn't be helped much by that. He'd just get out and start drinking again, especially without a job or a place to live, and then we'd all be right back to square one again. Dr. Wheeler told Mr. Barton the best thing for Clyde and everybody else would be to get Clyde admitted to the state mental hospital for a while."

"Did Mr. Barton think that was a possibility?" asked Mary.

"Yes," said Velma. "He said with the governor right here in town, he thought he could pull in some favors and get the papers signed so that Clyde would be on his way to Columbia by the beginning of the week. He was headed back to the courthouse to work on it after he left here." Velma teared up. "I haven't been this touched since Rosa gave Pauline the letter inviting us to come live with her."

Pauline hugged her mother again. "I know, Mama."

When Hattie and Mary walked back to the school to clean up her room from the cakewalk, Reverend Fitts met them at the door.

"We've gotten a lot done, but with all the confusion, we decided to call it a night and finish cleaning up tomorrow. I sent Mr. Larke on about fifteen minutes ago and he is dropping off Mr. Stanton and Miss Downey at their respective homes. Mr. Jenkins was waiting on you, Miss Robinson, but I told him to take Charles home and I'd give you a lift in my car when you got here. The rest of the high school students who stayed to help live in town and were able to walk together."

"I'll ride with you," said Mary. "We can tell you all about our discussion with Velma Jeter on the way."

They reached the Barton estate just as Charles Barton was driving up. Eager to get the latest word on Clyde Jeter, all three rushed toward him as he got out of the car. Charles Barton insisted that they come inside, heedless of the late hour. *He really is the consummate gentleman*, thought Hattie.

"I suppose if Clyde Jeter was going to cause a ruckus, he did it on the ideal night," Charles Barton explained once they were all seated in the parlor. "With the governor, the judge, the sheriff, the doctor, and the mill supervisor all attending the festival at the school, and with the school only a block from the courthouse, I was able to call them all together within the hour.

"After Dr. Wheeler attested to Clyde's deteriorating medical condition, Governor Ansel agreed to sign papers to expedite Clyde's admission to the state mental hospital. Judge Givens agreed to waive a sentence of jail time on the condition that Clyde go directly from the county jail to the mental hospital and stay there until he is fully rehabilitated. Sheriff Bonner agreed to drive Clyde to Columbia just as soon as there is a place for him at the hospital. Paul Godfrey at Calhoun Mills said that for all Clyde's faults, he could card more cotton than two men his size when he was sober, and he would promise him a job when he got his life turned around."

"A miraculous effort on your part, Mr. Barton!" said Reverend Fitts. "You succeeded in assembling the resources of the state, the county, and the town to rescue a poor soul who is drowning in his own vices and threatening to bring down his family with him in the process. A man of lesser stature would have written Mr. Jeter off as a lost cause."

"Thank you, Reverend Fitts. The Clyde Jeter who intruded on our gathering in the library tonight was a broken shadow of the man I met up in Spartanburg County and brought down to save my uncle George's cotton crop. He clearly needs help and I am grateful that we were able to throw him a lifeline. I believe he deserves a second chance. But Clyde won't thank me just yet for what he will be made to go through in the process of gaining sobriety. He has a tough battle ahead."

"Indeed he does," said Reverend Fitts. "But you have given him a reason to hope, and if he is as strong as you say, he may survive this."

"What do you think possessed Mr. Jeter to come to school when he clearly knew that he was trespassing?" asked Hattie. "Velma Jeter mentioned something about a phone call he received at Jakes Grocery."

"Clyde was under the illusion that he had received an urgent call from the governor summoning him to come at once. Of course that would have been impossible, as the governor was shaking hands with the crowd on the school grounds at six o'clock, the alleged time of the call. Dr. Wheeler said Clyde appeared to be suffering from alcohol poisoning and could be hallucinating, but Sheriff Bonner contacted Perle Jakes just to see if there had been some kind of prank call made."

"What did Mr. Jakes say?" asked Hattie.

"Perle got called out to make a delivery to a customer around that time and locked the front door of the store. He left Clyde in the back room and asked him to answer the phone while he was gone. He said Clyde was expecting to get up a poker game later in the evening. By the time Perle returned, the poker game had started and Clyde was gone. The men around the table said he must have left before they arrived."

"Did Mr. Jakes by any chance mention where he made the delivery?" asked Hattie, who was too curious to let things go.

"Why, yes. I believe he did. He said the Hicks boy called and asked if Perle could please bring five pounds of flour by their house. He said his mother was baking a surprise birthday cake for his father and wanted to do it while he was out. Perle doesn't usually make deliveries that late in the evening, but being the good-hearted person he is, was eager to help out."

"So I guess there is no way to corroborate whether or not the alleged call from the governor was made to Mr. Jeter," said Hattie.

"Probably not. Sheriff Bonner has a hunch that it was the result of some type of prank and suspects the Hicks boy could be in the middle of it, based on a fire in the Hicks's backyard he was called on to investigate last year. But there is really no way to prove any of it and Sheriff Bonner thinks it's useless to pursue it, although he does plan to keep a close eye on Jimmy Hicks. Besides, it would not have any bearing on this case. Clyde came of his own volition to the school in a drunken and disorderly state. Even if he did receive a call, that would not override the restraining order he was served with last spring."

Hattie breathed a sigh of relief. Clyde Jeter was out of their lives and he had been given a lifeline to recovery.

She recalled Charles's words that if Jimmy Hicks had a plan to make Clyde Jeter go away that was not hurtful or against the law, he was all for it. Hattie agreed. Everyone was safe and better off now, including Clyde Jeter. No one had been hurt and she was pretty sure no laws had been broken—or at least she did not know of any that had.

Hattie had learned one thing, though. She was never going to keep secrets again. It was too much of a strain.

19

The holidays approached, and Aunt Sudie commented to Hattie that it would be an especially difficult time for everyone in the Barton household.

"I've arranged for Bailey to host everybody at Thanksgiving and then George and I will take Christmas Day. Since the family will still be observing the customary period of mourning, we won't decorate as lavishly as in the past, but will only hang wreaths on the doors and arrange the mantels with greenery."

"I'm sure that Miss Willie Mae will be thrilled to help with that. She is so good at arranging anything that grows."

"Yes, that will keep her busy, and Alice, too. But you know, Hattie, the one George and I worry about is Charles Sr. He stays to himself so much. George is going to try and persuade Charles to join him up at Barton Ridge, our family's hunting lodge, the week after Christmas, just to provide a bit of distraction. Charles Jr. is old enough to go now, too, but I suspect he would rather stay in town to be with his brothers and cousins and that cute little Jeter girl."

Hattie smiled. "Yes, Charles keeps quite the social calendar these days. But he seems to look up to his father so and craves Mr. Barton's attention. And he loves his uncle George. I expect it would be a real dilemma for him to decide between going to the lodge and staying home."

Hattie returned home to Greenville for the holidays and found the mood to be much improved from last Christmas, with another year's distance from her father's death and her breakup with Will. It was a relief to be out from under the cloud of bereavement that permeated the atmosphere at the Bartons' and enjoy time with her own family. Lottie had been granted a scholarship to study at the Boston Conservatory and she was home for the Christmas holidays, and there was great excitement over little Frankie, whom Maudie and Frank brought home to meet the whole family for the first time.

Frank handed Hattie a Christmas card from Phillip. Tucked inside was a railway pass for a round trip from Greenville to Atlanta and a note that read, "I'm still looking forward to our night on the town." Hattie remembered Phillip's kiss on their last evening together and blushed.

"Well? Are you going to take him up on his offer, Hattie?" asked Maudie.

"I might," said Hattie. "I'll have a few days off around Easter. I could go then."

Mary Posey repeated her offer to room with Hattie second term, and Hattie would have jumped at the opportunity if it were not for the attachment she felt to the Barton children and to Georgia. If she left, it would be like abandoning ship and leaving them there with an absentee father and two aunts who clearly did not have their best interest at heart.

When Hattie returned to the Bartons' on New Year's Eve, she found on her bedside table an envelope addressed to her, with Will's return address. They had corresponded from time to time since his visit a year ago, but still the sight of one of his letters stoked the coals of bygone feelings and caused her to wonder if that fire would ever completely burn out. As she traced her finger over his name and lifted the corner of the flap, she noticed that it came apart easily, as if it had been opened previously. However, in her haste to read the letter, she thought no more about it.

December 23, 1908

My dear Hattie,

You are much in my thoughts and on my mind today as I recall that it was exactly two years ago that I asked you to marry me and you agreed to become my wife.

My joy was unsurpassed when you said yes. It was even greater than the joy I felt on that memorable day when I heard Miss Lottie Moon speak of her work in China and realized that God was calling me into foreign missions. My joy was multiplied because now I not only knew my calling, but I had gained the consent of my soul mate to accompany me on life's journey and to share in my life's work.

As a result of my father's treachery, my fortune changed in the blink of an eye, dashing our plans and wrecking our common dreams, like a small boat tossed by a storm upon the rocks. We have both survived the tumult; however, it is with the knowledge that we must now mend our dreams and chart our courses in different directions.

For me, that means finding the strength and resources to complete seminary and prepare for the mission field. I am happy to report that I will finish my course work in May and will seek ordination in my church in June. I have petitioned the Foreign Mission Board to serve in China, where, God willing, I can join Miss Moon and her fellow missionaries and take up her work there.

Even if I am not sent to Shandong, I will somehow make a visit there on behalf of my mother and personally present the sum of money that I have saved to replace the offering that my father took from the church. I believe that it will give my mother great comfort to make restitution for my father's actions.

Beyond that, I have no plans and will only go where the spirit leads. I doubt seriously that I will marry. From the news we receive, there are reports of widespread famine and a great deal of political unrest. The mission field in China is presently a difficult place to bring a wife and to raise children. I will take great joy in serving God through my work, and though you will not be with me in person, I will always carry you in my heart. That will be enough.

You, dear, dear Hattie, have found your mission there in Pickens County, as a teacher of young children. But you must open your heart to the potential of marriage. For, if it cannot be me, it must be some fortunate man to take you as his wife. You must have a loving husband to provide you with a home and the children you so richly deserve. You will be a wonderful mother.

My prayer is that the day will soon come when you will find a man who is worthy of you, and that together you will create a happy and loving home. I will rejoice with the news of that day.

Devotedly,

Will

Hattie sat on her bed and wept. Will truly was a remarkable man. Never had anyone understood her as he did. Never had she known anyone so unselfish. He had declared his undying love for her and, in the same letter, had commended her into the arms of some unknown man who could give her what he could not. He really did mean what he had said about loving another person enough to let them go.

Hattie wished she were that noble; however, she had to admit to feeling a perverse satisfaction in the notion that he would always carry her in his heart and might never love another woman again. She suspected that another woman would come along one day and that Will would marry, but the mere thought of it made her heart surge with jealousy.

"Hattie Robinson," she chided herself aloud. "Your thoughts are unworthy of a man like Will Kendrick." She folded the letter, returned it to the envelope, and laid it down on the bedside table next to a tiny vase of fresh forget-me-nots that she had not noticed earlier. She recalled thinking that the letter had already been opened, but knew that Georgia, the only other person who would have had reason to be in the room, would never do that. However, the presence of the arrangement brought to mind someone else, someone versed in the language of flowers. Hattie lifted the tiny vase and touched one of the fragile petals. She smiled and shook her head. "Remember me forever."

20

As the year progressed, Hattie could see that the Barton children were adapting to the changes wrought by the death of their mother. Charles Barton, on the other hand, seemed to draw deeper and deeper into himself and became more aloof from the family. Aside from their occasional dinners together and his infrequent appearances with them at church, he rarely sought out his sons or showed any interest in what they were doing.

Whenever he did have anything to say to them, it was usually to correct them or remind them of some duty that they had not performed. Hattie thought Mr. Barton was especially critical of Charles Jr. Yet he seemed to expect everything else to go on as if nothing had changed. He deferred to Alice on all matters concerning the running of the household, with the exception of Elizabeth's room, which he forbade her to tamper with in any way.

Hattie was grading papers in the sitting room one evening and overheard a dinner conversation. "Brother, I wish you would let me go through Elizabeth's belongings and have them stored. It is just not natural to keep everything like it was, and it gets harder and harder every day you wait to do something about it," Alice said.

"Sister's right, Charles," Willie Mae echoed.

"Leave it alone, Alice. I'm not ready," said Charles. And he disappeared into his study and closed the door.

Hattie was sympathetic at first, but as time passed, she came to resent Charles Barton's behavior. In her view, he had clearly made the choice to let his grief for the loss of his wife suck him under rather than to attempt to rise above it and comfort his children.

She confided her feelings to Georgia one day when the two of them were at the kitchen table, stringing green beans for dinner. "You know, Georgia, Mama lost her spouse three years ago, and never for one minute did she feel sorry for herself or walk around with a sad face. And I know she was hurting over her loss every bit as much as Mr. Barton. I'll bet if he had been the one to go instead of Mrs. Barton, she would have done the same."

"I know. I guess the Lord jes' built men diff'rent. And they call us women the weaker sex. Po' Mr. Charles. He pretty useless without Miz Lizabeth."

"Mr. Barton should take a lesson from George's teacher, Byron Stanton. Byron lost his wife two years ago and he is raising Bye and Anna all alone. His wife's folks offered to take the children, but Byron refused to be parted from them because he said that caring for them was the only thing that gave him comfort and solace."

Alice was relentless in her determination to "see Brother through his bereavement," and she appeared to be convinced that the children were at the root of the problem. One evening before dinner, the boys were in the parlor, having been forced inside by a bout of rainy weather. Hattie was sitting on the carpet, Richard in her lap, playing a board game with Charles, George, and Gene. George and Gene began laughing and tussling good-naturedly on the carpet and accidentally knocked over a stand full of African violets. The potted plants catapulted several feet into the air before they crashed and deposited shards of ceramic containers, dirt, and uprooted violets on the floor. Hattie handed Richard to Charles and began picking up the broken pieces when Alice appeared in the doorway.

"What on earth is going on in here?" Alice scolded. "You boys stop this foolishness this minute and go upstairs and wash up for dinner." She stood there like a traffic cop, her arm pointing rigidly toward the stairway. Charles scooped up Richard and followed Gene and George, who had run ahead to keep from bursting out in nervous laughter. They held it in until they were out of Alice's sight; however, Hattie heard them explode before they reached the top of the stairs.

Georgia came in with a broom to clean up just as Alice was telling Hattie, "These children are always underfoot, running and knocking things over."

"Oh, Miss Alice, they really are good children. They just have a lot of pent-up energy, with it raining and them having to stay inside."

"Well, they are simply too much for Brother to say grace over now that Elizabeth is gone. Why, no wonder he has become so quiet and withdrawn. At the least, he must consider sending Charles and George off to Pitford Military Academy. And it certainly would not hurt for him to let Sudie and George keep Eugene and Richard with them for a while."

"Miss Alice!" Hattie's voice was pleading. "Surely you don't mean that."

"Don't contradict me, Miss Robinson. I've known my brother since long before you were even born. I think I know what's best and I intend to discuss this issue with Brother tonight."

"But Miss Alice—"

"Enough, Miss Robinson." Alice consulted her watch and said on her way out of the parlor, "It's five forty-five. Georgia, you need to get the rest of this mess cleaned up and get the children fed and upstairs to their rooms so that everything will be calm and peaceful when Brother gets home." Hattie and Georgia exchanged shocked glances.

Hattie was determined to hear what Alice had to say to Mr. Barton that night at dinner. She lingered in the hallway, holding her breath like a sleuth, eavesdropping on a crucial conversation. Before long, Alice broached the dreaded subject.

"Brother, you must begin thinking of sending young Charles and George to Pitford Military Academy. Why, by the time you were George's age, you had already boarded there for a year. It made a real man of you and was a foundation for building a distinguished career in business and law. I am certain that with your contacts there, if you explained the situation, the headmaster would agree to take them right away, even though the term has already begun.

"It would take such a load off you. You would have time to work through your bereavement while they pursue an excellent education—much superior to what they are getting here in the public system. And they would be well supervised. Now, I have written to request applications. When they come, I want you to promise to consider filling them out. Perhaps the boys could even attend the summer session." Hattie had no difficulty hearing Alice, but she had to strain to hear Mr. Barton's response.

"I don't know, Sister. Elizabeth was determined that they remain at home through high school. That was why she made me promise to work toward high school accreditation for Calhoun School."

"Well, given the circumstances, I am certain that she would not hold you to that. It is simply too difficult for you right now to have all of these children underfoot. And you really should take Sudie up on her offer to keep Richard and Eugene for a while. They spend most of their time down with her and George anyway. You could see them whenever you feel up to it, and it would be such a relief to you not to carry the responsibility for them.

"If Charles and George were off at Pitford, and Richard and Eugene were with Sudie, why, then Willie Mae and I could devote all of our time to you. Then, when this dreadful period of mourning ends, you will be ready to get back into circulation and resume your social life. Goodness knows there's a host of lovely widows of your standing down in Columbia to whom I could introduce you and who will be eager to entertain you when the time comes. Any one of them would offer excellent companionship. At some point in the not-too-distant future, you will want to consider taking another wife. You know that Willie and I will be here to run things for as long as you need us, but that should not stop you from seeking the comfort and companionship of a woman of similar social background."

Mr. Barton had grown silent.

"Honestly, Brother, you have eaten hardly a bite of your dinner. You must keep up your strength."

"Sister's right, Charles," Hattie heard Willie Mae say. "You're looking right peaked around the eyes. We don't want you getting sick."

Mr. Barton's voice sounded drained. "Please, excuse me, sisters. I am feeling a bit tired and I have work to finish in my study before I turn in for the night."

"But you will think seriously about what I have said and at least take a look at the applications when they arrive?"

There was a long pause and then Hattie heard Mr. Barton's weary reply. "Yes, when they arrive, I will have a look at them, Alice."

Hattie heard Charles Barton's footsteps toward the study and ducked quickly into the kitchen to find Georgia.

Incensed, she began unloading the anger that she had suppressed since the incident before dinner. "What in the world is she thinking? They lost their mother, and now she's talking about splitting them up and sending them away. It would kill Charles to be separated from Richard. And to send him and George away from Calhoun School and their friends would take away the only thing that makes them smile and forget their loss right now. Elizabeth Barton must be stirring in her grave. And what in the world is wrong with Mr. Barton? Why can't he see it? See how much they need him now that she is gone? He is such a wonderful provider in every other way."

Georgia shook her head. "I knowed Mr. Charles for a long time, an' he as fine a man as they eva' was. He smart. He charmin'. He honest. He got the manners of a prince. But Mr. Charles neva' did have a lovin' home like the one Miss Sallie and Mr. James made for you or the one Miz Lizabeth made for her children.

"According to Miz Lizabeth, his mama was sick most of the time and his daddy—Law me, all he eva' talk about was the war and how he fought for the South with General Wade Hampton. He sent Mr. Charles off to military school to learn all about soldiering, even tho' they wadn't no war going on. Miz Lizabeth used to say she b'lieve if

Mr. Andrew Earl Barton had the power, he would have started one jes' to give Mr. Charles the experience."

"How did he and Mrs. Barton ever get together? Byron Stanton said that they met in Columbia."

"Oh, Law, chile. Miz Lizabeth and Mr. Charles was drawn to each other like a fly to molasses. She was a beauty. Could have had any man she wanted, but once she met Mr. Charles, she neva' had eyes for anybody else again. And he was a handsome thing. But it wadn't jes' his looks that 'tracted her to him.

"Way she tell it, she was at a friend's house in Columbia. She was at the college and he was in law school. He was all alone, standing by the fireplace, jes' staring into the flame like it hold some kind of deep secret. She say she knew right away she jes' had to meet that man. She say she determined to find out jes' what it was he was brooding about. An' Mr. Charles, he knew he had a good thing in Miz Lizabeth. Ain't nobody could understand him like she could."

"Do you think he will ever get over her?"

"Naw, I don't spec' he eva' will. But in time, he gonna hafta find a way to move on anyway."

"That's a good way to put it," said Hattie. "That's exactly how I feel about Will. I didn't know him half as long as Mr. Barton knew Mrs. Barton, and I never was married to him. But he understands me like nobody else, and I'll never forget him. Even so, I am finding that time makes it easier and easier to move on."

Alice became temporarily distracted from her plans to place the boys in boarding school when she received word that her home in Columbia had been vandalized and that she would need to return to work with the police in recovering any damaged or stolen items. She had acquired a rather enviable art collection and was anxious to see for herself that it was intact. Georgia answered the phone and when she called Alice to come, Willie was right behind her, eager to get the news. Alice placed the earpiece back onto the receiver and turned to Willie in dismay.

"Sister, I do so hate to leave you alone with Brother right now when he is in such distress, but I declare, I must check on my house and make certain that everything is all right, and it just would not do to leave him alone under the same roof as young Miss Robinson."

"Now, Sister, don't worry," said Willie Mae. "I'll just take charge while you are gone and see that everything runs smoothly."

Georgia rolled her eyes and shook her head. "Ain't that the inmate running the asylum," Hattie heard her mumble under her breath.

"Well, if you are sure you are up to it, I'll leave in the morning on the ten o'clock train. I can take care of things in Columbia and be back by the first of next week. But I'll worry about you taking your medicine like you're supposed to. I'll have to write everything down so you'll know just when to take it and what to do to keep the house running and up to standard."

Hattie saw Georgia perk up, as if she liked the idea of having Alice out of the house. "Don't you fret none, Miss Alice. I'll see to it Miss Willie Mae gets her medicine and take good care of her. You jes' go on stay long as you need to."

"I can drive you to the station, Aunt Alice," Charles said eagerly, making eye contact with Georgia.

"Oh no, Charles. You'll be in school. I'll just have Lonnie take me."

When Alice was finally out of the house and on her way to the depot, there was a notable lift in everyone's spirits. The boys spent less time at Aunt Sudie and Uncle George's while she was gone. One evening, Charles Barton arrived home early with a brand-new Model T Ford to replace the Model A he had been driving. It was shiny and slick, and he took everyone for a spin in it, including Georgia. Charles Jr. was overjoyed with the car. "Will you teach me how to drive it, Father?"

"Perhaps. But first you will have to demonstrate that you can be responsible for keeping it up. You will need to wash it regularly and keep it free of dirt."

He just seems to lecture Charles on responsibility at every turn, thought Hattie.

"Don't worry, Father. I'll keep it just like new. Is it okay if I practice by myself if I keep it in the driveway?"

"I suppose so."

It was almost like a vacation, having Alice out of the house. They ate dinner when it was ready and not according to the bell. Alice called that evening to check on things and let Charles know that she was finishing up her business in Columbia and would be home by the end of the next week. None of her paintings had been disturbed, and the police had been successful in retrieving the stolen items. She was surprised to find that Charles was home early and taking his meal with the family.

The children took advantage of the beautiful spring weather and Hattie watched them enjoy every moment of their freedom. *When the cat's away, the mice will play,* she laughed to herself.

21

With Alice still in Columbia, the boys were passing the afternoon in the backyard. Hattie was sitting close by, grading papers, while Georgia was keeping an eye on Richard from the kitchen window. Richard was being entertained by Gene, who had lined up his miniature metal soldiers on the grass and was reenacting the Battle of Cowpens, accompanied by sounds of musket fire and cannon. The sun was beginning to find its way to the west, casting shadows over the grove of cedars at the far corner of the property.

Charles stood at the end of the driveway, tenderly washing the Model T touring car. Hattie could tell that he was itching to drive it and show it off to Pauline.

George came from the barn with an armful of soft rags. He handed one to Charles, and the two of them dried and buffed until the shine returned and the car looked as if it had just rolled off the assembly line.

"I'm gonna drive it into the barn. It looks like it may rain later on tonight."

"You better be sure the goat can't get to it. He's likely to make himself a meal of those new tires," said George.

"I'm pretty sure I've got his number now." Mr. Barton had bought the goat to keep down the weeds in the backyard. He had put Charles in charge of him. Charles had come up with the idea of a stake and a ten-foot line. He'd tether the goat to the line, and when the goat had chewed up most of the weeds in the area, he'd move the stake twenty feet so that the goat could chew up the next section of weeds. It worked fairly well as long as Charles remembered to rotate the goat and as long as he pulled the harness tight enough to keep said goat from gnawing through it.

Charles slid into the driver's seat and started the engine. George hopped in on the other side.

"I ride, I ride," called Richard, leaving Gene and the soldiers behind and running toward the car.

"Okay, come on." Charles laughed, pulling his little brother up and setting him down between his legs behind the steering wheel. Georgia must have seen that Richard was with Charles and she turned from the window and began to dredge the chicken and get it fried up for dinner.

Charles pulled the automobile the short distance into the barn with Richard helping to steer and acting like one of the big boys. Charles shut off the engine and lifted Richard onto the ground. From the stall, Hattie heard old Boots snort as if she were feeling crowded out by the newfangled buggy that had invaded her space and was belching exhaust and creating such a commotion nearby.

Hattie thought about how the oldest and youngest boys were especially close. Richard idolized Charles, and Charles had infinite patience with Richard.

"I need to go rotate the goat," she heard Charles say. "And George, you need to make sure that Boots has plenty of oats and water. I don't see Gene. He must be feeding the chickens. Richard, you go on in and find Georgia. She will be looking for you."

Charles rounded the barn door and turned toward the back fence and the stretch of grass where he had last tethered the goat. He found the stake and the line, and a few feet farther, the halter, but no goat. Charles called out to Gene and George to stop what they were doing and come help him find that Satan of a goat. The goat had clearly left the yard for greener pastures. As the boys split up in three directions to form a search party, Hattie called out, "Do you want me to help?"

Charles called back. "No, Miss Robinson, you just relax and finish grading your papers. We'll find him." And then he said to his brothers, "Hurry up, it's getting late and Father will be home soon. We need to have all our chores done and pin that goat in the shed before he gets here. I'll have to fix his harness tomorrow."

Within the hour, George had found the goat in the cornfield down the road, and Charles had helped to pin him in the shed. The boys finished feeding the chickens and watering the horse as Georgia was calling them in for dinner. Hattie put the papers back in her tote bag and joined them to go inside. As they passed through the kitchen, Charles snitched a crisp piece of fat from the mound of fried chicken draining on a paper bag and waiting to be served. He popped it into his mouth and the other two boys followed suit.

Georgia seemed ready to scold but stopped. She and Hattie asked simultaneously, "Where's Richard?"

"Oh, I sent him in to you after he had his ride in the new car," said Charles.

"No, he ain't in here. I saw him with you and figured you was looking after him."

"He was headed inside when we went off to find the goat, and he sure isn't out there now, 'cause Miss Robinson was out there grading papers."

"Well, he ain't come in here, 'cause I been right here in the kitchen 'cept for jus' a few minutes when I went to take Miss Willie Mae a tray. She got one of her terrible headaches and has taken to her bed. Lawd, where is that chile?"

"Okay, let's stay calm," said Hattie. "We need to divide up and canvass the area before it gets dark. Richard must have wandered off. He can't have gone very far, but he's probably scared. Did he have his shawl last time you saw him?"

"Yes," said Gene. "He was holding it when we were out playing war with my toy soldiers under the tree, but it wasn't there when I went back to pick them up."

"He didn't have it with him when we were in the car; I am sure of that," said Charles. "He must have gone off to look for it before he went in to find Georgia, and maybe he got lost."

"Well, we need to act quickly. I'll check in the front and then go next door to see if he wandered over to your uncle George and aunt Sudie's place. He loves their big black dog. He might have heard her barking and started in that direction.

"Charles, you go down to the creek and look around down there, and George, you take Gene and y'all look around the other side of the property in the back. Georgia, you stay here in case Richard comes in and wait for Mr. Barton to come home. He should be here soon and somebody needs to be here to let him know what is going on.

"Hopefully we'll find Richard before he gets here and save Mr. Barton from having to worry. I'll also check the nursery on the chance that he got sleepy and decided to put himself to bed. Now that he has given up his afternoon nap, he gets tired early. He loves to stretch out in his crib."

Hattie searched the front yard and then ran over to Uncle George's to inquire after Richard. They had not seen him, and she came back empty-handed. It appeared that the boys had not found Richard, either, because she could hear them in the kitchen along with Georgia, explaining to Mr. Barton how Richard had gone missing.

"Where is that little boy?" She tried to get inside his mind and figure out where he had gone. Then she remembered she had not checked the nursery. Before she joined the others, she grasped the rail and began to climb the stairs.

She heard Charles call out from the front door and turned to see what he wanted. He was holding the silk shawl, tattered and dusty. "I found it by the shed. The goat got it and had already eaten off the fringe. Richard must have gone back for it, and it was gone. And he was looking for it and probably wandered off. But where would he have started looking?"

In that instant, a light dawned for Hattie. "Of course. Where else would he go?" She continued up the stairs with Charles following behind.

They reached the master suite, and the door that was usually shut tight stood slightly ajar. Hattie's heart quickened. Charles hesitated at the door, obviously reluctant to invade the room that his father had closed off and made into a sanctuary. He let Hattie go ahead.

"Could he be in there?" Hattie tiptoed in and surveyed the room. It was exactly as Elizabeth had left it. It looked as if not one of her possessions had been removed. It smelled of her lavender and roseship sachets and lotions. Hattie looked toward the window, the only source of brightness in the otherwise darkened room. The rays of dusk shed light on a small form curled up on the window box. Richard lay there in deep sleep. He had found another of Elizabeth's shawls and was clutching it tightly.

When Charles saw him, he almost collapsed from relief. The weight of self-reproach from letting his little brother go unattended was seemingly more than his fourteen years could bear. He called down to the others, "Come upstairs. We have found Richard." Charles must have temporarily forgotten that he was on forbidden ground and rushed through the door to see for himself that Richard was all right.

Hattie lowered herself to the window seat and gently scooped Richard up in her arms. He roused for a moment and opened his eyes. "Mama?" Hattie was touched to the heart and kissed him gently on his warm cheek.

"No, darling, but I know your mother is right here in this room looking over you. And so are the rest of us." Richard fell back into a depth of slumber that only a toddler could reach.

Charles bent down and traced his fingers over Richard's hair as if touching would confirm the reality. "I was so scared we had lost you," he whispered. "I just couldn't stand it if we lost anybody else. I was so stupid to get distracted and be so careless as to not see you all the way to the house to Georgia."

Hattie put her hand on Charles's shoulder and shook her head. "Don't be so hard on yourself, Charles. You are a wonderful brother, and there is not anyone who could blame you for what happened today."

In that moment, they both felt Elizabeth's presence as they breathed in her fragrance of lilac, surrounded by the pastel fabrics and rich mahogany, a mixture of elegance with soft and gentle tones.

The noise from the hallway distracted them, and they looked up to see George and Gene, followed by Georgia, who had hurried up the steps when they heard Charles call and had come quickly to see for themselves that Richard was safe. The two boys paused in the doorway as Charles had done, seemingly unsure of whether to go against Father's will, but Georgia pushed past them. Hattie knew Georgia was determined to get to her little charge and see Richard with her own eyes.

Never one to wake a sleeping child, Georgia bent over him and whispered, "Lawd, chile, you scared us so bad. This old heart couldn't take it if anything was to happen to you. I shoulda known you woulda come up here after that goat got yo' mama's scarf you so crazy about. You came up here to look for another one and you got up here and started breathing her in and you got so 'toxicated you done fell asleep. No use feeding you any suppa' now. You out for the night. But you'll be up with the chickens tomorrow morning, and I'll see to it you get a big breakfast to make up fo' it. Here, Miss Hattie, I'll take him on in to the nursery and let him stretch out in his bed. Suppa's on the table and it'll be getting cold. Y'all go on down now and get fed."

"It's okay, Georgia. I don't mind putting him in his crib. He's so sweet and innocent. He looked up and called me Mama and I thought my heart would break. He misses Mrs. Barton so. They all do. Anyhow, I'm not real hungry. Just make a plate for me, and I'll be down to get it later."

As she spoke, she was aware that Charles Barton had entered the room. He had that brooding look in his eyes that she had seen more frequently since Elizabeth died. He spoke quietly, but with an icy formality that any of them would have traded for a tirade of words, even a string of profanity.

"I am thankful that Richard is safe and unharmed. However, this never should have been allowed to happen. Charles, you are the oldest, and I expect you to look out for your brothers, especially Richard. I'm disappointed that you did not live up to my expectation. Miss Robinson, if you will please be so kind as to take Richard to the nursery as you have indicated that you were willing to do, and Georgia, you will get the boys fed, and then they are to go directly to their rooms and finish their studies before they go to bed. I will take my dinner in the study. Now please leave this room, which I have specifically requested remain off-limits to everyone."

The expression on Charles Jr.'s face would be etched indelibly in Hattie's memory. It was a collage of emotions displaying self-hatred, shame, and humiliation. However, some habits were ingrained and, for Charles, the habit of self-control was one of them. He was his father's son. Though Hattie could see his fists clench and his jaw tighten, his response was formal and civil. "Forgive me, Father. I will try not to disappoint you again." He left the room and disappeared down the hallway. There was little doubt in anyone's mind that he would not be down for dinner.

Georgia gathered up Gene and George and hustled them off downstairs, muttering, "Somebody's gonna eat that chicken I jus' fried and have some of those fresh beans and corn. You two growin' boys can't be missing a meal. No, sir."

Hattie could feel her cheeks redden. Lightning bolts of indignation flashed from her eyes as she, holding Richard, exchanged looks with Charles Barton Sr. on her way out of the room to the nursery. She kicked the door shut, and it closed a bit harder than she had intended. Richard was still asleep in her arms, oblivious to the drama that had played out only moments ago.

She passed the bedroom that George and Gene shared and noticed that the door to Charles's room was shut, and no light peeked under the door. He had no doubt gone to bed and was brooding over the incident with his father. She didn't blame him. She had been a mere witness and was still incensed at Mr. Barton's behavior toward his son. Charles had been the object of his father's insensitive words. He might never want to come out of his room, and she could understand why. He was a good boy. He did not deserve Mr. Barton's wrath.

When Hattie reached the nursery, she was still seething. Richard clutched the shawl as she gently deposited him in his bed. He stirred briefly and rolled over on his stomach, the shawl bunching up under him. Hattie watched him sleep for a long time, recalling the tiny, hopeful voice that had identified her as his mama. It tore at her heart again, and she felt the urge to distance herself from the troubling events of the evening.

She turned on the night-light and left Richard to his dreams. As she descended the stairs, she saw that the study door was closed and assumed that Mr. Barton was taking his dinner. Her anger flared again as she thought of him. She could hear Gene and George talking to Georgia in the kitchen. They were most likely sharing their dinner together.

She wasn't ready to face any of them and she was too stirred up to go to her room, and so she decided instead to go outside. Once in the fresh air, she walked briskly down the walkway toward the road. The night air was cool, and she sucked it greedily into her lungs. *"Deep, cleansing breaths"*—she could hear Dean Judson's words—*"will invigorate the body and calm the soul, and prepare one to articulate the message with confidence and with authority to the waiting audience."*

She had reached the road now and was still walking with abandon toward some unknown destination. "Somebody needs to talk to him," she said aloud. "Enough is enough. Somebody needs to set him straight and let him know what he is doing to himself and to those children. It's unacceptable, that's what it is."

She had been walking for twenty minutes when she realized she had absentmindedly taken her daily route to school. Just as she spotted the schoolhouse, the wind picked up and it began to sprinkle, and so she headed back in the direction of the Barton estate. By the time she returned, she had calmed down a bit and was feeling tired and ready for a few hours of rest. The downstairs was quiet, indicating that Georgia had gone to her quarters and George and Gene were in their rooms. She closed the front door and put on the bolt.

As Hattie passed by the study on her way to her room, the scent of cigar smoke filled her nostrils, and her pulse began to race. A strange impulse from deep inside propelled the actions she would take next. She felt as if she were watching herself from outside of her body, detached. Hattie squared her shoulders, lifted her chin, and grasped the doorknob. Opening the door, she saw him there, slumped into the leather wing chair, slanting away from his desk and toward the window. A snifter of brandy was on the edge of the desk, and a tray with his unfinished dinner sat on the floor beside the chair. The words spilled out like water in an overfilled vase as she moved toward him, confident and with purpose, on a mission.

"You think you are the only one who loved her? You don't think they miss her, too? You don't think they need you now more than ever? Well, they do. See how you have hurt Charles! He idolizes you and only wants to please you. He adores Richard and would never do anything to jeopardize his safety. He was so relieved when we found him, and you turned on him and humiliated him, as though he had no feelings at all and was uncaring and cavalier." Like a scolding mother, she continued, "I will tell you one thing, Mr. Barton. I am only a woman, and a very inexperienced one at that, but even I can see that Charles is behaving like more of a man than you are right now."

Charles Barton remained silent as he raised his eyes to meet her gaze. They were a sea of grief, remorse, and fear. As she stood looking down at him, he reached out like a scared child seeking safety. He raised his arms, encircled her waist, and buried his head into the folds of her skirt. His shoulders relaxed and tears flowed, followed by a symphony of sobs that played out the themes of rejection and loss that must have been pent up for years.

Her tirade spent, Hattie softened. She cradled his head in her arms and rocked with the rhythm of his sobs in a dance of shared grief. Neither of them spoke.

When the tears ran dry, Charles Barton pulled Hattie down into his lap and began to kiss her face and stroke her hair. He was no longer clutching her as a frightened child; he was responding to her as a man to a woman. His touch was tender and loving, and Hattie was stirred by feelings she'd never imagined she would have for him. He kissed her full on the mouth, and she kissed him back. She could feel his heart beating faster and his breath growing heavier. As his kisses became more passionate, she grew hesitant and pulled away. "Mr. Barton, I can't. I have to go now. I'm sorry."

"Of course," he responded as she stood up and slipped hastily away, down the dark hallway and back into her room, leaving him there in the study.

Not daring to turn on a light for fear of being noticed, she undressed in the dark, pulling off her shoes and stockings and throwing her dress over the chair. In her undergarments, she climbed between the cold sheets in her bed. She lay there, eyes wide-open, her body a riot of emotions, fighting to be understood, struggling to make sense of the events and her reactions to them. As the thoughts swirled in her weary head, her lids grew heavy, and it was as if a vortex had formed and was sucking her down into a deep abyss of sleep.

22

The next thing Hattie heard was Georgia rapping at her door. "You betta' get up, Miss Hattie, and get yo'self dressed for school. I got yo' breakfast ready and I've done fixed you a lunch to carry."

Hattie bolted from her bed, struck by the realization that she was woefully unprepared for her classes. She was grateful that it was Friday, and that meant test day for the older students. She would get some lesson plans together while they were testing. The events of the past evening seemed like a dream, which became more and more vivid as she awakened fully. How in the world would she face Mr. Barton? What would his frame of mind be today?

Pulling herself together, she washed up and dressed in her chocolate skirt and ruffled white blouse, gathered up her lesson materials and ungraded papers and hurried to the dining room for breakfast. She was both disappointed and relieved to find that Charles Barton had risen early and taken the train to Greenville on business and would not return until late that night.

Hattie went through the day in a fog. Her world upended by the events of the previous night, she hardly knew what to think or how to plan for what would come next. She fought to keep her focus on the students but lost her place during the reading lesson. She avoided Mary Posey, with the excuse of being under the weather, and said she would keep her children inside for lunch. She knew that if she spent any time at all with Mary, her friend would see right through her and demand to know what was wrong. Hattie was too distraught and confused to deal with it. When the day finally, mercifully, ended, she tidied up the classroom and started on the twenty-minute walk home.

Charles Jr. had gone to get a new harness for the goat, and George and Gene were finishing up their chores while Georgia was bathing Richard and putting him in his nightclothes. Aunt Willie Mae was feeling better and was sitting in the parlor, sipping a late-afternoon sherry, which she had used to chase her evening medication. The combination had the effect of loosening her tongue and making her more talkative and assertive than usual.

"Brother won't be back until later tonight. I've told Georgia to go ahead and serve us all at six. We can't wait up for him. He's likely to be midnight coming in. Besides, I haven't been able to eat all day with this headache and I need to go to bed right after dinner. I can't wait up for Brother."

"All right, Miss Willie Mae. I am glad you are feeling better."

Willie Mae continued, "I heard some kind of commotion going on last night, and Georgia told me that it was over little Richard going missing. That never would have happened if poor, dear Elizabeth were here. Honestly, this house has just gone to the dogs since she passed. And I don't know what Brother is thinking these days. He's so moody and unreasonable, closing her room off like that and not letting anybody go in there.

"Sister and I have tried to get him to let us dispose of her clothes and belongings, but he won't hear of it. He's such a queer bird. I never did understand him. Moody and private—that's Charles. He has been that way since he was a child. You know he does have family, and they could be helping him out if he would let them. But he simply shuts us out and won't let us do anything."

Willie Mae was the last person Hattie wanted to deal with right now. "Yes, ma'am. I'm gonna go put my things down and get washed up."

As Hattie left, she could hear Georgia's voice. "Now, Miss Willie Mae, you know betta' than to be taking yo' pills with sherry. Here, let me have that glass and get you some wata'." *Too late for that*, thought Hattie.

Charles Jr. was sullen at dinner and asked to be excused as soon as he had eaten. Aunt Willie Mae left soon after and took to her bed again. Hattie listened to Gene read and helped George practice his multiplication tables before they went up to bed. Finally, when everything had settled down, she went to her room and tried to correct a set of essays that she had assigned to the older students but had difficulty concentrating for thinking about Charles Barton.

She was anxious about their next encounter, about what he would say, what she would say. Would he behave as though nothing had happened? Would he regret his advances to her and try to make excuses? Or worst of all, would he chastise her as he had Charles for confronting him? Hattie was not certain what she felt, but she did know that she was not sorry for confronting him and she was not sorry that he had kissed her.

Charles Barton arrived home around eleven. He closed and bolted the front door and made his way down the hallway. From her chair, Hattie heard his footsteps into the study. She laid the essays on the side table and sat there hardly breathing. In the stillness of the night, he felt so near. The solid wall that separated the two rooms seemed paper-thin now. She was acutely aware of every sound, every vibration that came from the other side.

She sat there, waiting to hear him leave the study. She could not will herself to put on her nightclothes and go to bed until she was certain that he had gone upstairs. Presently, she heard the study door open, followed by footsteps, which sounded as if they were coming toward her room instead of the stairway. Shortly, there was a knock at her door, and she got up to answer it.

"Miss Robinson? Hattie? May I speak with you?" Hattie indicated for Charles Barton to come in and waited for him to say what was on his mind. He looked tired and spent, but there was in his manner a calmness, an expression of self-assurance, formality, and authority that drew her to him and subordinated her urge to speak.

"I am not a man to embellish things and so I will get right to the point. I have come to ask you, Hattie, if you will marry me." Speechless, Hattie sank down onto the rocker and stared at him in stunned amazement and disbelief as he continued.

"The events of last evening have convinced me that my children are in dire need of a mother and that I am in need of a wife. Although you are much younger than I, you have been more of a parent to the boys than I have and you have been a stable factor in their lives. I am certain that they would accept you readily were we to marry.

"I will be a good husband, and you can rest assured that you will be well cared for. I am a man of considerable means and will be an excellent provider. You will receive a generous allowance to manage the household and care for the children, and I, in turn, will continue to manage my businesses and provide a livelihood for the family. I can see that you are taken aback by my proposal, but I believe that when you have time to think about it, you will realize that it makes sense for us to marry."

It was the oddest proposal. Not at all like the one Will had made to her. Neither was it similar to any of the scenarios that she and her sisters had imagined and entertained one another with as girls, when they talked and giggled late into the night in the room they shared. There was nothing romantic about it, no mention of love or passion or lifetime commitment. It was more like a business offer or a contractual arrangement. And yet, there was something intensely exciting and stirring to Hattie about the prospect of it all.

A man of stature and means, almost twice her age, had taken her seriously, was asking her to take his name, to raise his children, and to manage his household. She would be stepping into the role of a woman whom she admired and loved, and caring for four boys who would need her and depend on her to take up where their mother had left off. Suddenly the pieces all came together for her, and she knew she had found the place where she belonged. Without further hesitation, she responded.

"No, Mr. Barton—Charles. I do not need time to think about it. I would be honored to marry you. I love your children, and your dear, departed wife was one of the kindest, gentlest women I have ever known. I will do my best to raise your sons as she would have done and to be a good wife to you."

He smiled and took her hands. "I am leaving again for Columbia on business tomorrow and will be back in the middle of the week. We can talk further when I return. As it has only been a year since I was widowed, and the traditional period of mourning is barely over, I think it prudent to have an intimate family wedding, perhaps in Greenville, and not to announce it until after we are married. When I return, I will pay a visit to your mother and ask for your hand in marriage. Then we will talk about how to tell the children and the rest of the family."

"I want to tell Mama first. I'll catch the train to Greenville in the morning and spend the weekend with her."

"As you wish. And now, I will leave you before my sister catches wind that we have been together unchaperoned. There is nothing she would like better than to sniff out a scandal and report it to Alice when she returns. We must make certain that as long as we are living under the same roof unmarried, all future contact is conducted openly and aboveboard to protect your reputation and to minimize gossip. Good night, my dear. Sleep well, and I'll see you at dinner on Wednesday." He kissed her gently on the forehead and left.

Hattie slept fitfully when she slept at all. Each time she dozed off, she would wake and think about what had just happened. The reality would hit, and she would shiver with excitement and anxiety. A gnawing in the pit of her stomach both terrified and thrilled, reminding her what she had just committed herself to do.

She rose early, dressed, and packed an overnight bag for Greenville. She would catch the eight o'clock train and be there in time to get Mama alone and tell her the news before the day got started.

The train pulled into the station in Greenville at nine. She took her bag from the porter and began the walk from the depot to East Washington Street, rehearsing what she would say to Mama all the way. She reached the drive and walked around back to the kitchen entrance, where she was most likely to find her. As she pushed open the screen door, Hattie could hear the sounds of female laughter and banter in the adjoining dining room.

"Oh my. Mama is having her weekly visit with her sisters, and they are all in there buttering up Mama's homemade bread and drizzling it with honey," Hattie muttered. Her news would have to wait until she could get Mama alone. Two of Sallie's sisters lived nearby. They had always been close, but since James died, they had made it a point to get together on a regular basis and visit.

She did not want her aunts to hear it first. They would go on and on, and each one would have an opinion. Worse still, they would have a million questions that she was unprepared to answer. She knew that in the end they would go along with whatever she wanted to do, but they would put her through the third degree first. She would rather postpone that until she could get Mama on her side.

Too late. Aunt Lucie came into the kitchen for more coffee and spotted her in the doorway. She was the tallest of the sisters, large boned, and with pale blue eyes and a frank manner, traits from their father's side of the family.

"Lord, Hattie. I didn't know you were coming. Sallie, why didn't you tell us Hattie would be here?"

Mama jumped up from the table and came to the kitchen. "Because I didn't know. Hey, suga', I'm so glad to see you. What a wonderful surprise. Can you spend the night?" That was the first question Mama always asked the minute any of her grown children came in the door.

She hugged Hattie and took her suitcase. "Come on in and have some coffee and rolls. They were freshly baked this morning." Mama's yeast rolls were the best in the world, flaky and sweet, and there was no one who could make them like she could.

Aunt Harriet hurried into the kitchen. "Well, there's my name-sake. Honey, aren't you a sight for sore eyes. How are things going over there in Calhoun, and what in the world brought you over here this early to Greenville on a Saturday morning unannounced?" Aunt Harriet had a sixth sense when it came to Hattie and she was an expert at reading her niece's expressions.

Hattie tried to look normal. "Oh, everything's fine. I just got to missing y'all and I decided to catch the train and come on over and spend the weekend."

Aunt Harriet persisted. "Hattie, you look all flushed and excited. Are you sure you don't have anything to tell us?"

Hattie caved and blurted out, "Oh, all right. I wanted to wait and tell Mama by herself, but since you are all here, I'll come right out and say it: Mr. Barton has asked me to marry him, and I have said yes."

"Lord," said Aunt Lucie. "I didn't see that coming. Let me get this straight. You mean Charles Barton? The same man who married poor, dead Elizabeth Cahill, who's the same age as Harriet? The one you are boarding with and the one who's old enough to be your father?"

"Lucie," Mama cut in. "That's a pretty straightforward way to put it. But Hattie, honey, have you taken time to think about this? Charles is a great deal older than you and he has four children, the oldest of whom is not too many years behind you."

"Yes, Mama, I have. Mr. Barton, Charles, is a fine man who suffered a tragic loss. I was devoted to his wife, Elizabeth, and I love the children like they are my own. I've taught two of them in school and have developed a very strong relationship with them."

"Hattie," Lucie persisted, "did that man force himself on you, and now you have to get married?"

"Lucinda," retorted Sallie. "What a thing to say. Go on and talk, Hattie."

"Well, Sallie, don't act so self-righteous. I just said what we all were thinking."

"No, Aunt Lucie. He never forced himself on me. He is an honorable man and has never been anything but a gentleman. Besides, Miss Alice and Miss Willie Mae are always there and they know everything that happens. Even if he'd wanted to, he could not escape their eagle eyes."

Harriet broke in. "Well, you have certainly given us a lot to talk about this morning, Miss Hattie Robinson." She gave Hattie a big squeeze and then took her by the arm. "Let's go back in the dining room and have a proper conversation."

Sallie followed with a basket of hot rolls and more fresh coffee. Lucie plucked a hot one, slathered it with butter and covered it in honey. "Don't you just wish you could make 'em as good as the bakery, Sallie," she said as she stuffed it into her mouth.

Lucie's remark broke the tension. "Oh, Aunt Lucie," laughed Hattie. "You are the only one in the world who would rather have something from the bakery than one of Mama's yeast rolls."

Mama sat down next to Hattie and took her hand. "Suga', you have always been my serious child and you have a good head on your shoulders. You know I love you and I will stand behind whatever you decide to do. But I want you to think about two things and make sure you are up to dealing with them. One is that you will be taking on a huge responsibility with all those children. The other is that Elizabeth was dearly loved in her community, and there are those who will not think much of a young thing like you taking her place with her husband and her children, especially so soon after she has passed."

"I know, Mama. I have thought of little else. But honestly, I believe this must be my place in life to make sure those boys are raised right. Nobody knows them like I do. And that Miss Alice, all she can talk about is sending Charles and George off to boarding school and sending Gene and Richard off to be fostered by his aunt. I couldn't bear it if that were to happen. And I know Mr. Barton, Charles, is much older than I am, and it may be hard for other people to accept me as his wife. But they'll come around in time. And some time, I want to have babies of my own, and I can't think of a better place to raise them than in that family."

"Oh, to see through the eyes of youth," quipped Lucie. "You're gonna regret the day you decided to take on that old man."

"Lucie, you're such a skeptic," said Harriet. She took a sip of coffee and continued, "You know, honey, Elizabeth Barton and I were friends way back when. There was not a lovelier person in this world, and when she found and married Charles Barton, I could not have been happier for her. He was a fine, upstanding member of the community, always had a good head for business, and inherited a grand estate from his daddy. He always took care of her in style. But as fine as he was, there was something kinda mysterious and brooding about him. Elizabeth once confessed to me that he was given to bouts of melancholy and that sometimes he would withdraw from the family and isolate himself for weeks at a time, burying himself in work.

"He's not like your papa was, rest his sweet soul, who thrived off being around his family. Lord, it seemed like the more children he had and the more activity there was around your house, the happier James was. He was just a social animal. Even in his last days when he was so sick, he still wanted to be surrounded by his children. Charles Barton's just not like that."

"Well, Aunt Hattie, it is true. He has taken pretty much to himself since Mrs. Barton died, but I expect he'll come out of it when he has someone to take care of the children and manage the house again permanently. And I know he can be pretty moody and detached. But it doesn't bother me too much. I'll just have to take things as they come."

"Honestly, my heart does go out to those boys," Hattie's mother said. "I know firsthand what it means when children lose a parent. There is no doubt you'd be a wonderful mother to them, honey, and if you have made up your mind, so be it. I just don't want you to rush headlong into something this important."

Aunt Lucie put down her knife and wiped the last crumb from her third roll from her chin. "Hattie, child, you're not a beauty like

Elizabeth Barton was, but you are a handsome enough girl and you did always have a good head on your shoulders. I'd say if this is what you want, go ahead and do it. But, Lord, I don't envy you takin' on that old man and all those children."

Harriet sighed. "Lucie, can't you ever say something nice without spoiling it. Hattie, I agree with your mama and Lucie, except that part about you not being a beauty. You are beautiful both inside and out, and Charles Barton would be lucky to have you. But, mercy, you are taking on a lot. Most girls your age start with falling in love and courting and then getting married and learning how to manage a house, and then having their children and raising them. You'll be doing all that at once. And I'm guessing you won't have a lot of help from Charles, other than the fact that he can give you anything you want and need in the way of material things. But you know, if you think this will make you happy, I am behind you all the way."

Harriet took one last sip of coffee from the porcelain cup before setting it down on the matching saucer with the gold band. Sallie always set out her best china for her sisters. "Ooh, this company china drinks good!" She turned to Lucie. "Lucie, go on and finish up that roll. We need to get out of here and let Sallie have some time alone with Hattie to take in all this big news. If we hurry, we can stop by the piece goods store and look at all the pretty spring fabrics. I want to get started again right away, sewing on Hattie's trousseau. We got interrupted last time and, anyway, the things we made before are out of style now. We'll need to make sure she has some real sophisticated, fashionable things, seeing as she is marrying into the Barton family and will be the mistress of an estate."

"I expect this will call for a trip to Atlanta to look for the wedding dress," said Sallie. "We can stay with Maudie, and she can take us to Rich's and Davidson's and all the good stores. She will be so thrilled about all this."

"Hold your horses before you get too far ahead of yourselves, sisters," Lucie put in. "We've seen hide nor hair of Charles Barton. It seems like we need to hear from the alleged groom and get a firm date set before we go off buying cloth and planning trips to Atlanta. You did say he was coming over to formally ask for your hand, didn't you?"

"Oh yes," Hattie assured her. "He wanted to be the first to come, but I persuaded him to let me break the news to Mama and y'all before he did. This has all happened so fast, and sometimes I have to pinch myself to believe it is even true. And Aunt Lucie's right. We need to keep everything quiet until Charles can talk to Mama. And then Charles and I will need to find the right way to tell the children, and Charles will have to break the news to his sisters. Lord, I dread to think how that will go. And I guess at some point, I will need to talk with Reverend Fitts about my teaching position."

"Well, all the more reason for Lucie and me to get on our way and give you and your mama a little time to talk things through. Come on, Lucie."

Lucie reached in and took the last roll from the breadbasket, wrapped it in her handkerchief, and tucked it into her handbag. "I'm coming, Harriet."

Alone in the house, Mama and Hattie had a few minutes to plan for Charles Barton's visit. Lillie and Minnie had taken John with them to the market, and Henry and Jamie had begged to drive them there, agreeing to carry their boxes and do the heavy lifting for them in return. They would be home soon, with the groceries to unload, and all of them would be hungry for lunch.

Hattie sliced a fresh loaf of homemade bread and helped Mama make up a plate of pimento cheese sandwiches while they talked. They decided that when Charles returned from Columbia and he and Hattie had had an opportunity to discuss things, Hattie would contact Mama about a convenient time for Charles to call on her.

Mama teared up. "Oh, Hattie, it's times like this I miss James so. He should be the one giving your hand to Charles, not me." She put down her knife and dabbed her eyes with a dish towel.

Hattie squeezed her. "I know, Mama. You have had to fill in for Papa in so many ways. And you are always so brave about it. We forget you miss him as much, or even more, than we do. Do you think Papa would approve of me marrying Charles?"

"Yes, Hattie. Taking into consideration all of the circumstances, I am sure he would. All he ever wanted for each of you children was for you to find happiness and a place where you could make your mark on the world."

Lillie and Minnie were thrilled for Hattie when they heard the news, and the three of them lay on the bed in Minnie's room and talked into the night about it. They had witnessed how much losing Will had hurt their sister and seemed genuinely happy for her. "Oh, I can't wait for Lottie and Maudie to hear it," Minnie exclaimed. "Let's call them right now long-distance and tell them."

"Lord, Minnie, it's almost midnight. If we call them now, they will think something's wrong with Mama, and it will scare them to death. Besides, with Maudie down in Atlanta and Lottie way up in Boston at the conservatory, there is no way we could keep the conversations short enough to afford the calls. They'll want to know every detail, and it would cost us a fortune to stay on the line long enough to answer all their questions. I'll write them each a long letter when I get on the train tomorrow to go back to Calhoun. School will be out soon, and both Lottie and I will be coming home, and Mama is already talking about a trip to Atlanta to pick out a wedding dress."

23

Having purchased her return ticket, Hattie reached the Greenville depot just in time to board her train back to Calhoun. As she hurried through the passenger waiting room toward the tracks, she spotted a familiar-looking gentleman reading the Sunday issue of the *Greenville News*.

Hattie froze in her steps as her mind raced to explain his presence. *Oh Lord. That is Charles Barton. What on earth is he doing here? He is supposed to be in Columbia. I knew this was all happening too fast. What if he has changed his mind and has come to break it off in private so that nobody will ever know and we will have to act like none of this ever happened? Two broken engagements! How unlucky can one girl be? Well, I won't cry. I'll stand up and take it, and he'll never know it mattered to me a bit.*

Charles had spotted her and he folded his paper and rose to greet her. He looked down at Hattie with an affectionate smile and seemed more relaxed than she had ever seen him. "That's a serious look. Please tell me you are not having reservations, now that you have gone and given an old man like me such hope."

Hattie let out her breath in relief, embarrassed that she had jumped to such extreme conclusions. "No, quite the opposite. When I saw you, I thought you had come to tell me that you were the one with reservations. But why *are* you here? I thought you were in Columbia."

"I've come to drive you home. It occurred to me that we have never been together alone, except for the brief moments the other night when you brought me to my senses and made me realize I needed to stop wallowing in my own grief and begin to live again. In those short minutes we were together, you turned my life around." He smiled and added jovially, "Imagine the influence you would have exerted had we spent more time together. Why, I would be completely reformed by now!

"I also thought the drive would give us time to discuss our plans in private, away from the ever-present and watchful eyes of my sisters. Thus, I rearranged my schedule and left Calhoun early this morning for Greenville. I thought we would take a leisurely drive through the countryside and I could still get you home in time to prepare for your classes tomorrow. I can take the train to Columbia in the morning and complete my business as planned."

"Won't Georgia worry when I'm not on the three o'clock train?"

"No. Before I left this morning, I told her not to expect you until late, and that you would explain it all to her when you get home. You know Georgia. She is always a step ahead of everybody else and has probably already figured things out for herself."

He took Hattie's overnight bag from her and offered her his arm. "How about it, Miss Robinson? Would you give me the pleasure of your company and spend the day with me?"

"Yes, Mr. Barton. I'd be delighted to spend the day with you." Hattie's heart fluttered as she took his arm and let him escort her from the station to his waiting car.

It was a beautiful May morning, and as the sun burned away lingering wisps of haze that clung to the mountains of the Blue Ridge, they became visible for miles across the horizon, their soft contours bathed in pastel blues and purples and pinks. Wildflowers dotted the road alongside the fields of tender green cotton plants making their way up from the soil.

They talked easily. Charles was a good listener and had an attorney's ear for detail. Hattie told him about her visit with Mama and her sisters, even the part about Aunt Lucie wanting to know if Charles had forced himself on her. On hearing that, Charles winced. "Oh my, I was afraid that's how my proposal might be interpreted by your family—the lonely widower taking advantage of the young, attractive boarder."

Hattie assured him that Lucie was always saying outrageous things and that Mama had not jumped to that conclusion at all. "In fact, Mama gave me her blessing and she said she thought Papa would have done so as well." Charles asked about him, and she talked all about Papa and his long illness. And then she told him all about Will. When Hattie realized she had been talking nonstop for over an hour, she exhaled and exclaimed, "Gosh! It feels good to get some of these memories off my chest. It's like opening up a dusty old chamber for spring-cleaning and letting out all of the stale air."

"Well, I know you meant that figuratively, but I suppose I need to do some very literal spring-cleaning of my own—one room in particular."

"You mean Elizabeth's room?"

"Yes. It has been closed up since May 8, 1908, and remains exactly as she left it when she went to Asheville."

"Oh, Charles," said Hattie, touching his arm. "That was such an awful day."

Charles nodded and fixed his eyes on the road ahead as he began to recollect. "Uncle George was the one who broke the news to me. Robert Simpson did not want me to be alone when I found out, so he called George first. I suppose George told me about the fire and all of the other details, but the only thing that I heard were the unthinkable words he spoke at the end. 'She's gone, Charles. Our Elizabeth is gone.'

"Thank goodness George was there, because I was immobilized. He took over and directed me as if I were a puppet. I just did what he told me. 'I've called Eugene and he is driving the hearse up to Asheville to transport her body. He will come by within the hour and pick you up, and you can ride with him. Sudie's on her way over to help you pick out the clothes for burial. Robert says that everything was burned in the fire and, of course, Elizabeth was in her night-clothes when all this happened, so they will need something nice to lay her to rest in. Since the hotel burned to the ground, Robert went ahead and had Elizabeth's body moved from the hospital to the mortuary down the street. Eugene knows the owner there and will go directly there to transport her back to Calhoun. Sudie and I will pick up the boys from school and take them home with us. Georgia can take care of Richard and bring him over after his nap.'

"George made all the funeral arrangements with Reverend Fitts, and Sudie planned the visitation. I went off with Eugene in the hearse to see the body of my beautiful wife one last time. When I returned, everything was arranged. I was numb to it all and simply went through the motions of memorializing and burying the dear woman who went off to Asheville, full of life and hope, and returned a corpse. The numbness gradually wore off and was replaced with a deep feeling of self-reproach and guilt for having allowed Elizabeth to make the trip at all."

"You couldn't blame yourself, Charles. I was there the night she decided to go, and nothing in the world would have dissuaded her from making that trip. It was a part of who she was and why you loved her so much."

"That is all true in hindsight, but nothing would have convinced me of it then. When Sudie asked me what I wanted to do about Elizabeth's belongings, I told her to close the door to her room and leave everything untouched. Then I plunged headlong into my work and tried to block out anything related to my past with Elizabeth. The children were a constant reminder. I could see her smile in Gene's face. Charles's determination for things to be fair and just, that was Elizabeth through and through. I knew that Alice would keep the house running like a well-oiled machine, and so I turned things over to her, as I always did as a child. I retreated into a kind of survival mode, into the safety of routine and order, a world that required little thought or emotion.

"It was not until you confronted me in my study last week that I realized how selfish I had been in my grief and how much I had neglected to tend to the grief of my children. I can see that it is time to open up Elizabeth's room to the light. She is certainly not in there anymore and would want her earthly possessions to be enjoyed by those she loved. Hattie, you may have anything from Elizabeth's wardrobe that you want, and I will have Alice dispose of the rest to charity."

"If it's all the same to you, Charles, I really don't want to keep any of Elizabeth's things. I could not wear her clothes because she was much more petite than I. However, I know someone who could. Pauline Jeter is about her size, and I bet she would be thrilled to have some of them."

"I think Elizabeth would have approved of that. I remember that the two of you were discussing Pauline the night before the trip to Asheville. Elizabeth also had a number of fine pieces of jewelry, which will certainly be yours if you want them."

"No, Charles. I think those should be divided out among the boys so that they will have them as a remembrance of her. They will be able to pass them on to their wives or daughters someday."

"What a good idea. I think Elizabeth would have liked that as well. Besides, it will give me an excuse to spoil you with some jewelry of your own."

They found a nice area along the way to get out and stretch. Charles pulled over, and they hiked out across a grassy meadow and found a shady spot at the edge of the woods to sit and share the lunch of fried chicken and rolls that Hattie's mother had packed for her to eat on the train.

"These are the best yeast rolls I ever put in my mouth," said Charles.

Hattie laughed. "Mama's famous for her rolls."

"Can you bake rolls like this?" asked Charles.

"Lord, no," said Hattie. "All of us girls have her recipe, but she always said the secret of her rolls is not in the ingredients but in the way you make 'em. We have all tried but nobody can make rolls like Mama."

"Well, when I go to Greenville to ask for your hand, I'll make sure I get there around dinnertime. Seriously, though, I will be coming back from Columbia on Thursday morning. I could take the train to Greenville and call on her then. Do you think that would be convenient for her?"

"Yes, I think it would. I'll contact her when we get back and make sure. I'm kind of nervous about what will happen when we get back to Calhoun. I'm afraid Miss Alice will disapprove when you tell her you've proposed to me. I am certain that she had someone much grander in mind for you—someone with a more sophisticated background. After all, I'm just a farm girl from Anderson County."

"Yes, Alice always did have high standards for me. But remember, my first wife was also a farm girl from Anderson County. Come to think of it, she did not approve of Elizabeth at first, either. But you just leave Alice to me. She will come around in time. She can be controlling and interfering as hell, but she has always stood by me. And whenever Alice comes around, Willie Mae will fall in line as well."

Hattie thought of Willie Mae and the question she had been dying to ask about her strange ways. "What caused Willie Mae to have such dreadful headaches? It seems like everybody in your family is so vague about it. The only thing I've heard anybody say is that there was some type of accident when she was an infant."

Charles grew silent, and Hattie was afraid she might have gone too far. "You don't have to tell me about it if you don't want to. I wasn't trying to pry."

"No," Charles replied. "It's time to open up all the rooms and let in the fresh air. I don't want any secrets between us. I want to tell you about it. The truth is that I am responsible for what happened to Willie Mae."

"You, Charles? Why in the world would you say that?"

"Because it is true. Alice was seven, and I was five when Willie Mae was born in 1871, just months after Mother and Father had lost a beautiful little daughter they had named Rose. Rose had just learned to walk and was toddling all over the room. One night she was playing in front of the fireplace and a spark jumped out, igniting her little dressing gown into flames. They were unable to extinguish the flames quickly enough and she died from the burns.

"It nearly killed Father, and when Willie Mae was born, he and Mother were on pins and needles and overly protective about her care. Mother had never been a well person and spent a great deal of time confined to her bed anyway.

"Sunie Jenkins was the wet nurse for Willie Mae. She had just given birth to a baby of her own and had plenty of milk. She also looked after Alice and me and was the only person Mother would trust with us. Willie Mae was colicky and screamed all the time. Sunie had trouble keeping her satisfied and looking after her baby, Lonnie, at the same time."

"You mean the Lonnie who works for your uncle George?"

"Yes, the same. One morning she had to tend to Lonnie for a little while and she left Alice and me to look after Willie. 'Jes' leave her in her crib and don't bother her,' she said. 'She may cry but she'll be all right for a few minutes. I'll be right back.'

"Willie started screaming the minute Sunie left. I couldn't stand to hear it and finally I went over and picked her up. As I lifted her over the rail of the crib, she started squirming and I dropped her headfirst right on the floor." Hattie gasped.

Charles shook his head and buried his face in his hands. "It was horrible. She lay there as still and lifeless as death. Alice ran over, picked her up, and laid her back in her crib. We both stood there in shock, unable to speak, just staring at her. She did not move.

"Sunie came in, and when she saw Willie lying there, she screamed, grabbed her up, and ran to find Father and Mother to send for the doctor. In all the commotion, Alice and I were left there alone in the nursery for what seemed like hours. I started to cry and told Alice, 'It's all my fault. I dropped her on her head and now she's dead.'

"Alice was always the one in charge, even back then. She always knew just what to do. 'No, Charles. Do not say that. Sister is not dead and she will be all right.'

"'But I have to tell Father and Mother that I dropped her.'

"'No, you do not. Mother and Father are still in mourning over Rose and they would not understand. They would blame you and things would never be the same again. Nobody saw you drop her but me, and I put her back in her crib. If they blame anybody, they will blame Sunie. She was the one who was supposed to be taking care of her.'

"'But that's not fair for poor Sunie to take the blame.'

"'Well, it may not even come to that. They may not blame anybody, but right now, I want you to promise to keep your mouth shut and don't say a word.'

"Willie Mae did recover, but she was in a coma for over a month, and they were afraid she might never wake up and would live as a vegetable. And then when she finally did wake up, the debilitating headaches began and never completely went away."

"What happened to Sunie?"

"Nobody had to lay blame on Sunie. She had already done that herself. When she saw how bad things were, she went out and slit her wrists. They found her floating facedown in the creek at the edge of the property."

"How awful! Lonnie told me one time that his mother had died when he was only a few months old, but I had no idea it was because she had taken her own life."

"Yes, and as he was so young, he was spared the details of it all until he was a grown man. Alice tried to keep the news from me, but that would have been impossible, even for her. Sunie had been a trusted worker, and her death devastated everyone in the Barton family."

"Oh, so that's why Lonnie was raised by Ossie," said Hattie. Charles nodded and continued his story.

"When I heard about Sunie, I crawled under my bed and lay there crying with guilt. Alice found me and pulled me out.

KATHERINE P. STILLERMAN

"'It's all my fault. Sunie's dead and Willie Mae is probably going to die, and I want to die too.'

"'You stop that, Charles,' commanded Alice. 'That is no way for a Barton to talk. I told you this was not your fault, and you are not to tell anybody it is. It is one of those awful things that couldn't be helped, and you will not make it better by going to Mother and Father with that terrible confession. They have enough grief to say grace over with Rose dying and Willie being in a coma and Sunie killing herself. If you died, do you really think that would make it better?'

"'No, but I think I should at least tell them I dropped Willie.' Alice had a backbone of steel, even at seven. With her brown eyes flashing, she took hold of my quivering chin in one hand and pointed right in my face with the other.

"'You look at me, Charles. I am going to say this one last time. You telling Mother and Father that you dropped Willie will not make her better and it won't bring back Sunie. It will only make things far worse than they are right now. You and I are the only ones who know the truth, and we will take this secret to our graves. Do you understand?'

"I nodded.

"'Now, you get up and wash your face so we can go pay our respects to Sunie's family and see how Willie Mae is doing. And we will never speak of this again.'

"And we didn't," concluded Charles.

"What a terrible secret for a child to have to carry around. Did you ever tell anybody else?"

"Yes, I did finally tell Elizabeth. I was tormented by the secret and had nightmares for years that all involved an empty crib and a baby lying still on the floor. When Charles Jr. was born, the nightmares returned and became more specific, to where I would dream that it was his crib and Charles lying dead on the floor. I did not trust myself to pick him up and hold him, though there never was a prouder father of a newborn son. Elizabeth could not understand it. One night she came to me in tears and demanded to know why I did not want to touch my son. I told her then. She was the only other person who knew. She always said she was attracted to me for my brooding eyes and was determined to know what secrets they were concealing. That night, she found out."

"Well, if anybody would understand, it would have been Elizabeth. And that certainly explains why she was so tolerant and understanding of both your sisters' idiosyncrasies. But didn't you and Elizabeth lose a child named Rose?"

"Yes, and it was a cruel irony. She was our first daughter after three sons. We named her Elizabeth Rose after her mother and grandmother. Rose was four when she contracted scarlet fever. Elizabeth stayed by her bed night and day, trying unsuccessfully to nurse her through it. A few days after Rose died, Elizabeth was diagnosed with a severe case of strep throat that developed into rheumatic fever. She lost her will to live until the doctor discovered that she was four months pregnant, and that gave her the determination to get well. Although she recovered, she was left with a damaged heart and was ordered to observe complete bed rest for the remainder of the pregnancy.

"Richard was born that July, and she called him her miracle baby. Tending to him did wonders for her spirits and she rapidly improved, though the doctor warned her that any major exertion could cause heart failure."

24

"Well, Hattie. Now you know it all. There is still time to change your mind. You are very young, and I would understand your reluctance to marry a man with this much history, when so much of your own history is yet to be written."

Hattie moved closer to him and gazed directly into his deep brown eyes. "No, Charles. What you have told me has not altered my decision. You have put together the pieces that were missing and helped me to see where I fit into the picture. Right here with you and the boys is where I belong. I want to marry you now more than ever."

She lifted her chin and kissed him deeply as he pulled her to him, and they reclined onto the grass in full embrace. She could feel his heart beating against hers and she began kissing his neck and stroking his cheek. As she lay there in the warmth of his arms, her body conformed to his, she was stirred with desire. She reached up to loosen his tie, but he covered her hand with his.

"No, Hattie, my darling. We can't do this now—not if I am going to look your mother in the eye and convince her that my intentions to marry you are pure. Your aunt already suspects me of ravishing her nineteen-year-old niece, and I don't want to do anything to confirm her suspicions."

"I'll be twenty in October," Hattie responded in mock defense. "I suppose you are right. But I have to say, I am feeling a bit rejected."

"I assure you that this is not a rejection, and you have no idea how much self-control was exercised in prying myself from your arms. But the vision of your mother wanting to know if my intentions are pure was enough. Not to mention that if she were not to give her consent, I may never have another of those heavenly yeast rolls again. Now, I suppose we need to head back to the car."

"Okay," said Hattie. "But if you will excuse me for a moment, I need to go over that ridge and see if I can find a private spot. I haven't had a bathroom break since I left home this morning."

For the remainder of the ride home, Hattie sat near Charles as they continued to make plans. As it grew dark, she laid her head on his shoulder and snuggled up even closer to him, at least until they reached the town limits of Calhoun, when she resumed a proper distance, so as not to arouse the suspicion of any of the townsfolk passing by.

They decided on July 3 for the wedding, if that worked for Mama. Hattie would be out of school on May 28, and it would give her a full month to make all of the arrangements at home.

Out of respect for Charles's recent widowhood, they would have an intimate ceremony in the Robinson home, inviting only the immediate family—Hattie's mother, sisters, and brothers, her aunts, and Uncle Sam, who was Harriet's husband; the four Barton children, Georgia, Alice, and Willie; Eugene and Bailey and their wives; and, of course, Uncle George and Aunt Sudie. Hattie would ask Uncle Rufus—her father's youngest brother, who had a church up in Virginia—to come down to perform the wedding. Lottie would be home from the Boston Conservatory by then, and Hattie would have her play the piano and sing. Oh, and she wanted Willie to do the flower arrangements. "That is, if she and Alice are still speaking to me," Hattie added.

As Alice was not due to return from Columbia until Wednesday, Charles would stay at her house while he was there and break the news to her before he left for Greenville on Thursday to talk to Sallie Robinson. When Charles returned to Calhoun, he would stop by and tell Uncle George and Aunt Sudie. After that, Hattie and Charles would gather the children, and together they would tell them.

"I want to make sure the children know I'm not trying to take their mother's place. They don't even have to refer to me as Mother after we are married. They can just say Hattie, or even Mama. That's what Richard called me when I found him up in Elizabeth's room after he was lost."

"The children have always loved you, and I believe they will be thrilled when they find out that you are to become a permanent part of their lives."

"Still, I think it would be real nice, Charles, if you would go ahead and divide up Elizabeth's jewelry and make a box for each boy. We could give them out when we tell them about us. Then, let's pick a time and all go out to Elizabeth's grave and leave some flowers, let them have some time with her. They need to know it's all right to talk about her and remember her even as our lives are moving on."

"How did a nineteen-year-old girl gain such mature insight?" marveled Charles.

"I'm really closer to twenty than nineteen, Charles." She laughed, and then added more seriously, "But I guess the credit should go to Will Kendrick for that. He taught me that sometimes the only way to love a person is to let them go. But just because you let go, it doesn't mean you have to forget."

While Charles was out of town, Hattie would make an appointment with Reverend Fitts to let him know that she would not be returning to Calhoun School and that he would need to recruit a new teacher for fifth and sixth grade. Charles would not hear of her working outside the home. Hattie hated to leave her teaching but didn't argue with him about it because she knew she would have about as much on her plate as she could handle, taking on the roles of wife, mother, and lady of the estate. Still, she entertained the hope that someday she might return to the classroom.

When they finally reached the Barton estate, it was well after eleven. The house was dark except for a lamp left burning to illuminate the entrance hall. Georgia had waited up and met them at the door. "Lawd, Mr. Charles, I thought you was in Columbia."

"No, Georgia, I had a change of plans and am leaving in the morning."

"Reverend Fitts been trying to get up with you. He say he just got back from the Methodist conference. He have something important to talk to the school trustees about and need you to call a special meetin'."

"Okay, thanks, Georgia. I'll go look at my calendar now and will call the other trustees before I leave in the morning." Charles smiled at Hattie, and she touched his arm before he disappeared into his study.

Georgia picked up immediately on their exchange of intimacy. "Miss Hattie? What in the world's going on, you coming back here so late on a school night with Mr. Charles, and Mr. Charles supposed to be in Columbia?"

"Shh, Georgia. Come on back with me to my room. You won't believe the news I'm going to tell you."

EPILOGUE

As the sun beamed through the bedroom window, Hattie stirred from sleep. She could hear the familiar sounds of the birds chirping sweetly outside, and from the kitchen, she smelled the coffee and the country ham Georgia was frying. George and Gene were early risers; she heard them stirring overhead. Soon they would clamber down the stairs, two steps at a time, ravenous after a long night's sleep. Charles Jr. would take his time getting to the table. Hattie would need to get up and dress if she were to make it to town by eleven.

Ever since Elizabeth Barton had brought Hattie to that room almost two years ago, Hattie had slept alone every night and had arisen every morning from under the Martha Washington spread in that same bed in the same blue room. In her drowsiness, the routine sounds and smells of the house waking up lulled her into a false sense that everything was as it had been. And then she felt the mattress shift, heard the springs creak, and became aware of the steady breathing of Charles Barton, asleep beside her, lying with one arm crooked behind his head and the other by his side. Her body pulsed with excitement as she awoke more fully to the wonderful dream that had now become her life.

She turned and laid her head gently on Charles's chest, hearing his heartbeat and feeling the rise and fall of his ribs as he breathed in and out. She inhaled his sweet woody fragrance of cologne mixed with the scent of tobacco and felt his chest hairs as they brushed against her cheek. She raised herself onto one elbow, resting her head in her hand, and then leaned back over him and touched her lips ever so gently to his mouth, her hair falling like a curtain around his face. He roused and shifted from his back to his side, reaching for her with his free arm and pulling her to him. She kissed him again and then whispered, "Shh, it's early yet. You can sleep a few minutes more. I'll wake you for breakfast." Charles drifted off again and she slipped from under his arm and out of the warm bed they now shared together.

When they had returned only two weeks ago from their brief honeymoon to Charleston, they decided that Charles would move in downstairs with Hattie, at least until the master suite upstairs was renovated. Hattie was delighted with the arrangement. After all, her room had been the place where Charles had proposed and it held special memories. As Charles was a night owl, he said that the arrangement suited him as well. He could work late in his study and still be near Hattie, a habitual early riser who always turned in early. Charles had jokingly accused her of roosting with the chickens.

Hattie pulled on her negligee and hurried into the bathroom to wash her face and pin up her hair. She couldn't waste any time if she wanted to be on time to the garden party at Lila Givens's. She looked at her reflection in the mirror hanging above the porcelain lavatory and no longer saw staring back the face of the jilted, heartbroken girl who had come as a guest to the Barton home two years ago, intent on making a new start and finding her place in the world. The face beaming from the mirror was that of the young bride of Charles Barton and mistress of the estate. "Mrs. Charles Barton," she said aloud and shivered with delight at the mention of her new title, wondering if she would ever get used to saying it.

Hattie selected a pretty cotton floral morning dress from her trousseau and pulled it on over her petticoat. She put on her shoes and stockings and tiptoed over to the bed where Charles was still sleeping.

Bending over him, she stroked his face and whispered, "I'm going to join the boys for breakfast before I go into town. You were up so late last night. Why don't you sleep in and I'll tell Georgia to bring your breakfast in later?"

He opened his eyes, smiled, and pulled her to him. "Only if you'll stay and sleep in with me," he said groggily.

She laughed, kissed him, and pulled away. "No, I have to be at Lila Givens's garden party by eleven and I want to spend a little time with Richard before I go."

"All right. I'm awake now anyway and don't care to lie here all alone. I'll get up and join you for breakfast shortly. I have to be in court at one and I need to go over some papers before I leave."

Hattie blew him a kiss as she opened the bedroom door and made her way to the kitchen. Giddy with happiness, she thought to herself: *Here I am, leaving my husband in our bedroom, walking down our hallway toward our kitchen, where I will say good morning to our dear Georgia, who will have breakfast ready for our sons. If this is a dream, may I never wake up!*

Lonnie came by at ten thirty to pick Hattie up and take her to town. The garden party was to honor Mary Posey, who had recently become engaged to James Fitts. Reverend Fitts had been assigned in May to a new church near Spartanburg and had already moved there to assume his duties, which officially began on July 15. Hattie had not seen Mary since she and Reverend Fitts had become engaged and was anxious to congratulate her and find out the details of her nuptials. Charles had told Hattie that the trustees voted to appoint Byron Stanton as the new principal and that the news would be released to the paper for the next edition. Hattie knew that Susan Downey would be at the party and suspected that Byron's promotion would be good news for the two of them. She had missed the daily contact with Mary and Susan and could not wait to see them.

As usual, Lila Givens had organized a flawless event. In addition to inviting Hattie and Susan, she had invited Chester Larke's wife, Betty, and all of the women at Calhoun Methodist Church, many of whom she had recruited to make sandwiches and cakes and serve punch at the party. She had also invited the ministers' wives from the two other churches, as well as Mary's mother and two of her aunts from Walhalla. The guests were ushered down a brick walkway, which led around the house to the Givenses' beautifully manicured backyard. They sat beneath the shade trees in white wicker chairs arranged around a gazebo entwined in wisteria and banked with hydrangea bushes. Punch was served in crystal cups and plates of tiny cucumber sandwiches and chicken-salad tarts were passed, along with dainty teacakes iced with almond-flavored frosting and decorated with pink rosettes.

Hattie and Susan Downey arrived at the same time. They embraced and began chattering away at once as they walked around to the backyard.

"Look at you, Hattie. You're radiant! Marriage must certainly agree with you. I can't wait to hear all about the wedding."

"Oh, Susan, I'm besotted with happiness. I don't know what in the world I did to deserve it all. But what about you? How are things with Byron? I'm just thrilled that the trustees have made him the new principal."

Susan's face seemed to light up in response to the sound of Byron's name. "Byron is a love and we could not be closer. And yes, isn't it wonderful that he's been appointed principal? He has so many good ideas about how to continue the work that Revered Fitts started with accreditation. He is so smart and dedicated, and I am so proud of him."

Mary Posey was talking with her mother and aunt as Hattie and Susan came into the backyard. When she saw her friends, she turned from her conversation and broke into an undignified gallop to get to them.

"*Hattie!* How's the bride?" She hugged Hattie and twirled her around. "You look wonderful, *Mrs. Barton.*"

"It feels so strange being called that," said Hattie. "Good strange, though." Hattie grasped Mary's hands. "What is that sparkling on your ring finger, Mary? Is that what I think it is?"

Mary held up her left hand and spread her fingers wide, displaying to Hattie and Susan the pearl solitaire ring encircled with tiny diamonds. "Isn't it beautiful? It belonged to James's grandmother. James was so romantic. I know you don't believe it, Hattie. But the day before he left for Spartanburg, he took me on a long drive up toward Table Rock for a picnic, and he dropped down on one knee and gave me the ring while we were looking out over the most gorgeous view below."

"Have you set a date yet?"

"Yes. December 28. I'll finish up the semester at Calhoun School and then join him after the wedding."

"Byron is happy you aren't leaving right away," said Susan. "Filling Hattie's position, as well as finding a Latin teacher to replace Reverend Fitts and getting the building ready for the opening of school, will be about as much as he can handle. Oh, Hattie, things won't be the same without you across the hall!"

"Well, look on the bright side, Susan," said Mary. "Hattie is now the mother of four boys, all of whom will go through Calhoun School. In a few years, she may even supply the school with one or two more little Bartons." Hattie blushed and Mary added, "She may not teach there anymore, but she will make a wonderful volunteer."

Susan laughed and lowered her voice to a whisper. "Maybe if you're good enough, Lila Givens will let you take over as chair of the library committee, or even run the fall festival. I'm sure that Byron would be happy to see that happen."

Just then, Lila Givens called to Mary to take her seat for a presentation. Hattie had heard that the women of the church had purchased a silver tea service as a wedding gift for James and Mary.

"You're the honored guest, Mary. We'd better stop talking and let you go on over there," Hattie said.

Before she left, Mary handed Hattie a package she had been carrying. "Here, Hattie. This is just a little wedding gift I wanted you to have to remember me by. You can open it with Mr. Barton when you get home." She squeezed Hattie tightly and hurried off to take her seat.

"She's such a wonderful friend," said Hattie to Susan. "And I owe it all to a little bird who set things straight between us."

Susan smiled and gave Hattie a hug. "It was my pleasure."

Hattie rocked on the porch swing with Richard that evening, while Charles sat close by reading his newspaper. Hattie was holding the package that Mary had given her, which she had waited to open until she and Charles were together. Richard helped to untie the satin ribbon and unfold the tissue paper wrapping to reveal a handsome leather-bound scrapbook. Opening the cover, Hattie found that Mary had already pasted in the first entry, a clipping of their wedding announcement from the *Calhoun Sentinel*.

Charles had put down his paper to watch her open the package. "How thoughtful," he said. "I suppose Elizabeth was right in predicting that Mary would be a good match for James Fitts. She had a sixth sense about those things." Hattie nodded and smiled. She was glad that Charles felt free to talk about the past with her.

"Let me see," said Gene, who was playing with a set of wooden blocks that George had outgrown and abandoned. Hattie showed him the book and the clipping and helped him find his name, which was listed in the wedding announcement as one of Charles's sons. It was the first time he had seen his name in print.

"Show my name," said Richard, pulling the book from Hattie's lap.

Hattie laughed and found his name. "Master Richard Cahill Barton," she read. "You were named after your mother's father."

"I'm not Master, I'm Richard," he insisted.

They were interrupted by Charles Jr., who had come from the house onto the veranda to say that he and George would be leaving for town. It was Pauline Jeter's birthday and Rosa Greer and Velma had invited a group of her friends to come for cake and homemade ice cream.

"Don't forget to take Pauline the little gift I bought for her. And be sure to give her a big hug and kiss for me," Hattie said. And then she amended her request when her husband peered at her with raised eyebrows. "I mean, wish her the happiest of birthdays for me and tell her I'll see her soon."

"I'll make sure to give her the package and the message," laughed Charles.

"Preferably the latter message rather than the former one," said his father. "And don't you boys be out late."

"Yes, Father," said Charles as he hurried off to find George.

Hattie turned her attention back to Mary's gift. "Look, there is an inscription on the inside cover. Oh, that's just like Mary to find the perfect quotation for us."

"What does it say?" asked Charles, reaching for Hattie's hand and squeezing it.

"Nothing is really lost to us as long as we remember it." —L. M. *Montgomery*